MURDER ON PEA PIKE

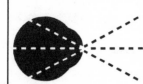

This Large Print Book carries the
Seal of Approval of N.A.V.H.

MURDER ON PEA PIKE

JEAN HARRINGTON

THORNDIKE PRESS
A part of Gale, a Cengage Company

GALE
A Cengage Company

Farmington Hills, Mich • San Francisco • New York • Waterville, Maine
Meriden, Conn • Mason, Ohio • Chicago

LIBRARY OF CONGRESS CIP DATA ON FILE.
CATALOGUING IN PUBLICATION FOR THIS BOOK
IS AVAILABLE FROM THE LIBRARY OF CONGRESS

ISBN-13: 978-1-4328-4878-1 (hardcover)

Published in 2018 by arrangement with Camel Press

Printed in the United States of America
1 2 3 4 5 6 7 22 21 20 19 18

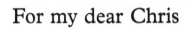

For my dear Chris

ACKNOWLEDGMENTS

My sincerest thanks to fellow writer, Doris Lemcke, a former Florida and Michigan real estate agent, for her many helpful insights into the world of real estate sales; to critique partners, writers Joyce Wells and Brenda Pierce for their skill and honesty (you were relentless!); to Dawn Dowdle of Blue Ridge Literary Agency and Catherine Treadgold and Jennifer McCord of Coffeetown Enterprises for their confidence in me and their enjoyment of this story. And, of course, to John for all the times he has said, "Where are you? Oh, at the computer. It'll wait. I'll talk to you later."

CHAPTER ONE

I knew she was trouble the minute she stepped in. It wasn't just her big hair. In Eureka Falls, Arkansas, big hair's a tradition, kind of like pecan pie. Her shoes, like some I used to wear, were the giveaway. Silver stilettos with ankle straps that criss-crossed up to her knees. Those boots were made for mischief. I ought to know. So was her little scrap of a skirt.

As I watched through my open office door, she strolled over to Mrs. Otis at the reception desk by the plate-glass window.

"Morning, ma'am. I'm Tallulah Bixby, and a while ago I dropped my car keys nearby. I'm hoping someone here in Ridley's Real Estate may have found them."

"As a matter of fact, I did find a set of keys earlier. Right next to an automobile." Mrs. Otis opened her desk drawer and paused. "You live here in town?"

"No, I'm from Fayetteville."

"Oh, I see. Well, what kind of car do you drive?"

"A big ol' Caddy. A present from my daddy."

"Color?"

"The prettiest sapphire blue you ever did see."

"That's right where I found them." Mrs. Otis reached into the drawer, took out a set of keys, and handed them over to the girl.

"Thank you, ma'am. If ever I can return the favor, I surely will."

"I appreciate the offer, young lady," Mrs. Otis said with a sniff, "but I've never lost a key."

"Neither have I," Tallulah replied, quickly adding, "except for now."

The "except for now" sounded like a hasty cover-up, and though Mrs. Otis was trusting enough to believe the story, I wasn't so certain this Tallulah girl owned that Cadillac. If she did, the "daddy" she mentioned might be made out of sugar, a subject I had no business messing with. A stolen car, however, meant a lot of grief for somebody.

I came out of my office, and acting on that uneasy feeling, jotted down the Caddy's license plate number. Wasting no time, Tallulah pulled out of a parking slot and shot down Main Street going ten miles over the speed limit.

"What's a sweet girl like that doing in those shoes?" Mrs. Otis wanted to know.

Pretending I didn't hear the question, I went into my cubicle and closed the door. Problem was, Mrs. Otis thought everyone was sweet, maybe because she was so sweet herself.

Out of loyalty to me, she'd quit Winthrop Realty when I did and came to work at Ridley's. The last thing I wanted was to upset her. But as office manager and sole sales agent — other than my boss, Sam, of course, who happened to be in New Orleans for the week — I felt responsible for what had just happened and wasted no time dialing Sheriff Matt Rameros.

In his own calm way, he'd been hitting on me since my Saxby Winthrop days ended. I'd never encouraged him and didn't want to give him the wrong idea today either. But with a possible car theft in the works, I figured I'd better make the call.

"Honey Ingersoll," he said the instant he picked up, "as I live and breathe."

"Mighty glad to hear you're alive and well, Sheriff. I have a number here for you to check out."

"Your phone?"

"You wish."

"No wishing about it, Honey. I've had your number for over a year now. Memorized it too. One of these fine nights I may give you a ring. Most likely between midnight and three a.m."

"Why three a.m.? So I'll think somebody up and died?"

"No. That's when the longing for you gets intense."

I took a deep breath. We weren't having what you might call telephone sex. That was against the law, and Matt was a law-abiding man. But the conversation was heating up in a way I didn't quite favor. "Here's that number, Sheriff."

"Oh, we're getting formal, are we, Miss Ingersoll? Well, let's have it, and then suppose you tell me what this is all about."

The wheels of justice moved slowly in Eureka Falls, which didn't seem to matter much since we had next to no crime. Whether that was due to Matt's efforts, or because peace-loving folks lived here, I hadn't a clue. But I gave him Tallulah's license plate number, refused his offer of a beer after work, and said goodbye. Just in time.

We'd no sooner hung up when Mrs. Otis forwarded a call to me. Always hoping an incoming call meant a prospect, I hurried to answer. I'd learned a lot under Saxby, including sales techniques. I'd give him that much. All sugar, I drawled, "Good morning. Ridley's Real Estate. Honey Ingersoll speaking."

An indrawn, shuddery breath echoed through the line. Then another. I was about to hang up on a crank call when Amelia sobbed out, "Honey, I'm so scared." I gripped the phone and sat up straight.

"What is it?" I asked, not sure I wanted to know.

"We're being thrown out. Onto the street."

"Explain, Amelia, please. Is Joe back? Has he threatened you?"

"No." Though her voice wobbled, I was real glad to hear that "no." Her ex-husband, Joe, was bad news, always had been. Sad to say, Amelia married him before she found out just how bad, and left him after he gave her two baby boys and four broken ribs.

I paced my cubicle. If Joe wasn't the problem, I was afraid I knew what was. "Are you losing the house, Amelia?"

"Yeeess." She was still wobbly voiced but getting stronger. "I'm going into foreclosure. The bank's evicting me. We'll be out on the street, the boys and me and the fridge."

Next to the boys, that stainless steel beauty was her pride and joy and, foreclosure or no foreclosure, she'd never leave it.

"We can't let that happen."

"But what can I do?"

"There has to be an answer. Why don't I stop by after work and we'll talk about it? I'm sure we'll think of something."

She was my friend, and I wanted to help her. We were both about the same age, twenty-four, and though I'd had my share of bumps, Amelia had been through far more.

"If only we could," she said. *Crash!* "That's little Joey. He flung his truck against the fridge. See you tonight."

The phone went dead. Just as well. Amelia and her boys were in deep trouble, and though I'd tried to sound comforting and all, there was little to nothing I could do to help them.

Except. . . .

CHAPTER TWO

Like a bloated king of the hill, Eureka Falls First Federal Savings & Loan, the holder of Amelia's mortgage, sat perched at the very top of Main Street. A sturdy, rough-cut limestone building with lots of walnut paneling inside, the S&L was no fly-by-night enterprise. It sure was ugly, though, and had proudly been so since 1912.

Last year, thirty-year-old Cletus X. Dwyer, considered Eureka Falls' biggest catch by every unmarried female in Yarborough County, had replaced his granddaddy as president of the bank. When I walked in, he was chatting away with a man I didn't know but could swear I'd seen somewhere. A tall man, forty maybe, with a dark suit and a stern, pock-marked face. They looked to be tight as ticks, but when the heavy, carved doors whooshed closed behind me, Cletus excused himself and hurried across the marble floor to take both my hands.

"Well, my day is now complete." He beamed his glittery Cletus smile. He had a healthy set of molars, and a man with a great smile usually made my heart beat faster. But somehow Cletus didn't, and for the life of me, I didn't know why not. His cheeks were chubby but pinchable, and the elastic garters he wore on his shirtsleeves weren't all that bad. If he'd say good riddance to them and those lavender shirts with the white collars, he'd look a whole lot younger, not so much like somebody's grandpa.

"Your timing is perfect, Honey." He gave my fingers a quick squeeze. "There's someone here I'd like you to meet. Someone you might find valuable to know."

He led me across the bank to the stern gentleman. "Honey Ingersoll, this is Trey Gregson, Senator Lott's aide."

Ah, up close I knew where I had seen him. On the TV. I held out a hand. "You're mighty well-known around these parts, sir."

His smile was cool and didn't quite reach his eyes. "Delighted to meet you."

I doubted it, but that was all right. Anyone close to an important man like the senator met people every day of the week. Saying he was delighted was a polite way of talking, no more, and his next words proved it.

"Cletus, I believe our business is complete, so I'm going to say goodbye and leave you with this lovely lady."

A final nod of the head for me, a quick man-to-man handshake for Cletus, and he was off.

As Cletus watched him stride away, he whispered in my ear, "The senator's aiming for the White House. Trey just confirmed it. Unofficially, of course." He cleared his throat. "But that's not why you're here today, and whatever the reason may be, I want to hear it."

With a wave of his hand, he pointed to his office, pleasing me to no end. That was just where I wanted to go.

"So, how are you these days, Honey?" he asked as we walked into his walnut cave. "Good as you look in that pretty blue suit?"

"Well, I'm just fine, Cletus. Thank you for asking. From that great big smile of yours, I don't need to inquire how you might be."

"Inquire, darlin', inquire. I love it when you do."

I shook my head. "My eyes are telling me everything I need to know, and while I don't wish to be rude, I'm here on a delicate matter." I fluttered my eyes. "May we speak privately?"

"I was hoping for that very thing." He

17

closed his office door behind us and took a seat in the leather swivel chair behind his desk.

"I'll come right to the point." I settled in the armchair across from him. "We have a problem."

"A mutual one?" Up went an eyebrow.

"A fiduciary one." I hoped I'd said it right.

He bent forward and rested his elbows on his desk blotter. As long as I'd known him, I'd never seen a single ink stain on that blotter. Like his garters, a useless frill.

"Tell me about this problem of yours."

"Ours."

He ignored that little correction. "Tell me what's bothering you."

"It concerns Mrs. Amelia Swope."

"Oh, I see." He withdrew his elbows and slumped back in his chair, swiveling like crazy. To ease his guilt, maybe, or his tension over what I was about to say.

"We can't let her lose her home, Cletus. She has two little boys and a devil of an ex-husband. She needs that house."

He stared at the wall behind me as if it held some kind of artwork, instead of all that dark ol' walnut.

Time for Plan B. I fanned myself with my left hand. "My, it's warm in here today. In all this heat, I can't seem to catch a deep breath." With my right hand, I undid the top button of my blouse. Well, the top two, but no more than that. Sometimes two were enough. Anyway, having captured Cletus' attention, I leaned over the desk. "Oh, that's better. Now tell me, darlin', what earthly good will it do you to throw an innocent woman and two helpless babies out into the cold?"

His eyes stayed glued to my cleavage. "You don't understand."

"Then help me do so." I leaned in a little farther. "It's a tragedy in the making."

"That's extreme language, Miss Honey."

I sat up straight and borrowed his fancy way of speaking. "As you know, I'm not given to exaggerated phrasing. Unless the situation warrants it. And this one does."

He sighed and dug his elbows into the blotter. "My hands are tied." He locked his fingers together.

Drawing in a shocked breath, I placed my right hand over my left breast. "Stop right there, Cletus. I know you don't mean that. You're the most powerful man in town" — scarily close to the truth — "so I can't believe, not for a teensy little second, there's nothing you can do. Why," I paused and let my hand slide from my breast to my lap, "when your mind is set on a goal, you can perform miracles."

His eyes were following my hand's every move. "Miracles only happen in the Bible. Make no mistake. I'm a true believer, but there are limits."

"None a man like you can't overcome."

He pushed his chair back from the desk and stood. "Sorry to refuse, but like I said. . . ."

I stayed seated and rebuttoned my blouse. "I'm not through yet." Every trace of sugar was gone from my voice.

His eyes flared wider than they had when I bent over his desk. "No need to take that tone."

True, getting vexed with Cletus would do no good. I was on an errand of mercy and had come dangerously close to forgetting that. So, I sweetened right up, and dripping syrup, murmured, "I do apologize. I'm afraid I misspoke, but it won't happen again. So, please take your seat and let me finish."

He cleared his throat. "Very well." Holding his tie against his belly, he sat. And waited.

"My employer, Mr. Sam Ridley, sends a great deal of business your way. Isn't that true?"

A shrewd man and a far cry from a fool

— after all, Cletus X. Dwyer had inherited his granddaddy's horse sense — he narrowed his eyes. "Go on."

Wanting to get all the words right, I steadied myself with a gulp of air. "Well, I know Mr. Ridley plans to continue sending prospective mortgage clients to the Savings & Loan." I paused. "And to no other. He's been happy with the arrangement. So much so that Ridley Real Estate hasn't created the same kind of warm and . . . and, ah, beneficial relationship with any other banking establishment. However. . . ."

Cletus threw his arms, garters and all, in the air. "Stop. This is blackmail, pure and simple."

"True."

He sat there frowning but didn't offer a solution. I guess for that I'd have to strip, and I knew without asking that even though Amelia was desperate, she wouldn't expect me to show that much skin.

He fiddled with a paperclip for a while. "The woman's six months behind in her monthly payments, and she has no visible means of support."

"Correct. Joe Swope's left town. No one knows where he is. At least no one who's willing to up and say so. Amelia's looking for employment, but with two little boys to care for . . ." I let my voice trail off.

Cletus flung the paperclip across his desktop. "A client's marital complications are none of my business."

I was perched at the edge of my chair. "What a downright silly thing to say. I've seen the mortgage forms you require people to sign. They're asked to tell you every detail of their private lives."

"Not quite." He smiled, right up to his black banker's eyes.

"Oh, this is funny, is it?" I was losing my temper again. Couldn't be helped. Couldn't be reined in, not a second time. "What Amelia has gone through is partly your doing, Cletus. You've known Joe Swope since grammar school. You knew he was a bully with a mean streak. What did you think was going to happen on that property? That he'd build a white picket fence and live happily ever after? You owe Amelia for letting her sign your documents without warning her what Joe was like."

His brows meshed together in a single, jagged line. "How on earth could I have done that? Get between a man and his woman? It's not possible."

I could have argued, but instead, with a sigh, I softened and tried a little sweet talk. "Well, perhaps not then, but you can help *now* if only you'll try. After all, who's to say you can't? You *own* the bank."

"Aren't you forgetting the board of directors? I report to them."

"No, I'm not forgetting, but if anybody can win them over, it's Cletus X. Dwyer. And when word of how good you've been gets around town. . . ."

He slapped his palm on the desktop. "I'll have every deadbeat in the county clamoring for the same treatment." He held up a warning finger, the one flashing his great-granddaddy's diamond signet ring. "If Mrs. Swope can show she's actively seeking employment, perhaps the bank can forgive her payments for three more months."

"Six."

"Four, but only with your guarantee of absolute silence in the matter." He paused, and up went his eyebrow. "And a dinner date. Saturday night at seven."

"Done! But dinner only." I stared him straight in the eyes. "No dessert." I stood, and after smoothing my skirt over my hips, bent over the desk and gave him a soft peck on the cheek.

He flushed bright pink, a shade that went well with his lavender shirt.

"Thank you, Cletus darling. You won't regret it."

What I didn't add, as I strolled out of his office with a happy little goodbye wave, was I hoped *I* wouldn't regret it. I'd saved Amelia's home for a few months, but if Sam Ridley learned how I'd threatened the wealthiest, most powerful man in the county, I might be the one out on the sidewalk.

CHAPTER THREE

After making a quick call to Amelia with the good news, I checked my watch and gasped. No point in worrying about what might happen when Sam Ridley came back from New Orleans. Right now I was in a worse fix. I had an appointment in fifteen minutes at the old Hermann farm out on Pea Pike, a twenty-minute drive away.

Speeding wouldn't help. If either Matt or his deputy, Zach Johnson, stopped me, I'd never make that appointment, and I had to, just had to. I needed the sale. Otherwise, Sam might think all I'd done since he left was babysit the office. He liked results, and when you came right down to it, so did I. The way I looked at it, a girl like me, with no family to speak of, no formal schooling and no money, had only two paths in life: marry and depend on a man or stay single and depend on herself. From what I'd seen of married life, my vote was to stay single, unless Mr. Wonderful came along. I slid behind the wheel of my car with a sigh. Problem was, he had come along but didn't know I existed. So, what good was that?

Yes, her own wits were all a girl could count on, though in my business, she also needed good wheels. And in that I had lucked out. With last December's year-end bonus, I'd bought a nearly new, big ol' Lincoln Town Car. A Harley Hog would have been better by far, but I didn't buy the Linc for fun. It was a sales tool I kept waxed and polished. Never knowing when a client might ask to see a listing, I had to be ready at a moment's notice to take him to his dream house.

Today, though, the voice on the phone, a Mr. Charles Ames, had said he'd meet me at the property. He used to live here in Yarborough County and knew where it was located. Ten miles out of town and set on a hilly ridge off the pike, the Hermann farmhouse had a sweeping view of the valley, a pump handle in the kitchen for water, and an outhouse in the yard for necessities.

I hoped Mr. Ames had deep pockets. Anyone who bought the place would need them to upgrade it to twenty-first century standards. For someone with the means to do so, the pretty view alone would be well worth the cost.

At the edge of town, I rolled down the windows and let the spring air waft through the car and play with my hair. Without clients along to impress, I didn't have to listen to that Beethoven music again. Instead, I put Miranda on so she could rip out "The Fastest Girl in Town." I sang along with her loud enough to jar my teeth, enjoying the scent of newly mown grass and the breeze with its promise of summer. Before long, wildflowers would carpet the hills and. . . .

An empty car parked by the side of the road caught my attention. I drove by too fast to catch the license plate number, but unless I was mistaken, it was that girl's, Tallulah Whatsername's, sapphire blue Caddy. *Hmm.* If that didn't beat all. There wasn't a house or a store within walking distance, not in a pair of silver stilettos. Maybe she'd had engine trouble, and some good ol' boy had picked her up. Strange, though, she hadn't used a cell phone to call for road service. Or maybe she'd changed her shoes and gone for a tramp in the woods, but I doubted it. She hadn't looked like the type of gal who was into nature trails.

I nearly stopped and backed up to make sure she wasn't in trouble, but I was already late and couldn't afford to botch this deal. Besides, Tallulah had struck me as a girl who could take care of herself. But just to be sure, as soon as I got to the farm, I'd call 911.

Five minutes late, I turned off the pike onto the rutty lane that led up the rise to the Hermann place. The house, an unpainted chink-walled log cabin, had a saggy shake roof, its only bragging point a fireplace somebody had built by hand years ago, one stone at a time.

In the gravelly patch fronting the house, a rusted-out Ford pickup sat on four bald, flat tires. So, Mr. Ames hadn't arrived yet. At least I didn't think he had. He'd sounded too interested in the place to have driven off in a huff over a five-minute delay. Fairly sure he'd be by in a little while, I parked, made the 911 call, then strolled across the scruffy yard to the cabin door. The double wide I grew up in had been bad enough, but this was worse, far worse.

Hoping the splintery boards would hold a hundred and fifteen-pound woman — well, one eighteen — I ventured onto the porch and pushed open a squeaky door that had never known a key. Something small and furry scurried out of a moldy chair in the front room and disappeared into what passed for a kitchen. A mouse. I shuddered and told myself to toughen up. Selling houses in rural Arkansas wasn't for sissies.

No one had shown an interest in the place for over a year, and that was easy to understand. It was damp and dirty, with cobwebs hanging in the corners and tattered rags at the windows. Worse, an outhouse odor rose above the dampness. A squirrel maybe. Or a 'possum.

I tiptoed across the creaky floor. How would I explain the odor to Mr. Ames? I hoped it wouldn't matter. He might be planning to tear down the cabin and build a brand-new house. Or he could have an interest in history — it was my understanding some people were keen on it — and planned to take the warpy old place apart, board by board, and rebuild it as a tribute to the past. No matter. Whatever his interest might be, I'd base my sales pitch on the beauty of the scene, the acreage, the privacy.

Phew. That odor was mighty strong. I left the door open to the fresh air and, with my pulse revving up a bit, peered into the back room to see what critter might have died in there.

Omigod. No, no, no!

I couldn't believe my eyes. They were lying to me. They had to be. But then I did believe, and a scream ripped from my throat.

Stretched out on her back, the silver stilettos still crisscrossed to her knees, Tallulah Bixby lay in a puddle of blood with a bullet hole in the middle of her chest.

CHAPTER FOUR

For a frozen moment, I couldn't move. Then I came to in a rush, and with the scream still throbbing in my throat, I whirled around and raced like a madwoman out of the cabin, onto the porch. Wild with fear, paying no mind to where I was going, I ran willy-nilly right into a man's chest, whacking the both of us off our feet.

The breath knocked from my body, I landed in a patch of weeds and came to, gulping the air. An arm's length away, the man I'd plowed into lay spread-eagled on the ground. A frail little guy, he was as quiet as dirt, his eyes closed, glasses bent and hanging off his nose, and his hat knocked halfway across the yard.

My heart pounding overtime, I scrambled to my feet. Who was this man? The killer? Or . . . ?

"Mr. Ames?" No answer.

I bent down and patted his arm, but he

didn't move a muscle. He looked so small and skinny, I doubted he was the killer, come back to polish me off. He was just a man who needed help. As for poor Tallulah, the only one who could help her now was Matt Rameros.

In no time flat, Matt's cruiser, with Zach behind the wheel, careened into the yard, sending up a cloud of dust that settled over me like dirty confetti.

Zach had barely cut the engine when Matt's boots hit the gravel. "Honey," he hurried across the yard, "are you all right?"

"I think so." Now that help was here, I was feeling more certain by the minute.

As Zach bent over the unconscious stranger, Matt held me so tight his gun pressed against my thigh.

"Tell me what happened," he said.

I loosened his hold. Backing up a step, I pointed toward the open cabin door. "Like I told you on the phone, there's a dead woman in there. She's been shot." I hiccupped. "In the chest. It's the woman I saw drive off in that blue Caddy."

"He's out cold," Zach called across to Matt.

"Have 911 send an ambulance," Matt said. Turning to me, he added, "Stay here,

32

Honey. You'll be safe with Zach."

Though I could have told him that Tallulah, except for a scampering mouse or two, was alone in the cabin, he slipped his gun from its holster and disappeared inside. While Zach made his call, I slumped onto the edge of the porch and leaned against a rickety post.

I'd never been so low before, not even on the day Billy Tubbs slugged me. He never got to do it a second time, though. I walked out on him that same day. Nobody knows, except for Matt Rameros. I'm so ashamed of it. Anyway, what happened back then was nothing compared to what happened to Tallulah today. Poor thing, she'd met a horrible end, killed and dumped in an abandoned house like a piece of trash. Why? There had to be a reason.

The stranger moaned, his voice mingling in the soft air with the twitter of the birds. Zach closed his cell phone, helped him to sit up, and after a while, to stand.

Shaky-kneed, barely conscious, the man fingered his right shoulder. "I think I've broken something."

"Come, sit down." Zach walked him over to the bottom step. "An ambulance is on the way."

Leaning heavily on the deputy's arm, the

man squatted beside me and managed a smile.

"I'm so sorry I banged into you," I said. "But there's a dead body in the house, and it scared me plumb out of my wits. I didn't know what all I was doing. I ain't . . . I mean, I'm not usually like this, but it was so awful I lost —"

"Understandable." He patted my hand. "No need to go on."

Zach picked up the man's briefcase and hat, shook off the dust and handed them to him.

"Are you Mr. Charles Ames, by any chance?" I asked.

"The same. May I assume you're Miss Ingersoll?"

"In the flesh."

He smiled, a real one this time. "I can see that. Pleased to meet you."

"Is that a fact? Under the circumstances, I. . . ."

Footsteps sounded on the cabin floor, and Matt reappeared, grim-faced. "We need the coroner."

Zach didn't waste a second in reaching for his phone

One boot on a step, one on a patch of gravel, Matt jutted his chin at me. "You think the girl inside is the same one who came into Ridley's earlier?"

"Yes. She said her name was Tallulah . . . Bixby, I think, and she drove off in a Cadillac. The one I believe was stolen."

He shook his head. "No, it's not stolen. It's registered to a Tallulah Bixby."

I gasped. "Then it really is hers. So why did she leave it by the road?"

"A good question." Matt glanced down at Mr. Ames.

Before he could ask his name, I said, "This is my client, Mr. Charles Ames."

Matt nodded. "Glad you're awake, sir. I have some questions for you." His glance cut over to me. "For both of you. Which of you arrived here first?"

"I did." I raised my hand like I was back in Miss McGinty's third grade class.

I'd never seen Matt so serious. He sure didn't act this way the times he ate apple pie at Josie's Diner.

He strode over to the cruiser, returning with a handheld recorder. He pressed play. "Are you Miss Honey Ingersoll?"

"Well, for goodness sake, Matt Rameros, you know perfectly well who I am."

With a sigh, he turned off the recorder. "Cooperate, will you, Honey? This is a murder investigation. The basic facts have to be stated."

"Oh. Sorry. I've never been involved in a police procedure before." Though, truth be told, a few times there when Daddy was around, I wished I had been. His voice still echoes in my ear, *See this strap, gal? It's got your name on it.*

"That's all right. We'll start again. Just answer the questions to the best of your ability. Okay?"

I nodded. If Matt wanted to speak to me like I was a little off in the head, I couldn't blame him. So I womaned up, and the rest of the interview went down nice and easy.

Mr. Ames's interview did too, though his was short. All he said was, "I walked up onto the porch, and this young lady, Miss Ingersoll here, knocked me senseless."

His questions finished, Matt turned off the recorder. "You'll both need to sign your statements. Any time this weekend will be fine. The station's open twenty-four seven. Will that be a problem for you, Mr. Ames?"

"Not at all. I'm planning to be here for several days."

"Excellent. And, Miss Ingersoll, I know you're," he cleared his throat, "available."

Oh, he did, did he? Anyway, he'd barely finished speaking his piece when a siren shattered the quiet of the Hermann hilltop. A few minutes later, an EMS vehicle roared up the rise, followed by the coroner's black panel truck.

Two medics rushed over to us.

"These are your patients." Matt pointed to Mr. Ames and me. To the coroner he said, "The body's inside."

As the doc went in to examine Tallulah, the medics took a look at us. Except for being shook up and nervous, I was fine, but Mr. Ames needed an X-ray.

"My car . . ." he began.

"Deputy Johnson will drive it to the hospital for you," Matt said.

Mr. Ames nodded. "Very well, I'll go with the medics. But first I must complete my reason for being here." He unzipped the briefcase he'd been holding on his lap, took out a legal-sized envelope, and handed it to me. "For you. Or to be more specific, for this property."

I gaped at him. "You still want it, even though a woman was killed here?"

He smiled. "I still do."

"You must love the view."

"Indeed. Now, would you please make certain the payment is in the correct amount?"

I took the envelope, slid a finger under the flap, and removed a certified check. Drawn on the Fayetteville Federal Trust

Bank, it was made out for the full amount of the sale. I stared at the check. No question about it. Mr. Charles Ames had bought the farm.

CHAPTER FIVE

That same afternoon, I deposited the certified check in the Eureka Falls S&L. The teller stared at my soiled suit with questions in her eyes, so I explained I'd been showing a neglected property. Sort of true, sort of not, but close enough.

By evening, Sam Ridley hadn't yet returned or called the office, and I'd about decided he wasn't lingering in New Orleans to admire the French Quarter. More likely, cruising a bayou and having him a red-hot time with some floozy.

Though the thought gnawed at me, I took comfort in the notion he'd trusted me with his business for a whole week. To clue him in on what had happened, I sent a text message describing the murder and saying both Ridley's Realty and I were just fine, thank you very much.

Friday, the day after the murder, the *Eureka Falls Evening Star* plastered Tallulah's death all over the first three pages. Except for weddings and crop failures, Kelsey Davis, the editor, seldom had exciting news to report. With a murder to tell about, he went on as long as a Sunday preacher. He even beefed up the account with photographs of the cabin, Sheriff Matt, and me. He got in a snapshot of the coroner's truck, too. None of Mr. Ames, though. I guess Kelsey couldn't find one in time to include it.

I scanned the article quickly; just as I suspected, Ridley's Real Estate was mentioned. Four times. What would Sam think when he read all this stuff? I stopped worrying about it. I could have been killed in that cabin, in the line of duty, and no way was that part of my job description.

At noon, I dashed out to buy BLTs and shakes for Mrs. Otis and me. When I got back to the office, she said, "You just missed Sam's call."

"Oh, no." I dropped the deli bag on her desk.

"You need him for something?" she asked.

"Yes . . . no . . . what did he say?"

"He spoke with Sheriff Rameros, who told him there's no need to rush back. So he's going to stay on for the weekend. Has a commitment or something." She handed me a memo slip with some numbers scrawled on it. "You can reach him here if you have to."

I tucked the slip in a pocket and resisted the urge to kick over the wastebasket. I would have loved to talk to him, hear his voice, tell him the whole story of yesterday. Lunch. Who needed lunch, anyway? I should have skipped it like I usually did.

On the plus side, the old saying that there's no such thing as bad publicity did seem to be true. Due to poor Tallulah's death, Mrs. Otis and I were kept busy all day answering calls. Most were curiosity seekers with a nose for news, but Mrs. Otis had a talent for filtering those out, and by day's end, I had a solid list of appointments all set for Saturday and Sunday.

Working people like to look for real estate on weekends, a plum time for walk-through showings and open houses. On the down side, a weekend schedule with no set hours and appointments, often running into the evenings, makes it hard for a girl to date. As a result, since I'd ditched Saxby, I'd been living like a nun in my little garden apartment. I didn't mind.

Between Billy Tubbs *Whaddya mean you don't want to do it again? What else you good for?* and Saxby Winthrop *If my momma was to find out we're cohabitatin', it would just*

41

about kill her, my choices in men had been mighty poor. When it came to dating, I guess you could say I'd pretty much chickened out, a phrase I understood most poultry farmers hereabouts hated.

Anyway, business kept me busy, and on Saturday, I showed six properties to three different couples. One pair warmed right up to a cozy little ranch house on a quiet, dead-end street. I'd give them time to think about it and call back around Tuesday to see if they had any questions.

In the meanwhile, I put away my worries and sorrows and hurried home to get ready for my payback dinner with Cletus.

When I walked up the Inn's broad front stairs, Cletus leaped off a rocking chair on the veranda and hurried over to me. "Well, aren't you something? Has anyone ever told you that you're the prettiest girl in town?"

"If I'm not mistaken, Cletus Dwyer, someone just has. Thank you."

He offered an arm. "May I escort you into the dining room?"

I tucked my arm in his and, despite my misgivings about the evening, I found myself perking right up. I'd been to the Inn before, for Rotary Club breakfasts and such, but never this late in the day. The most expensive restaurant in Eureka Falls, the Inn dated from before The War and was where the town's rich people ate supper when they weren't at the country club. In the three years I'd lived with Saxby, he had never once invited me here, and I had to admit, being escorted in like a lady on the arm of a gentleman — even one wearing a lavender shirt with a white collar — felt mighty fine. I hoped the outfit I'd copied out of a magazine, a sleeveless black silk dress and a single strand of fake pearls, looked right. The skirt was kind of short and the heels kind of high, but it was too late to fret about that now.

At the sight of me, the hostess squealed out a surprised little "oh," but Reba Fuller recovered fast and led us to a white-topped table in front of a glowing fireplace. She handed me my menu with a wink.

"How's the new house treating you?" I asked her.

"We love it. Every inch."

"I'm so glad," and I was. A few months ago, I'd sold the Fullers a small bungalow, a fixer-upper off Main Street. Reba worked at the Inn nights and weekends to help pay for the repairs.

"This table is perfect," I said to Cletus when she left us. The warmth of the fire felt wonderful on my bare arms.

"That's what I was aiming for. A perfect evening for a perfect woman."

Uh-oh. "I hate to disappoint you, Cletus, but no one is perfect."

"You come darn close. White or red? Or something stronger?"

Oh shoot, wine. I would have loved a Bud Lite instead, or even one of those fuzzy drinks, Lambrusco, I think they call it, but that might be the wrong thing to order in a place like this. "White would be elegant," I fibbed.

While the waiter hovered, Cletus took his time studying the wine list. Apparently, nobody hurried Cletus. Or pushed him around. I heaved a mental sigh. On that point, I still had Sam to deal with.

"You're a thousand miles away," Cletus said.

"Oh, sorry. It's so elegant in here that for a moment I got lost in a dream."

"What are your dreams like?" he asked softly, eyes fixed on mine.

My face warmed. His voice, the way he asked the question, the way he reached for my hand on the tabletop, struck a chord in my soul. Usually I could sleep through his conversation and not miss a thing, but so far tonight wasn't shaping up like one of those occasions. Maybe that was partly because he was wearing a suit coat, so I couldn't tell if he had on his sleeve garters or not.

Our server returned and made a fuss out of opening the wine. Cletus took a test sip before nodding at him to pour mine.

"Do you ever make them take one back?" I asked.

He smiled. "When I have to."

"When does that happen?"

"When I'm not pleased."

Ah, a peek into the mind of Eureka Falls' biggest wheeler-dealer. He must be pleased. At all costs? My jaw tightened. Not tonight. Though Cletus didn't know it, my pleasing days were over forever. At least in certain departments. For a change, a mutually enjoyable experience would be welcome.

A heavy drift of musk, followed by, "Well, if it ain't Miss Honey Ingersoll, of all people."

I glanced up, though there was no need. I'd know that heavy scent and sugar voice anywhere. "Hello, Saxby." Matching his sugar with my own brand of syrup, I raised my glass and took a sip. He ran his glance over me, making me glad I'd worn a dress with a high neckline. Saxby'd had enough free peeks. And then some.

He'd gained weight in the six months or so since I'd last seen him. And lost more of his hair. A girl hardly out of her teens, with long black curls and long white legs, stood holding his forty-five-year-old hand.

"Nice to meet you, Mrs. Winthrop."

"Oh, we're not married." She reddened. "We're just —"

I waved a hand. "No need to explain. Some men hate the very thought of marriage. To the likes of them, wife's no more than a four-letter word."

Saxby's quick, sucked-in breath was my reward. "Do tell me," I continued, "how is Miss Eloise, Saxby's beloved mother?"

"Oh, I haven't met Miss Eloise yet," she said, in the same voice you'd use to refer to the Almighty.

"I never met her either." I gave out a little tinkle of a laugh, the kind that sounded like breaking glass. "Sometimes I wonder if there really *is* a Miss Eloise."

That she existed, living in a big, antebellum mansion surrounded by acres of groomed lawn, I knew only too well, but Saxby always had an excuse as to why I couldn't meet her. When I finally understood he didn't want his momma to know about me, I realized I had to change into the kind of girl a man didn't hide behind the barn like a pile of manure.

Out went my big hair, platform stilettos, and cherry-flavored chewing gum. To try and figure out how society girls dressed, I studied the pictures in every style magazine I could lay hand to. Still did. I even stopped having Cindy Mae color-streak my hair, and I tossed all my tube tops. Didn't buy another one, either, not even when Belinda's Boutique put them on sale. Instead, I bought a navy-blue suit, the kind where the skirt matched the jacket, and a white cotton shirt I kept buttoned at all times . . . well, almost.

And when dealing with people looking for upscale houses, I said far fewer "y'alls" and far more "How are yous." Though I admit, on a few occasions, when flustered or something, I am liable to forget some of the niceties.

None of this was exactly a college education, like going to Emory or anything, but it helped. As a result, here I was tonight, sitting across from the most prominent citizen in Eureka Falls and gloating a little, I'll confess, when Saxby said, "Momma exists all right, but I'm guilty of forgettin' the manners she taught me. You two lovely ladies haven't met, yet, have you? Well let me correct that failin' right now. Honey, this is Mindy, my secretary."

47

I arched a bitchy brow. "New title?"

He flushed but otherwise didn't let on I'd been uppity. Smooth as buttermilk — Saxby could be smooth when he chose to be — he said, "Now, if you would kindly excuse us. We've been working late and need a bit of reinforcement." He stepped away then suddenly swiveled back. "Oh, by the way, Honey, I heard you sold the Hermann farm. Congratulations. I've been trying to unload that run-down place for years."

"I'm not surprised you heard about it. The *Star* had the story all over yesterday's paper."

"Not the details of the sale. I got those from the buyer."

I darn near dropped my glass. "Mr. Ames?"

"The same. He was inquiring about Sloane's acres, that parcel of land next to Hermanns'."

"I didn't know the Sloane family wanted to sell."

"They don't, not yet, but Ames is hellbent on bringing them around to that way of thinking." Saxby lowered his voice. "He asked me to keep his interest quiet, but I know you and. . . ."

He knows me. I ignored his smirk. "Interesting." *And loose-tongued.* So typical of the

Saxby I knew and detested. Also somewhat strange that Mr. Ames hadn't asked me if those acres were for sale. Perhaps knocking a man senseless wasn't the best way to build a clientele list . . . still. . . .

Mindy coughed, a delicate clearing of her throat, just enough to tell Saxby she'd tired of our shop talk.

His hand tightened on her elbow. "Sorry we can't have the pleasure of conversin' longer, but our table is ready."

"Of course, you must run along." Cletus reached for my hand across the tabletop and, with that gesture, dismissed Saxby.

I loved him for doing that. I positively did, whether he had garters hidden beneath his jacket sleeves or not.

"Well, well, quite the hostile exchange," he said as they strolled away. "No doubt about it, you jerked a knot in Saxby's tail." He smiled. "I don't think that happens to ol' Sax very often."

I tossed back my wine and pointed to the bottle cooling in the ice bucket. It wasn't a good, cold Bud, not even a fuzzy Lambrusco, but it was growing on me. He poured what amounted to a tumbler full. "The truth is, I'm far from perfect. For a while there, Saxby and I were, uh, together."

I'll take care of you, missy, but you'll work for

me. Understand?

"So I heard." Cletus' gaze was on me, his voice unruffled. "You were waitressing at Josie's Diner, and he offered you a job. With strings attached."

To avoid his searching gaze, I stared into the fire. "So he did, and I accepted his offer. My apologies for how I up and sassed him just now. I have no right to be bitter."

"You have every right. Saxby's more than twenty years older than you and a wealthy man. He took advantage of a beautiful, distressed young girl."

Forgetting about the fire, I snapped my gaze back to him. "You know the whole story?"

He nodded and poured a little wine into his glass. "The town banker hears everything."

"Yet you asked me out." I managed a smile. "For a night without dessert."

"Of course."

"Can I ask you a personal question?"

"Ask away. For you, my life's an open book."

"Has anyone ever told you that you're very cool?"

"If I'm not mistaken, Miss Honey Ingersoll, someone just has. And now, what do you say we summon our waiter and order something mutually enjoyable?"

Ha! How cool was that?

Chapter Six

On Monday morning, a hint of aftershave cologne floated in the air of Ridley's Real Estate. A new, expensive scent, not Sam's usual Old Spice.

Is he back?

Giving Mrs. Otis a skimpy little nod, I hurried over to the corner office, hoping, hoping . . . *yes!*

The soles of a pair of size twelve loafers stared me in the face. I didn't care; it felt perfect walking toward him. Tilted back in his swivel chair, Sam had planted his long, chino-clad legs on his desktop and rolled back the sleeves of his white, oxford-cloth shirt. His cowlick was blonder than ever, and the hair on his arms shone like gold against his newly tanned skin. The sun on those bayous must be powerful strong.

He glanced up from the newspaper spread out on his lap and beamed me one of those smiles that showed off his high, angled cheekbones.

"Good morning, Honey."

"You're back." *Duh.* Couldn't I think of something else to say? Something smart, for a change?

"Yes." He swung his feet off the desktop. "Sorry I couldn't get here sooner. My date left midweek, but I really couldn't. An old college pal had big plans for the weekend, and I didn't want to let him down. Especially not after I heard you were okay."

"I understand."

"Now why don't you close the door, have a seat, and tell me all about it? Begin with the Hermann sale and don't leave anything out."

When I finished my tale, he said, "Let me get this straight. You knocked a client unconscious —"

"I couldn't help it. It was an accident."

"I know," he waved the apology away. "My point is, after you knocked this guy on his behind," a mischievous smile lifted the corners of Sam's lips, "he needed medical treatment, but he insisted on buying the property before seeking help? Then this same guy approached Winthrop about buying Sloane's acres."

"So Saxby told me," I said.

He rocked in the swivel for a moment. "I

don't like the sound of this. Nothing's moved on that side of town for years. Now, out of the blue, someone wants to buy two tracts of stony farmland. The question is why. Did this Mr. Ames give you a reason?"

I shook my head. "The view, I thought."

"No, not that alone. My ol' salesman's instinct tells me something's up."

Old? He's only thirty-two, for Pete's sake, a fine age.

"We need to find out what it is."

We.

"Should you hear anything, anything at all, let me know. As soon as I go over my mail, I have a notion to pay a little call on Cletus Dwyer. He hears all the latest rumors. We give him so much business, he should be willing to clue me in."

Uh-oh. Well, Sam would likely hear the Amelia story sometime, so better sooner than later. Though, after our cozy Saturday evening, Cletus might soft-peddle my meddling visit to the bank. On the other hand, I *had* turned down his offer of a second dinner date next Saturday. For an Arkansas gentleman, it was a handshake on the first date, a kiss on the second, and on the third . . . I couldn't go there with Cletus, as sweet as he'd been all evening. Especially not with Sam sitting across from me, tanned and smiling, his deep voice playing up and down my spine like music on a keyboard.

As I stared across the desk, drinking him in, I saw a frown flit across his face. "We'll have to rethink your role here at Ridley's. You put yourself in danger going into that abandoned house alone. In fact, the whole concept of a female agent needs to be reassessed."

My heart nearly stopped. "Why? Haven't I done a good job? My sales have gone up for three years in a row. As you very well know, I'm in the top ten percent of all realtors in Yarborough County. There's no reason for —"

"Whoa, little lady." He held up a palm. "You're an excellent agent. Have been right from the beginning. Your safety's what concerns me, not your sales ability. Suppose you'd walked in on the murderer? You could have been killed too. From here on in, I don't want you . . ."

Oh, God, he's going to fire me.

". . . going into these abandoned properties alone." His soft blue eyes warmed as he glanced over at me.

I was glad that today, instead of a business suit, I'd worn a new outfit to celebrate spring, a cotton sweater in the same robin's egg blue my granny favored, and a flowered skirt with flouncy little pleats all around. At first, I'd been afraid the skirt was a tad too fluttery. I'd stood staring at it in the changing booth so long, Belinda came knocking on the door. But in the end, I decided I loved it so much, I went ahead and bought it.

"From now on," Sam was saying, "we'll call on these isolated places together, or I'll go alone. I don't want anything to happen to you, Honey."

He didn't? My heart leaped up . . . too soon.

"The day you left Winthrop's to come over here was one lucky day for Ridley's. You're the best agent a realtor could have."

Agent. "Thank you, Sam." My heart fell back to its normal pulsing. "Well, I'd better get over to the station and sign my witness statement. Then I have an appointment to show that small ranch near Dolby's Corners. It'll be a second callback. I think the buyers are really interested."

"Excellent," he said as I got up from my chair. "But before you go, I have some news for you. You might as well hear it from me, instead of reading about it in the *Star.*"

No doubt about it, he was excited over something. That edge in his voice. . . .

"What is it?"

"I'm engaged."

"To be married?" My question came out as a squeak.

He laughed. "What other kind of engagement is there?"

Some news you could take standing up. Some you had to take sitting down. I fell back into the chair I'd just left. "Congratulations. Who's the lucky girl?"

His eyes gleaming, he sat there at ease, a happy man just swiveling away. Kind of like Tarzan, ready to pound his chest and roar at the jungle.

"Lila Lott." His tongue played with her name as if it tasted as sweet as, well, honey.

"The senator's daughter? The beautiful brunette who's always in the society pages sitting on a horse or something? *That* Lila Lott?"

"None other." Pure satisfaction rolled off his words.

He shifted in his seat but didn't put his feet back up on the desk. Good thing. *Let him try, let him just try, I'd. . . .*

"She's coming in later today. While we were in New Orleans, I spoke so highly of you and Mrs. Otis, she can't wait to meet you both."

The hired help. No, no, and no.

"I'd love to meet her, Sam," I lied, "but I

do have to get over to the station and sign my statement. After that, there's the callback I mentioned. Sorry. Maybe some other day real soon."

Forcing my rubbery knees into action, I hurried from his office and dashed into my cubicle. I grabbed my purse and ran past Mrs. Otis without a word.

As the door slammed behind me, she exclaimed, "Well, I never."

CHAPTER SEVEN

"Well, I never either, Mrs. Otis." I stomped toward my car. "I never had a chance with him."

Not surprising. Why should a man as successful, handsome, and well-connected as Sam Ridley bother with a girl from a double-wide? A girl who ended up in Eureka Falls for only one reason? Billy Tubbs' motorcycle had run out of gas and so had Billy.

I shoved the key in the ignition and drove along Main Street, tears streaming down my cheeks and cussin' like mad. Finally, as I rounded the corner from Rolly's Hardware, I was crying so bad, I had to pull over to the curb. Snatching a tissue out of my purse, I blew my nose good and strong, clearing my head for further reflection.

Why was I so upset, anyway? I'd known all along Sam would never fall for me. As traffic whizzed by, I snorted, blew again, then wound down my window and flung the tissue into the street. A new low. Worthy of a citation or something. Well, what could you expect from somebody like me? Lila Lott would never do such a thing. Not Lila, the product of Chambliss School and Yale University. Not Lila, the glamorous hostess at her daddy senator's garden parties. Not Lila, who rode horses not Harleys. Not Lila, who lived on a plantation outside of Eureka Falls and in a townhouse in Washington, D.C. No more tissues, dammit.

I snuffled up my nose and risked a peek in the rearview mirror. A forlorn-looking face with red eyes and a red nose stared back.

"Know what your problem is, Honey? You're jealous, plain and simple. Things could be worse, far worse. Think of poor Tallulah Bixby, whoever she was. At least you're alive, and this isn't the end of the world. Just the end of your silly dreaming."

Three years ago, when I broke up with Saxby, I promised myself no more substitutes for the real thing, no more talking myself into believing love was in the air when it was just a drift from the outhouse. Now was the time to remember that promise and the night I swore it.

Not that I could ever forget the very first

time I met Sam. Every minute of that night was etched in my brain. Saxby had dragged me to the Bijou to see some kind of action film with lots of explosions and body parts flying in the air. That was bad enough. Worse, he had a flask in his jacket pocket and kept nipping at it throughout the film. When the show was over, I refused to get in the car with him. After an argument on the sidewalk outside the theater, he let me drive us to Josie's for coffee.

Later, rowdy and mean drunk, despite two black coffees and a Danish, he snatched his keys off the tabletop and lurched to his feet. "Come on. Let's get outta here."

"I'm not going with you, Saxby. You're not fit to drive."

His eyes got small and kind of slitty. "The likesa you is tellin' me what's fittin' and what ain't? I took you out of the gutter. 'Member that, Missy. Now get the hell outside and into the damn car."

That's when Sam came to the rescue with nothing more than his strong right arm. One tap on Saxby's chest and ol' Saxby collapsed, useless as a flat tire.

"You heard her," Sam said. "The lady isn't going anywhere with you. You're drunk. Josie, call the police."

"Why you —"

Saxby went to rise up but didn't quite make it. Instead, he landed back on his rear end and passed out on the leatherette cushion. After he'd been hauled off to the hoosegow, Sam and I had a long talk. Seemed he'd been following my sales record through MLS, and, liking what he'd seen, he offered me a job right there on the spot. Needless to say, I grabbed it.

Ridley's realty business rivaled Winthrop's, and best of all, Sam was the first honorable man I'd ever known. He was always calm and levelheaded, always in control, so unlike my daddy or Billy Tubbs or Saxby the Rat. I was sure I could do a mighty fine job for him, and deep in my heart, hoped that someday he'd. . . .

After a blind search, I found my compact and slapped some powder on my nose.

"Better," I told the face in the rearview mirror. "Not good, but better." I stared into those red eyes. "So far, I've kept vow one. Now, here's vow two. The day Sam Ridley marries Lila Lott, I'm quitting my job and moving out of Eureka Falls."

"Oh no you're not." *Lord Almighty, I'm hearing voices now.* "That's your jealousy talking. I thought your momma didn't raise no stupid children. Leave Eureka Falls and you'll be throwing away your contacts and a town that's become home to you. And what about all the friends you've made?"

"If they're true friends, they'll understand."

"You'll walk away with nothing."

"Not so. I have five years' experience in the real estate business. When I leave, that'll go with me. It's more than I had when I rode in here on the back of Billy's bike. And besides, Sam isn't married yet." Tamping down the little voice that whispered, "Forget it, he soon will be," I put the car in gear and drove over to the Eureka Falls Police Station.

Ellie, the dispatcher, looked away from her keyboard long enough to shrug a shoulder in Deputy Zach's direction.

He stood as I approached his desk outside of Matt Rameros' inner office. "I'm on my way out, Honey. You here to sign your statement?"

I nodded.

"Have a seat." He upped his chin at a row of molded plastic chairs against the wall. "Matt has somebody with him, but he shouldn't be long. Ellie can get you a cup of coffee."

"No thanks. I'll just wait."

"Suit yourself." He gave me a two-fingered salute and left.

I studied the wanted posters for a while then opened my cell and texted my clients to firm up our noon appointment. A murmur of voices came through the thin, plywood partition of Matt's office. A minute or so later, chairs scraped against the floor and the door opened. Out popped none other than Charles Ames. As he hurried toward the front entrance, I jumped off my seat.

"Mr. Ames!"

He stopped and turned around to see who had called his name. At the sight of me, he winced and glanced about as if he needed an escape route.

"Remember me, Honey Ingersoll? Your real estate agent? Or maybe I should say, one of them."

"Of course I remember you."

I pointed to his sling. "How's your poor shoulder?"

"Fine. It's fine." Holding a briefcase in his good hand, he stood shuffling his feet as if hell-bent to get away. But I wasn't about to let him go yet.

"I understand you have an interest in Sloane's acres out near the Hermann place. That parcel hasn't been listed yet, but when it is, Ridley's Real Estate would be happy to accommodate you. I only hope the accident I caused wasn't the reason you turned to another agency."

He shook his head. "I have no idea what you're talking about. Now, if you'll excuse me."

"But I have it on very good authority" *ha!* "that you. . . ."

He stepped away from me so fast the briefcase slapped against his thigh. Nodding a curt farewell to Ellie, he hustled out of the station without another word.

Hmm. Somebody had lied to me. Either Saxby Winthrop or Charles Ames. But which one? The man with the teenage girlfriend or the man with the sling? Sam was correct. Something was going down over at Pea Pike.

"Honey, want to come in my office?"

I whirled around.

"You been crying?" Matt peered into my eyes.

"No, Sheriff, 'course not. I just had a speck under the lid earlier."

"You shouldn't lie to a cop. Didn't your daddy ever tell you that?"

I suppose I could have been a Savannah-style lady and said my daddy never had a reason to say any such thing, but it came out, "Hell no."

He laughed, and with a hand on my elbow, escorted me into his office. Lined with locked steel filing cabinets, the cramped space held a desk, two chairs, and except for his family wall art, not much else. Born in Arkansas, Matt had a warm-toned Mexican complexion. To prove both facts, not that he had to or anything, he kept a copy of his parents' immigration papers of twenty-nine years ago on the wall, along with his birth certificate dated a year later.

After riffling through some papers on his messy desktop, he plucked out one and handed it to me. "You might want to read this before you sign."

When I took it from him, our fingers accidentally touched. Or if not accidentally, I could have told Matt he was wasting his time. My sexy vibes weren't even on autopilot; they had completely conked out.

Anyway, I scanned the statement, signed it, and slid it back to him. "This looks about right."

Frowning, he placed it face down on his desk. "Since you're involved in this Bixby case, I want you to know something."

Another man with news.

"I've called in the state police. I would have preferred not to, but it's the only way. Eureka Falls doesn't have the manpower or the forensic backup to investigate a murder. Not one like this, with no witnesses and no obvious motive."

"None at all?"

"Not at the present. Without a sign of forced entry, we can't tell if the victim went into the house willingly or not. And we found no weapon. That fact plus the blood spatter pattern eliminates suicide."

"Blood pattern?"

He nodded. "The killer shot from about two feet away." He laid his muscular arms on the desktop and leaned in. "You sure you never met the victim before that morning at Ridley's?"

"Never."

"Do you know anyone who did? In your job, you meet a lot of people. Maybe you ran into a high school friend of hers. Or a distant relative or a neighbor."

"A neighbor? She was from Fayetteville, Matt." To citizens of Eureka Falls, Fayetteville was the moon, and Matt knew it.

He grinned, a tad lopsided, but still a grin. Except for hunting season, the local townsfolk didn't do a lot of traipsing around the countryside. At least not countryside that involved big cities.

"Haven't you found out anything about her?" I asked. "Where she lived? Why she was here in the first place? Anything?"

"I'm not at liberty to say."

The abandoned Caddy had been registered in Tallulah's name. That meant he did know who she was and where she lived. Stood to reason. He knew far more than he was letting on. So, why pump me for information?

"There's something else." He hesitated like he didn't want to tell me what it was. "To the state police, you're a person of interest."

The muscles in my neck tensed. "What does that mean?"

He pointed at my report. "Your signed statement says you were first on the scene. You arrived there before Ames."

"That doesn't mean I killed her."

"I couldn't agree more. That's one reason I didn't want to call in State. But I had no choice. A girl's been murdered. Until you're cleared of suspicion, they'll be checking into your background, looking for a motive. When they don't find one, they'll move on." He stared at me, his troubled dark eyes darker than ever. "I probably shouldn't be telling you all this, but consider it a warning from a friend."

A warning from a friend who happened to be the town sheriff. Not the same as a warning from your granny. I stiffened on my hard wooden chair. To be considered a person of interest in a murder case was worse than Daddy's temper, worse than Billy's abuse, worse than Saxby's drunken fits. This was being dumped on big time, and I'd be damned if I'd just sit and take it. Little Miss Real Estate Agent needed to fight back. For my sake and for Tallulah's too. You might even say the time had come to kick ass, but not if you were as elegant as Lila Lott. Or me.

CHAPTER EIGHT

For what I was conjuring up, I needed darkness, not noon sun, so I reined in my impatience and did what I had to do next, meet my clients.

"Knock six hundred dollars off for a new water heater and y'all have a deal," Dexter Jones said an hour later.

"Sounds mighty fine to me," I replied, "but I'll have to check with the owner. I can call her right now if you like."

"No, I'm not convinced this is the one, sweetie," his wife said. "I don't like these Formica countertops. My heart's set on granite. You know the kind with little flecks of color sprinkled through it."

"Emma, we've already looked at over two dozen places." His voice tinged with irritation, Dexter upped his chin at me. "This lady's running out of houses in our price range."

True! I wanted to shout. Either that or kiss

Dexter on both cheeks and knock off his John Deere cap while I was at it. In all our viewings, he'd never once removed it. Probably bald as a fireplug.

Anyway, the time had come for me to do what Cletus Dwyer found distasteful, jump between a husband and wife. So, I squared my shoulders. "Mrs. Jones, I do believe your husband's right."

Dexter's eyes widened as if he didn't hear that very often.

"Look at it this way. You can replace the counters at a later date, but once you buy a house, you can't change the location." I pointed out the kitchen windows. "See that beautiful grassy yard? What a wonderful place for your children to play, and best of all, this street's a cul-de-sac. No through traffic, ever." I paused to let her think that over, then hauled out my big guns. "Your little ones can ride their bikes around here and you'll never have to fear for their safety. What do countertops matter compared to that?"

"Well, when you put it that way," she hesitated for a long, breathless moment, "I have to agree." She beamed a triumphant smile at her husband. "Let's take it, Dexter."

He tugged off his cap, revealing a mop of

curly black hair, and gave my hand a firm shake. "Thanks, young lady. Now don't forget about that water heater."

"I surely won't, Mr. Jones." I reached into my purse for the cell.

Sounding happy, and without bothering to make any counter offers, the owner agreed to the sale. As soon as Dexter gave me a check for the down payment, I wrote Cletus Dwyer's name on the back of my card and handed it to him. "For your mortgage, I suggest you apply to the Eureka Falls Savings & Loan. Feel free to say I sent you and deal directly with Mr. Dwyer. No one else. You'll get the best rates from him."

In truth, mortgage rates were pretty much fixed, but I knew Cletus would do everything possible to help me complete this sale.

As the Joneses headed for the bank, I headed for my apartment, though my day was far from over. But going back to the office and facing Sam so soon after he'd dropped his bombshell was more than I could bear right now. When I got home, I'd check my calls and try to relax until the witching hour.

Twelve a.m.

I parted my living room curtains to peek out onto Hillside Avenue. No moon tonight.

Good. I slid into some clothes that, if a body was so inclined, were dark enough for rum-running. Black jeans and turtleneck and a black headscarf. Sneakers, keys, a flashlight, and I was ready to go.

I stepped out into a night filled with the scent of spring. Night-blooming jasmine maybe. And lilac. Yes, lilac. Pulling some of that sweet air into my lungs, I put the Lincoln in gear and purred across town. As I eased along deserted Main Street, nothing moved in the light cast by the streetlamps. In the darkness between the lights, the velvet night lay eerily still. Just what I wanted.

At the corner of Briggs and Main, I turned right and coasted into the parking lot behind Winthrop Realty. For old time's sake, or maybe from force of habit, I parked in the slot that had been mine when I worked, in more ways than one, for Saxby.

Key in hand, I padded over to the back door. With any luck, Saxby hadn't changed the locks. Why would he? Crime was rare in Eureka Falls. Besides, what did he have to fear from two female ex-employees?

Heart pounding, I inserted the key. With a click that sounded like a rifle shot in the silence, the tumblers slid back. *Bingo.* I stepped inside, closed the door, then stood still in the dark for a moment. Had Saxby changed things around, moved the office furniture?

No. Everything was where I remembered it. Even the glowing green eyes of the printers were in their familiar locations. I tiptoed over to the wall of steel filing cabinets behind the new secretary's desk. I'd start with A for Ames. If nothing came up, I'd try S for Sloane. If that failed, P for prospects. Surely one of the files would yield some useful info.

Hoping the light wouldn't show from the street, I aimed my flashlight into the A drawer. I didn't have to look far. There it was, Ames, C. I lifted the folder out and laid it on a desk. Bending over for a closer look, I beamed the ray of light onto the file's single page. *Ah! I knew there had to be more to this than. . . .*

Was that the back door creaking open? Didn't I lock it? I froze as a footfall sounded behind me. Then another. Someone who meant no good was heading straight for me. *Oh, Lord in heaven!* Before I could whirl around or even let out a scream, a large, callused hand clamped over my mouth. Seizing me in a body lock, a hard arm wrapped around my waist. The flashlight flew out of my fingers and rattled along the floor.

"Don't move," he said, and my thundering heart slowed to its usual steady beat. Matt Rameros. *Phew,* at least an arm of the law had me in its grip, not a killer. "If I let you go, no noise. Understood?"

When I nodded, he loosened his hold. I stepped away and spun around to face him. "You nearly scared me to death."

He picked up my flashlight and flipped it off. In its brief glow, he hadn't been smiling. "What are you doing in here?"

"Well, I —"

"Breaking and entering," he said before I could dream up an answer.

"What a thing to say. I want you to know I have a key."

"And I want you to know you have a problem. You're under arrest."

"You're kidding."

"I never kid." He handed me the flashlight. "Keep this off. No need to attract undue attention. Your Lincoln out there's making enough of a statement."

That was when I knew there'd be no arrest. A flood of relief washed through me.

"So, to repeat my question, what are you doing here in the middle of the night? Make it good."

Since he'd caught me arm deep in Saxby's cookie jar, I figured honesty was the best policy. Also, on a gut level, I trusted Matt, something I hadn't realized until that very moment.

"I think Saxby Winthrop is up to something. Some kind of land deal he was supposed to keep secret but couldn't help boasting about. It's a property out near the Hermann place."

"An illegal deal?"

I shrugged, though he probably couldn't see it in the dark. "I don't know. That's what I'm trying to find out. It involves Charles Ames. Whether legal or illegal, whatever they're doing is sneaky."

"Like breaking and entering?"

I sensed more than saw his smile. "I didn't break in. I used a key that's my legal possession."

"Hand it over, and I'll call this escapade a draw. I'll even go one better. Put the file back where you found it, promise you won't pull this stunt again, and we'll forget this ever happened."

"You leave me no choice."

"No, you leave *me* no choice. At least none I want to make. As I tried to warn you this morning, the state police will be taking a good, hard look at you. You don't want to prejudice your case."

"*My* case?"

"All right, your situation. The point being this isn't the time to do something stupid. Like repeating this little caper. Now put the file back."

I returned the folder and shut the cabinet drawer.

"Did you remove anything?" Matt asked.

"No."

"Sure?"

"Would I lie?"

"I could frisk you to find out."

"Don't you dare!"

He laughed, and together, like two empty-handed thieves in the night, we left Winthrop Realty. After locking up and pocketing the key, Matt followed me home in the cruiser but was thoughtful enough to leave off his blue lights.

I hadn't exactly lied to him about not removing anything, for I hadn't taken a single thing, not really, just noted the name of Mr. Ames' client, the one interested in Sloane's acres.

International Properties, LLC, Fayetteville.

CHAPTER NINE

Ring, ring. The phone jarred me out of a deep, beautiful dream. Astride a Harley Goldwing, racing down the highway, fast and free, the wind blowing in my hair, the sun shining on my face, nothing but. . . . *Ring, ring.*

Eyes still closed, I groped for the phone. "Hello."

"Oh, Honey, did I wake you?"

"No, no, Amelia, I've been up for hours." I eyeballed the clock. Noon. And on a Tuesday. I groaned and fell back on the pillows.

"Mrs. Otis said you hadn't come in yet, so you must be out on a showing. But I took a chance you'd be home. Joe's back."

Wide awake of a sudden, I sat up. "Back where?"

"In town."

"The nerve of him. When did he get here?"

"He said sometime last week."

I was afraid to ask but had to. "Where's he staying?"

"With his cousins out on Suggs Road."

"Omigod." I gripped the phone. "He came by."

"Yes, last night. He wanted to see the boys."

"You let him in? But you have a restraining order."

"How could I deny him his sons?"

"Easy." I perched on the edge of the bed, swinging my legs to the floor. "Did he threaten you?"

"No." She paused. "Not this time."

But the next.

"So what did he want? You know Joe always wants something."

"He said," her voice trembled, "he wants his family back."

"Oh, God." I flopped down, flat out on the mattress. "What did you tell him?"

"I'd have to think about it."

"You did? Remember what your therapist said. Once an abuser, always an abuser."

"I know." Panic had crept into her voice. A bang echoed in the background. A dropped sippy cup or a plateful of lunch?

"I have to go," she said, the standard closing to most of our phone conversations.

"Hold on a sec. Why don't I take the

afternoon off and we all go out for a while? Have a picnic by the creek. Let the boys run around and play. It's a gorgeous day." *I think.*

"That would be wonderful. They'd love it. So would I."

"Pick you up in an hour."

Alone with two little bundles of mischief and practically no money, Amelia didn't get out much. This would be a chance for her to have some fun and for me to help stiffen her spine. Joe Swope had already proven what he was, and if Amelia went back to him, anything could happen. None of it good. Then where would her boys be?

I closed the phone, leaped up, and got dressed. After pulling on cutoffs and my favorite U of A T-shirt with "Never Yield" scrawled across the chest, I scrunched my hair into a ponytail and washed the midnight hour off my face. In no time at all, I'd tossed together some peanut butter and jelly sandwiches, cut apples into chunks, and loaded bottled water and juice drinks into my picnic cooler. A half hour later, humming "Redneck Woman," I hopped into the car.

My bedside squint through the blinds had been a good guess. The day was sunny bright and carpeted with grass as fresh as a new parlor rug. Even the dogwood bloomed pink and pretty.

At the Norton farm, as soon as Amelia unbuckled their car seats, Joey and Jimmy zoomed up the meadow like little blond bullets.

"I'd better go with them." Amelia laughed, some of the weariness lifting from her face. She reached into the trunk for a tote stuffed with bath towels, toy pails, and shovels and hurried off.

As she ran after the boys, I grabbed the cooler and a blanket and followed along. At the top of the slope, I took a deep breath of sweet spring air and glanced down at the creek that curled like a narrow blue ribbon around the base of the hill. On both sides of the sandy bank, tanning teenagers on blankets and families with little kids were enjoying the day too.

Joey was tearing at his sneaker laces. "Sneaks off, Momma. Sneaks off!"

"Off, Momma, off," two-year-old Jimmy echoed.

Within seconds, they raced barefoot to the creek's sandy edge.

"Wonder if the water's cold," I said as they waded in.

"It's so shallow, I doubt it." Amelia laughed as Jimmy plopped down and let the water wash over his chubby legs. "Now let's see if he can get up." She toed off her sandals, ready to go after him.

Though Jimmy had nothing to hold on to, and the creek bottom was soft and squishy, the little guy didn't cry or ask for help. He got to his knees, one at a time, then tottered upright, took a few steps and dropped back down. This time he wailed his head off. Like a lioness to the rescue, Amelia dashed in after him.

"Fishies, Momma, fishies!" Joey squealed.

"Ooohh look, Jimmy, fishies." Amelia planted him back on his feet.

"There are minnows in here," she called to me. "What fun!"

No way could I miss the first minnows of spring. I hurried down to the water, and feeling like a young'un again, waded in and gazed down. Darting among the reeds and pebbles, tiny silvery shadows wound their way south. Even Joey and Jimmy were quiet as they watched.

Finally, the show over, the boys went back to digging up the sand. Amelia and I waded out of the creek and sat on the bank in the sun.

Eyes on her children, Amelia hugged her knees to her chest. "What am I going to do, Honey?"

"Well, for one thing, how about telling Sheriff Rameros Joe violated the restraining order?"

She shook her head. "If I call the police on Joe, he'll get back at me somehow. Some way."

"If you don't, you know what can happen."

She picked up a handful of pebbles. One at a time, they dropped from her fingers.

"Did Joe say when he'd be back?" No point in even asking "if."

"He wasn't sure. He has to borrow his cousin's car."

"Good. I'll pray it gets four flats."

She laughed, warming my heart.

Pail in hand, Joey struggled out of the creek and up the bank to us. He flipped the pail upside down, dumping its contents like a love offering at his momma's feet.

"Thanks, sweetheart." She kissed his wet cheek. "Want to get me another one?"

Eager to please, he dashed back into the water.

Tears shone in Amelia's eyes. "I'm worried, Honey, and not over Joe alone. I've got to find a job. My money's about run out."

I understood how worried felt and squeezed her hand. "Something you could do from home might be good."

She nodded. "That's my thinking too. All I know how to do is waitress and take care of little ones. So I thought maybe I'd open a daycare center. You know, take care of some tots for pay. Put an ad in the paper."

"Why not? Sounds good. When I get back to the office, I can check to see if your street is zoned for business. And if the town has any licensing restrictions."

"Oh." Her face fell. "I never thought of all that."

"No, no, it's a good idea. Just let me do a background check first."

"Or I could work nights at the roadhouse. If Joe's mom would sleep over or something. Either way, thanks to you, I don't have to worry about the house for a while."

"Oh, I was happy to. . . ."

She tore her eyes away from the boys for a moment to send me a sly little grin. "Mr. Dwyer may be helping me, but he's doing it for you."

"Me?"

"Yes, you. Showing what a good man he is, and you know something? He is. The next thing, he'll be asking you out."

I laughed. "You're late. He already has."

That grin of hers spread ear to ear. "You went, I hope."

"Once."

"And?"

"I turned down a second date."

"Oh, no. He's a great catch. Go for it."

Jimmy came toddling up from the creek. A shiny stone sitting atop a creek-side boulder caught his notice, and not to be outdone by his brother, he plucked it off the boulder and laid it, like a cherry on a cupcake, atop the pile of sand.

"For me?" Amelia asked.

He stuck a finger in his mouth and nodded.

"Give me a hug."

He did, pressing his chunky little body into hers, soaking her shirt up to the neck. She didn't seem to mind. If anything, she hugged him tighter.

As I glanced over at them, I noticed the sun's rays were running through Jimmy's yellowish cherry stone as if it was glass. Curious, I picked it up and held it out to Amelia.

"Look at this."

She turned the pebble over in her palm. "You can almost see through it."

"Yes." Near the boulder where Jimmy found it, half sunk in the sand, another stone like the first caught my eye, and I reached for it. Like the first, this one shot out pinpricks of light each time I moved my hand.

If polished, these pebbles would shine like stars. Hey, wait a minute. My heart skipped a beat. No, they couldn't be. Not possible. That was downright silly, still. . . .

"You ever hear of anybody finding diamonds around here?" I asked.

"Never." Amelia chuckled. "That's a funny question. Why do you ask?"

"Because I have a crazy idea that's what these might be."

"You mean it?"

We stared at them, held fast by the possibility hidden in each lump of stone.

"Cleaned up, I wonder what they'd look like?"

"I don't know. There's never been a diamond sighting in these parts, though down in Murfreesboro, folks have been finding them for years. It's kind of a tourist attraction. You pay a few dollars for some panning equipment and anything you find, you keep." She shrugged. "But Murfreeboro's a long way from here."

"True, but suppose, just suppose, these are real diamonds. Why, people would be pounding on Violet Norton's door, begging her to sell the farm to them."

Amelia nodded. "That would be a good

thing. The poor ol' soul's been living hand to mouth for years. Her husband passed last month. He wasn't much, but he was all she had. Sad to think about."

"Maybe Violet's luck has changed. But no point in getting her hopes up for nothing. So if it's agreeable with you, I'll take the stones to a jeweler before we say anything."

"I don't object to that."

A sudden scream shattered the calm.

"Momma, blood!" Joey yelled. "My foot, my poor foot."

"Uh-oh." Amelia leaped to the rescue. "He's hurt."

I dropped the stones into the pocket of my cutoffs and hurried after her, not caring just then whether or not I had a fistful of pebbles or a pocketful of diamonds.

CHAPTER TEN

The following morning, I called Amelia to see how Joey was feeling.

"Just fine. He's back to rocketing through the house."

Cheered by that good news, I phoned Mrs. Otis to say I wouldn't be in until tomorrow. Since I'd chalked up two sales in less than a week, I figured taking another personal day wouldn't be too upsetting to Ridley's Real Estate. Also, I needed time away from the office to get used to my new normal. Employment by a soon-to-be-married Sam Ridley.

Then I combed my closet for city clothes. Black skirt suit, an ivory silk shell, and patent-leather heels. At Christmas I'd splurged on what the consignment shop called a "gently used" Kate Spade bag in wide black and ivory stripes. The one bitty spot hardly showed. With my hair brushed straight to my shoulders, pearl studs and a fake tank watch, the outfit was as city as I could manage.

Not far from the University of Arkansas campus, Franconia Jewelers turned out to be a small store with a glittery front window. As I peered in, I'll admit all the sparkly stones had me a tad frazzled. A salesman in a double-breasted suit with a red silk handkerchief peeking out of his jacket pocket saw me looking and buzzed me in. He was all smiles until I took the little cloth sack from my Kate Spade and shook the two unpolished stones onto the glass countertop.

"These are?" He arched a brow.

"My goodness, I haven't the faintest idea." I laid on the Southern. "That's what I was hoping an expert like you could tell me."

He smiled again, briefly, and held a jeweler's glass to his eye. While he made a study of first one stone and then the other, I stared at the sparkling gems in the display case. It was all I could do not to tap a toe.

Finally, he set down the glass and placed the stones on a velvet mat laid out for that purpose. "Uncut gems like these aren't a household item. Do you mind telling me where you got them?"

Gems. Fluttering my lashes to soften the blow, I borrowed Matt's favorite line. "I'm afraid I'm not at liberty to say."

"I see." He drew himself upright and looked at me down the long shaft of his nose. "Well, in my opinion, they are diamonds. Yellow. Not of the first quality. And the smaller stone contains a few flaws. But that said, they're the real deal."

Not wanting him to know my knees had gone to mush, I leaned on the counter for support. "What might they be worth if polished and cut and everything?"

He cleared his throat. "We don't do that kind of work here."

"I'm just saying. . . ."

"It's hard to establish a price, with accuracy that is, until after they're cut. Cutting releases the color and clarity, and both affect value." He raised the glass to his eye and gave the bigger stone another peek. "I see no major flaws." He lowered the glass and the stone to the countertop. "If you're lucky, and this turns out to be a fancy yellow, it would probably fetch several thousand dollars, retail. And the other one?" He shrugged. "Every jeweler has a cupful of small diamonds. They have many uses."

"That's wonderful news."

"Indeed." He tore his gaze from the stones to rivet it on me. "Do you wish to sell them?"

"You'd be interested?"

"I could be."

"That's very kind of you." I scooped up the stones and dropped them into the little sack. "But they're not for sale. I'm acting on behalf of the owner." I put the pouch in my bag and zipped it. "Should she be inclined to sell, though, I'll ask that she contact you first."

"And you are?"

"Miss Smith. Miss Molly Smith."

Though a shadow of doubt filmed his eyes, like any good salesperson, he wasn't ready to give up on a possible customer. "Until that happy day, may I interest you in something else?" He glanced at my wrist and sniffed the way you do when you detect a rank odor. "A new watch, perhaps?"

"Wouldn't that be lovely? But my daddy gave me this one years ago, and I'm not happy unless it's on my wrist." I waved a hand at his glittering display cases. "Y'all are in the love business, so I know you understand my sentiment."

"Completely, Miss, ah, Smith."

I think he understood only too well, but he shook my outstretched hand and escorted me to the front door, smiling all the way. I really didn't feel guilty telling him that lie about the watch. No need for him to know Daddy never gave me much of anything except maybe a backhand to the fanny. But would he have been as smiley if he knew I had kind of swiped them . . . those diamonds?"

CHAPTER ELEVEN

I hurried to my car, excited as all get out to know the stones were diamonds but still wondering why they were out on that boulder by Norton Creek. Washed up by a winter storm? Or proof of a new Arkansas diamond field? Unlikely answers, both of them. The winter had been mild, and besides, Eureka Falls wasn't on the same glacial ridge, or volcanic pipe, or whatever force of nature had created the Murfreesboro diamonds. *Hmm.* And to think we found them right by the path everyone took to get to the water.

My heels pounding the sidewalk slowed to a crawl as the same nasty thought from yesterday popped up stronger than ever. Suppose someone playing head games had planted the diamonds right where they'd most likely be found? A crazy notion, but I couldn't shake it.

People brushed past me while I plodded

on, unable to keep denying the question when the answer seemed clear. To sweeten a land deal. Which meant little ol' Violet Norton was likely mixed up in a swindle. At that, I balked. Surely not Violet. But if my hunch was correct, somebody had done the dirty.

A woman carrying a heavy shopping bag knocked into me, bringing me back to the moment. I'd never solve the problem standing on a Fayetteville sidewalk. Anyway, I didn't have time to dwell on what Momma would have called my "troubles." I still had to find International Properties, LLC.

I unlocked the car, slid in, and set the GPS for IP. The lady with the bedroom voice led me down Razorback Road, through a bunch of confusing turns and more traffic than Eureka Falls saw in a month. Finally, "Take your next right, Downtown Square is five hundred feet ahead."

The Square was a flower-filled block crisscrossed with brick walkways and lined with Victorian-era buildings that had shops on the bottom floors and what appeared to be offices above. My target, 1990 Center Street, a modern office complex snugged in the middle of all the stone gingerbread, was easy enough to spot. Inside, the lobby had an atrium with a soaring ceiling and the State of Arkansas logo embedded in its marble floor. Like an island in the middle of a sea, an information desk sat plumb in the center of the space.

"Good morning, I'm looking for International Properties," I said to the gorgeous receptionist.

"Yes, ma'am." She pointed a crimson nail at a bank of hammered bronze elevators against the far wall. "IP is in our penthouse. That last car will take you directly there."

"Oh, good. Like I always say, an express is better than a local, don't you agree?"

She gave me a blank stare. "Yes, ma'am."

Another ma'am. Maybe it was the black suit.

I rode alone to the top floor and stepped out onto a hall carpet so thick my patent leathers sank in halfway up the heels. Straight ahead on a sleek dark door, International Properties, LLC, was printed in gold and below, in slightly smaller letters, C.T. Ames, President. In the anteroom, another supermodel sat behind yet another information desk. This one had a glass top that allowed visitors to ogle her legs, should they be so inclined.

Busy on the phone, she glanced up and raised a forefinger for me to wait. When the call ended, she asked, "May I help you?"

"Yes. Mr. Ames, please."

"Do you have an appointment?"

Uh-oh. The hurdle I've been expecting.

"No, but I've come all the way from Eureka Falls just to see him."

"Sorry, but —"

I plucked a business card from my purse and handed it to her. We were alone, but I lowered my voice anyway. "Mr. Ames and I were involved in a murder case last week. We really need to talk about it. There's been a new development."

"A murder?" Her full, pouty lips parted. "That's a highly unusual reason to —"

"Oh, I know, but if you give him that message, I'm sure he'll spare me a few minutes from his busy schedule."

"Well, for a murder, he just might. I'll go ahead and ring his personal assistant for you."

"Thank you so much."

"You're welcome, ma'am."

Ma'am. *I give up.*

While she murmured into the phone, I took a seat and flipped through a copy of *Forbes* magazine, settling on a piece titled, "What Is Your Financial Future?" *Lordy, wouldn't I love to know?* But it was hard to concentrate on tomorrow, what with wondering about today. After Mr. Ames practically ran away from me in the Eureka Falls Police Station, I couldn't be sure he'd give me even a moment of his time. The uncertainty had my pulse revved up a bit, but I had no intention of leaving without speaking to him. The woman I'd found shot to death was from Fayetteville and so was he. A shaky connection, but the only one I had. As a person of interest in a murder, a *murder,* I had questions and every right to ask them.

Besides, to be honest, I was curious about something else. Why did Mr. Ames buy the Hermann farm from Ridley's and then go to Winthrop's for Sloane's acres? Not for a minute did I believe it was because I had accidentally knocked him out. And now, Violet Norton's farm, which happened to sit next door to those very Sloane acres, was sprouting uncut diamonds.

The office phone rang. Mr. Ames saying he'd see me now? I glanced over at the receptionist, hoping . . . but no. In that oh-what-a-delightful-surprise kind of voice, she cooed, "Wonderful to talk to you, Senator. For you, sir, he's always in. Oh, I'm just fine. So nice of you to ask. I'll ring him immediately, sir." Smiling, pink in the cheeks, she worked her keyboard. "Mr. Ames, the senator is on line one."

The senator. I set the magazine on the coffee table and strolled over to her desk.

"Excuse me." Still pink-cheeked, she looked up. "Honest to Betsy, I wasn't eavesdropping, but I couldn't help overhearing. Was that our handsome Senator Prescott Lott you were just speaking to?"

She sent the closed corporate doors a quick glance over one shoulder before nodding. "Yes, ma'am. The same."

"Isn't he wonderful?" I gushed.

"Oh, I couldn't agree more. So charming. So down-to-earth." She lowered her voice to a whisper. "He never has his aide put me on hold. Always places the calls himself. How many important people do *that*?"

I shook my head.

"He's the only one I know of."

"Imagine."

"Exactly. The man has my vote forever." As she leaned over to whisper a little more, her low-cut top gaped open. We were wearing the same style bra, though the straps on mine weren't under nearly the same strain.

A little more girl talk and I returned to my chair to try and figure out the meaning of what I'd just heard. Interesting that Senator Lott did business with IP. Placed all the calls himself too. A good way to keep them quiet.

One of the mahogany doors at the rear of the reception area swung open. A short, balding man with gold-rimmed glasses stepped out and strode over to me. Was he or wasn't he? They looked much alike, yet not quite the same. Unsure, I stood and held out a hand. "Mr. Ames?"

"Yes." His handshake was so brief, I knew he hadn't wanted to touch me. "You're Miss Ingersoll?"

"Yes, Honey Ingersoll. We met last week, remember?"

He sent me a tired, I've-done-this-before kind of smile. "No. We've never met, Miss Ingersoll."

"But you —"

"You met my brother, Charles. I'm Chester Ames."

Ah. "His twin."

"Very perceptive." He managed another weary smile. "People are constantly making that mistake. It stopped being amusing years ago." He checked his watch, though I could have told him it was two fifteen. "How may I help you?"

I guess this was what some folks would call a city type of question. Kind of cold with no invitation to step into his office and

99

no polite request to please take a seat, ma'am. He wanted to brush me off like lint on his Sunday coat. All right, I could play a game with those rules. So I went all wily on him, like folks do when a stranger comes down the pike.

Using big words, I said, "I'm just paying a neighborly call, Mr. Ames. After Charles bought a Eureka Falls property last week, I learned that a nearby parcel is going on the market. It's an outstanding opportunity, so I thought I'd give him, and you, the chance to acquire it."

Not certain the Sloane family's land was even on sale, I was way out of line here. Risking my realtor's license, too. But the possibility of a link between Tallulah's murder and the fact some rough acres nobody had wanted for years were now sought-after property made me press on.

"I have no idea what you're talking about, Miss Ingersoll. Charles is not employed by this firm."

"Oh, my goodness, how embarrassing." I allowed my jaw to go slack. "Don't tell me I'm plumb wrong."

He sent me one of those snippy smiles, the kind that tells someone she's stupid without saying a thing. "Charles occasionally consults for us, but that's the extent of his involvement."

"Since you're kin and all, I imagine he told you what happened in Eureka Falls."

He hesitated. "He told me something of it, yes."

"Then you know why I want to reach him."

"You did business together. Didn't he give you any contact information?"

"A cell phone number and a P.O. box address is all."

"That's perfectly legal, Miss Ingersoll, when a piece of real estate is sold for cash."

So he knows the terms of the sale, does he?

I stiffened and drew myself up to my full five-feet-five inches. And that was without heels. "If it hadn't been legal, Mr. Ames, I wouldn't have sold him the Hermann farm."

He bristled at that. Had he been wearing a pair of work pants, I do believe he'd have given them a hitch. "Is there a problem concerning the sale?"

"Glory be, of course there's a problem. We're both persons of interest in a murder case. That's another reason why I need to talk to him."

"Whatever he has to say, he'll tell the police." His voice took on a hard edge. Too bad. I wasn't about to leave yet.

"Just before the victim was killed, she told me she was from Fayetteville. Charles may have known her. It's a slim chance, but —"

"Impossible. Charles hasn't lived here in thirty-five years." Then he clamped his lips together as if he'd already said too much.

"That's strange. His P.O. box has a Fayetteville address."

"I'm a busy man, Miss Ingersoll, so you'll have to excuse me. I'm afraid I can't help you."

"There is one way you can."

Half turned on his heel, he glanced back and frowned. "How?"

"Would you kindly have Charles call me? He has my number."

"I'll see what I can do." With a brief dip of his head, he stomped past the reception desk, hurried through the mahogany door, and slammed it behind him.

I picked up my purse, said goodbye to the supermodel, and left International Properties, sure Chester would tell Charles I'd been looking for him and equally sure Charles would never call.

No matter. I'd learned a lot today. For one thing, if Charles knew Tallulah any better than I did, that was what my daddy would call a long shot. For another, IP had regular dealings with Senator Prescott Lott.

And, while letting on that he was acting for himself, Charles Ames secretly bought up properties for his brother's business. Then, to thicken the pudding, Violet Norton's farm up there on Pea Pike, with the Hermanns' and the Sloanes', was sprouting diamonds.

Something was afoot, maybe legal, maybe not, but darned interesting. I couldn't wait to get back to Eureka Falls and tell Sam and Matt what I'd found out.

As soon as I got to the car, I plucked the cell out of my purse and checked voicemail. Four were from Ridley's Real Estate. The first three were Mrs. Otis with routine office details. On the fourth, Sam's voice came roaring through the line. "Where the hell are you, Honey? I'm worried sick. Return this call as soon as you get it. The police are swarming all over town looking for you."

CHAPTER TWELVE

Thrilled that Sam cared enough to worry about me, I raced home, practically floating on air the whole way. Though I drove five miles over the limit, no sirens wailed along the highway and no blue lights flashed in my rearview mirror. I'd almost decided Sam had spun me a yarn when, on the edge of town, a familiar cruiser slid into traffic behind the Lincoln. It hugged that position until we both reached Ridley's parking lot. Matt Rameros and I stepped out of our vehicles at the same time, my door slamming shut in echo to his. He didn't waste a minute stomping over to me.

"Where've you been?" he demanded in a voice without a trace of Mexicali warmth. "I told you not to leave town without telling me first."

"I was on personal business."

He stood, legs apart, both hands on hips, the right cradling his holster. "I also told you not to do anything stupid. Don't you listen? The state police have been here looking for you. They're not happy you couldn't be found."

"I went to a jewelry store in Fayetteville, I didn't —"

"Jewelry store?" His dark eyes smoldered, angry hot. "At a time like this —"

"You don't understand."

"You've got that straight. I don't."

"Well, if you'd just listen up for a second. . . ."

He blinked as though I'd smacked him right between the eyes. "You get an engagement ring or something?" He stared at my left hand, looking so upset I smiled, even though I didn't want to.

"Would you care if I did?"

"I'm asking the questions. So what were you doing there?"

"Do I have to answer that?"

"No. I'm asking as a friend."

I pointed to the hand covering his holster. "Some friendly chitchat we're having. You've been cradling that gun since you stepped out of the cruiser."

"Reflex action." He let go of the Glock and folded his arms across his chest.

I sighed. "Better, but not by much. Why are you holding yourself like that?"

"My crossed arms indicate that I'm keeping a barrier between us."

"Whatever for?"

With an exasperated swipe of his hand, he tilted his uniform hat farther back on his forehead. "Otherwise I might wring your neck. Or . . ." his ruddy face flushed.

"Or what?"

"Kiss you." Without checking to see if anyone was watching, he grabbed me and pressed my back against the Lincoln. His mouth came down hard, crushing my lips against his. Then, softening, his mouth opened, and his tongue darted out, tasting, wanting, the surprise of his move stripping away my protest, along with my breath.

He let me go, finally, and stood panting in front of me.

I blew out a breath and sucked it right back in. Ignoring my trip-hammer heart, I glared at him. "I ought to have you up on charges."

"Yes, you should." He took off his hat and ran a shirt sleeve across his forehead. "My deepest apologies, Honey. I thought you were in some kind of trouble today, and that made me a little crazy. It won't happen again."

"No?" A stab of disappointment shot through me. It had been a long time since a man had kissed me like that, as if he wanted me, body and soul. Though I'd vowed to keep my life free of men and their demands, how could I not respond? After all, I wasn't dead. Far from it. Besides, I liked Matt. I liked him a lot, and seeing him so remorseful, I couldn't stay vexed. To show there were no hard feelings, I put a hand on his arm and squeezed.

He glanced at it. "No rings," he said softly.

"Not a single one."

"Am I forgiven?"

"Of course. What's a little kiss between friends?"

His face fell. "You know something, Honey, I've got a lot of friends. Josie, Zach, Mrs. Otis, to name a few, and I've never kissed a one of them, not once, and for damn sure not like I just kissed you." He jammed his hat on his head. "Now, let's go in and see your boss. You've had him half nuts all day too."

CHAPTER THIRTEEN

While Matt got on his cell phone to notify the Arkansas State Police that a person of interest in the Bixby murder had been located, I went over to give Mrs. Otis a hug.

"My goodness," she declared. "Wait till Mr. Ridley sees you. He's been beside himself all day."

With that music ringing in my ears, I knocked on Sam's office door, and at his quiet "It's open," I peeked in, not quite knowing what to expect.

He looked up, dropped his pen, and leaped to his feet. "Honey. You're all right!"

" 'Course I am. What's everybody so upset about, anyway?"

He came charging around the edge of his desk, coming to a halt a foot or so away from me. I could have reached out and touched him, but I didn't dare. One touch and I wouldn't have been able to stop.

"When the police tell you not to leave

town without notifying them, that's what that means. Instead, you skip off to Fayetteville, and nobody knows where the hell you are."

"I'm sorry."

"That's all you've got to say?" He stepped in closer, so close I could see every lash fringing his eyes. "Do you realize I've had cops in and out of here all day?"

"That couldn't have been good for business," I murmured.

"Screw the business. I thought you were lying in a ditch somewhere with a bullet in your head."

If he meant to kiss me, now was the time, and I swore he came close to grabbing me and sending me on a trip to the moon. But, like in a Grade B movie, someone knocked on his office door and the moment shattered like a piece of cracked glass.

"Come in," he yelled.

Darn. Matt's timing sure was off.

Wrong. Matt was out in the main reception area, pacing around, his cell locked to his ear. Sam's visitor was none other than his fiancée, Miss Lila Lott.

A stunning Lila Lott, smiling her perfect smile, her perfect hair dark and glossy to her perfect shoulders, her perfect designer dress hugging, not too tightly, her perfectly toned curves.

"Darling!" Arms open wide, Sam rushed to embrace her. I closed my eyes, opening up only when he said, "Honey Ingersoll, this is Lila Lott."

She held out long, tapered fingers beautifully manicured with colorless polish. In comparison, my ruby reds looked kind of shouty. Thank the Lord I hadn't let Mitsy at the salon put little razorbacks on the pinkies like she wanted to.

After wiping my sweaty palms on my skirt, I shook her hand. It was cool to the touch. What about her feet, say, on a cold winter night? Well, that I'd never know, but I couldn't help noticing she was everything I was not. Sleek and polished as a gem, the kind of girl life's down and dirty had never touched. I'd lay odds she'd never been punched in the face by a thuggy boyfriend.

"May I call you Honey?" she asked.

"Why I'd surely be delighted if you would," I answered, sweet as all get out. Then I waited. And waited. In vain. No sweet words came flying my way saying, "Do call me Lila." It figured. In her eyes, I was only Sam's employee, not someone she cared to have as a first-name acquaintance. I suppose I could have turned the question around and asked if I could call her Lila.

But I wasn't sure what a well-bred lady would do at such a time, so I didn't bother. Or dare. The truth? Dare.

Basic greetings over, she wasted no time switching her attention back to Sam. I couldn't blame her. "Darling, I was hoping you'd be free to join me for a cocktail. It has to be five o'clock somewhere." She gave a little carefree laugh.

I wanted to kill her.

"You know I never need an excuse to be with you. But you've caught me at an awkward time." He glanced up as Matt strode in. "We're expecting the state police any minute now. Isn't that right, Sheriff?"

Matt nodded. "Yes, but you've already spoken to them, Sam. So feel free to leave, if you wish. I'll keep Honey company until the officers arrive."

Looking doubtful, for which I wanted to leap over the furniture and kiss him everywhere, Sam grabbed his jacket off the back of his chair and shrugged into it.

Before taking Lila by the arm, he came up to me and stared into my eyes. "You have nothing to worry about, Honey. I'll back you all the way."

Matt spread his legs, big city lawman style. "You can count on me, too."

"Good." With a farewell nod, Sam escorted Lila out into the sunshine, her laughter floating in the air behind them like an odor wafting on the breeze. And it wasn't roses.

I sank onto the chair across from Sam's desk, aware that all the air had gone out of the room along with him.

Eyeing me carefully, Matt arched a brow. "What?"

"You outshine her a million to one."

"I don't know what you're talking about."

"You're such a lousy liar, I hope you tell the state police the truth and nothing but. Otherwise, they'll see right through you."

Out by Mrs. Otis' desk, the front door clattered open.

"Here they come."

CHAPTER FOURTEEN

I didn't lie to them. Not so's you'd notice. I said I'd gone to Fayetteville to do a little shopping and to call on a client, International Properties. My purpose? To see if they might be interested in Sloane's acres, a parcel of land I understood would soon be on the market. When they asked where I'd shopped, I supplied the name and address of Franconia Jewelers but didn't mention the appraisal. If they interviewed the jeweler, they'd find out, but by then the stones would be back in Violet Norton's hands.

Anyway, after thanking me for my statement and politely asking me to notify Sheriff Rameros if I decided to do any more traveling, they marched out of Ridley's Real Estate, setting the floorboards in the old building vibrating under their heavy boots.

Alone with Matt, I slumped in the chair, my brave front draining away like water down a gulley. "All those questions. Do they really think I killed Tallulah?"

"They're doing their job, is all. Like I said, once they eliminate you and Mr. Ames as possible suspects, they'll probe elsewhere. I don't see that you have anything to worry about."

He strolled behind the desk and sat in the swivel chair, the look on his face somewhere between a frown and a smile. "Can you take one more question?" His voice challenged like he was inviting me to a shootout. "You don't have to answer unless you want to."

"Ask away."

"How do I look in Sam's place?"

I tipped my head to one side, pretending to study him like he was a new client I was trying to size up. "A little darker, a little shorter, maybe a tad heavier, but every bit as handsome."

"Darker and shorter, true. Heavier . . . yeah, probably. But just as handsome, no way." As if sharing a secret he didn't trust anyone else to hear, he leaned in closer. "I've known all along Sam's the reason you keep turning me down. I don't believe for a second it's because you don't like the way I look. You're not that shallow." The hint of a smile flitted across his face. "Actually, you're not shallow at all."

"I wasn't lying to you. You *are* handsome.

It's just that. . . ."

He held up his hands, palms out. "No need to explain. This isn't an interrogation." He stood. "Since you've told the police everything you know —"

"Not quite."

"What?" He sank onto the swivel so suddenly the springs squealed in protest. "There's more?"

I nodded. Reaching into my purse, I removed the little cloth sack and emptied the diamonds onto the desktop.

Brows meshing, he picked one up. "This isn't —"

"Yes, it is."

"A diamond?"

"Um-hmm."

He placed it carefully back on the desk. "Where did you get these?"

"On the Norton farm. Out by the creek."

He looked up. *Bam.* His eyes flaring like headlights. "You stole them?"

"Not exactly."

Swiveling like mad, he listened to my story then brought the chair to a squeaky halt. "You should have told State everything. And I mean everything."

"But I found the stones on a different piece of property. Not the Hermann Farm. There's no connection."

"You don't know that. Even details that seem unrelated may be important. This isn't some kind of game we're playing here. We're looking for a murderer."

"But I didn't —"

A hand went up for silence. "I know you didn't do it. You're not capable of murder. More to the point, you have no motive. It's entirely possible, make that probable, the boys from State don't think so either. But the governor wants a conviction. And what about Senator Lott? The man's considering a run for president, for God's sake. If you think he'll tolerate having an unsolved capital crime in his own hometown, think again. Bottom line, the investigation's going to heat up, and when it does, it'll sizzle. Also," his finger jabbed the air, "do I have to tell you the fewer reasons to consider you a suspect, the better?"

"No, but —"

He waved an irritated hand, brushing away my protest like it was a mosquito. Too vexed to stop, he sucked in a quick breath. "Crap like having stolen diamonds appraised out of town is just plain foolhardy. And I'm using mild language here. You got that?"

I sat silent as anger turned Matt's jaw into concrete and his words into bullets. I'd never seen him this fired up, though that wasn't what scared me. I'd known angry men all my life. His words were what had me frightened. I must have turned as white as my momma's best bed sheet, for his jaw softened and he heaved a sigh. "You're scared now. Maybe that's not such a bad thing."

"I thought being innocent meant I wasn't in any kind of trouble. I had no idea —"

"You're not in trouble. Yet. The point is to stay out of it. So here's what you're going to do." He waited a second, no doubt for a protest so he could shoot it down, but my teeth were busy biting my bottom lip. "First thing in the morning, pay a call on Violet. Tell her about your find and leave these pebbles with her."

"Pebbles? They're worth thousands."

He ignored my outburst. "Should the state police interview this Franconia Jewelry guy, they'll likely learn the reason for your visit, and guaranteed, you'll be in for another quizzing. How that will play out, I don't know, but I don't think any laws have been broken. Not if you show good intent by returning the stones before the loss is discovered." He nailed me with a stern, no nonsense glance. "Have I made myself clear?"

"Yes."

"Excellent. Now, let's call it a day."

Mrs. Otis had already left, so he waited while I locked up.

"Violet, first thing in the morning," he said as I dropped the key in my purse.

"Right."

"Good. Get some sleep tonight. You look like you could use it." Without another word, he gave me a snappy, two-fingered salute and strode toward the cruiser.

I watched him walk away, and despite my worries, I enjoyed the view. Even though his legs weren't as long as Sam's, he did his uniform proud. Having caused him so much trouble today, I was glad I hadn't mentioned giving the clerk in Franconia Jewelers a fake name. AKA. Like in the wanted posters hanging on the police-station wall.

CHAPTER FIFTEEN

As soon as I got home, I kicked off the heels, hung up the black suit, and stood under the shower until the water ran cold. All day I thought I'd been slick as an old-time mountain man, but maybe I'd only been acting the fool. Matt seemed to think so. As for Sam, the bath towel slipped to the floor as it dawned on me. I hadn't had a chance to tell him much of anything.

Darn. I could call him at home, but the day's events were too prickly to go into over the phone. And what if Lila picked up? Why go there? My news would hold until morning. I'd call Amelia. She'd be anxious to know about The Big Find.

Shivering and squeaky clean, I tossed an old chenille robe over an outsized U of A T-shirt — the shoulders came to my elbows, the hem to my knees — and dug the cell out of my purse.

Before punching in Amelia's number, I

glanced at the kitchen clock. Eight p.m. With any luck, the boys would be in bed, or hunkered down in front of the TV, so we could talk. When she picked up, sure enough her "hello" was hushed.

"It's me," I said, keeping my voice to a whisper too, for some reason.

"Who?"

"Me," I repeated, my voice louder now. "Can you talk?"

"Just for a minute." Her voice was still low. "I have a guest."

"Sounds interesting."

"Uh-huh. Cletus Dwyer stopped by. Isn't that nice?"

"Lovely." *Hmm.* "Don't do anything I wouldn't do."

"Oh, for heaven's sake." That was louder. "We're talking about my business plan. You know, starting a daycare."

"Uh-huh."

"What's that supposed to mean? You forgot about my mortgage?"

"No, no. I know the bank won't wait forever."

"Exactly." Then she whispered again, "What are they? You know, the —"

"Diamonds. Not perfect but valuable. First thing in the morning, I'm bringing them over to Violet." As if Cletus could hear me, I dropped my voice. "Not a word to anyone, okay?"

"Certainly not." She sounded miffed, as if I shouldn't even suggest such a thing.

"Well, you know, girl talk and all."

"Come by for coffee when you have a chance, and we'll have us some real girl talk. I have to go now. Cletus is waiting."

"See you soon." I pressed End and lowered the phone slowly. Was I the only person in Eureka Falls who was alone tonight? I snugged the robe closer and tightened the belt at my waist. No! No way would I fall into the self-pity trap. My life was good, better than good. I had everything I needed, almost, and in a year or so, I'd have saved enough to make a down payment on a house of my own. If I never found anyone to share it with, well, a life lived alone was better than a life filled with woe. My momma knew that, God rest her soul, and Amelia. Though, as a reward for their suffering, both Momma and Amelia had children. I had no one. At least no one who mattered to me right down to the ground he stood on. No one I could lay claim to, that is.

One hand on the fridge handle, I swatted a tear sneaking along my cheek. "Suck it up, Honey." I yanked open the fridge door.

As Matt had made clear, I'd scrambled a few laws today, so why not complete the trend and scramble a couple of eggs? Tomorrow would be different. Tomorrow was Diamond Day.

The next morning, I suited up in a lavender outfit and put my hair in a French twist. The magazines said you couldn't go wrong with a French twist, so once in a while I rolled my hair into one, though I didn't like them much. For a color boost, I slid on my favorite shoes, red stilettos with open toes. They looked real good with the suit but — I couldn't put my finger on it — not quite right. So I switched to some plain beige pumps instead. Anyway, in the suit and pumps and my hair all knotted up like that, I drove out to see Violet Norton and share the good news.

The Norton house, a kissing cousin to the Sloane place one farm over, stood on a sandy rise. In the front yard, a big ol' rooster strutted around, pecking at the ground, and nearby, motor running, sat a Eureka Falls police cruiser. As I pulled up and parked, Matt got out from behind the wheel and strode over to me.

"You stalking me, Sheriff?" I stepped out of the Lincoln.

"No. I came by to see Miz Norton." He upped his chin at the house. "Feel free to go in. She's alone."

If he was checking on me, I didn't take offense. I'd said I'd be here this morning, and here I was. I strolled over to the porch. The hounds slung across it slit open their eyes a bit but were too lazy to leap up and scare me off. I patted the one draped on the top stair and climbed over him. Before I could rap on the door, it opened a crack. Tall and gaunt, with a soiled apron covering her cotton dress and a man's brown sweater over her shoulders, Violet peered out, staring at me without saying a word.

"Morning, Miz Norton, I'm Honey Ingersoll. I work for Sam Ridley. We sell real estate."

She pointed a gnarled finger at Matt. "That there po-lice officer told me you'd be by. Said he was waitin' to see you." She sniffed. "He's still lingerin' for some reason or other. Ain't he seen you?"

Ignoring her frown, I beamed a happy smile. "Yes, he has, but we'll talk later, after I show you something. Might I step in?"

"Wal, I don't know." She opened the door a bit wider, squinting to get a better look at me, the wrinkles around her eyes deepening into crevices. "Ain't you the gal that's mixed up in that murder? What all bidness you got with me?"

Beyond her, through the open door, I saw a tidy kitchen with a pump handle at the sink and two chairs near the eating table, its surface rubbed white from years of hard use.

"What I have to show you will only take a minute."

She hesitated, a lifetime of suspicion clouding her face.

"You won't be sorry," I coaxed.

"Long as I can remember, I been sorry for most things, so one more time won't make no difference either way." She turned and walked into the kitchen.

Taking that as my welcome, I stepped in and glanced around. A black monster of a wood-burning stove took up one wall and across from it stood the prettiest Welsh dresser I ever did see, its shelves stacked with rows of filled canning jars. Strawberry jam, onion relish, peach conserve.

"That's a mighty fine dresser."

"Yup," she said proudly. "My granddaddy made it hisself from pure memory. Said it was like his momma's back in the old country."

"Scotland?"

She nodded, having spoken more than she probably did most days. The poor ol' thing.

I'd be glad to give her some good news. Reaching into my purse, I pulled out the little cloth sack and walked over to the table with it. "Miz Norton, please come take a look at these."

Her expression blank, she came a few steps closer. I spilled the diamonds onto the tabletop. Streaming in through the narrow window, the sun's morning rays fingered the stones, firing up their dusty glow.

Eyes wide, she studied them long and hard, then glanced over at me. I could see why she'd been given her name. In their nest of wrinkles, her eyes were as deep a violet as any flower that grew.

"These are diamonds," I said, "and they're yours."

"What are you talking about, gal?" Her legs about to give way, she sank onto a chair at the table.

I took that as permission to sit too. "A friend and I found them over by the creek the other day. They were just lying there near a big boulder."

Excitement throbbed in her voice. "You found 'em on my land? They're mine?"

"Yes, ma'am."

With a shaky hand, she picked up a stone and held it to the light. "Reckon this is worth some money?"

"Yes, thousands." I fumbled in my purse for the card from Franconia Jewelers and laid it on the table. "This man said he'd buy them from you."

Clutching the stone in her fist, she smiled, revealing gaps where teeth had gone missing. "Well, slap me nekkid. I've got me a treasure, just like Henry claimed."

"Henry?"

"My husband. Before he passed, he always said we'd find diamonds on the land. Knew it in his bones." She opened her fist to gaze at the stones. "Reckon this makes the farm worth a lot more than I figured." Her glance snapped up. "Don't it?"

I shrugged. "Maybe. Maybe not."

"Maybe not? If this one bitty stone is worth thousands like you say, there's no telling how much a whole farm full of 'em might fetch."

"That's the problem, Miz Norton. You have to have the land tested, to prove these two diamonds weren't an accident, or washed up by a storm, or. . . ."

Cheeks flushed, she urged, "Go on. Or what?"

"Or planted. They were right by the path, on top of —"

She snorted. "Nobody's darned fool enough to leave diamonds sittin' around on

126

the ground."

"True, but —"

"No 'true buts' about it. I've got me diamonds on my land." Cackling with glee, she clutched my wrist with her gnarly fingers. "No more dillydallyin' around. I aim to sell the place." She waved a hand at the weedy fields outside the window. "With Henry gone, the land didn't get planted this year. And the way things are headed, it won't no time soon neither. So I can't see that I got much choice, and you strike me as an honest gal. So you want to bring the buyers to me? You and Sam Ridley?"

I slid my hand out from under hers. "Without proof, you can't put your farm on the market and tell people there's diamonds on it."

"You got something wrong. I'm not planning on telling nobody nothin'. If folks hear there's diamonds out here, it ain't going to be from me." She sent me a sly smile. "All's I plan to do is ask my price."

"Listing is one thing. Selling is another." I stared straight into those glittery violet eyes so there'd be no mistaking my intent. "If you spread a false story around, you'll be messing with the law. You want that kind of grief?"

Stony silence. Lord knows, this shrewd ol'

woman in a man's sweater looked like she needed every penny she could lay her hands on, inside or outside the law. But the scam I was pretty sure she was cooking up could land us both in prison.

I placed a second card, my own, on the table and used some fancy words so's she'd know I wasn't joshing. "If you agree to have the soil tested by a geologist, it's quite possible Mr. Ridley would be happy to have his firm represent you. Without one, however, I'm afraid we can't accept your offer."

"Wal, I never —"

I stood and picked up my purse. "Do let us know your plans, Miz Norton." I pointed to my business card. "I'm in the office most days. Or can be reached on my cell wherever I am."

"Cell?"

"Oh, right." No electronics. I should have remembered. Overhead a single bulb dangled from the beamed ceiling, along with bundles of herbs she'd probably collected in the fields and hung from the rafters to dry. "Well, suppose we leave it this way. I'll give Mr. Ridley your message, and if he's interested, we'll contact you. Will that work?"

"Makes no never mind to me. I'm set on selling, and that's what I'll do."

"You want to end up in jail?"

My only answer was the rock-like set of Violet's chin.

With a "thank you for your time," I said goodbye, and careful not to step on the dogs, I stomped off the porch. How on earth did the ol' girl manage to live way out here with no modern conveniences? That sure proved how tough she was. I guess she had to be tough to survive this long. And though little more than a bag of bones with a lined face, she looked like a woman who intended to live on for a good long while yet.

CHAPTER SIXTEEN

Matt was still standing by his cruiser, not looking like he was in a hurry to patrol the highways or anything.

"I'm surprised you're still here." I headed over to him.

He gave me one of those easy smiles, the kind that built sort of slow but was worth waiting for. "Thought I'd stay on for a while, tell you how much I like your hair that way. Nice shoes too."

I tapped one of those shoes in the dust. "Get to it, Matt."

He let the smile go and cleared his throat. "Until this killer is found, could you sell houses on the other side of town for a while?"

My foot tapping picked up speed. "Suppose the killer is never found? You said there are no clues, no evidence. In the meantime, I have to earn a living."

"The operative word is living."

I pointed to Violet's cabin, where a thin spiral of smoke rose from the chimney. "If it's dangerous out here, then everybody who lives on the pike's at risk."

"Some folks don't have the luxury of avoiding the area. This is their home. But you have options. And one of them is to act like you're smart." He touched a finger to his hat brim and spun on his heel.

"Matt."

He looked back, stony faced.

"I'll only come out here again if I have to."

He nodded, expression unchanged. "If and when you do, call me first."

I was grateful he was looking out for me, but damn it, I sold real estate. That meant I had to chase sales. Every day. Still, he was right. No need to be foolhardy about it.

After following Matt down the rise, I swung onto Pea Pike and headed back to town. As I passed Sloane's acres, I nearly lurched to a stop. There was Saxby Winthrop, wearing a blue pin-striped suit with a red bow tie under his chin, hammering a SOLD sign into the ground.

Damn. I needed to talk to Sam. Faced with this news, he might agree to handle Violet's sale, if he could talk her into having the soil tested first. Maybe he'd even offer to pay a geologist himself. Or, double damn, he might decide to forget about the whole rocky ridge and let Saxby outfox us one rundown farm at a time. I didn't like that idea at all, but either way, we needed to talk. Keeping one hand on the wheel, I dug the cell out of my purse.

Mrs. Otis picked up on the first ring. "The boss isn't here, Honey. Said he'd be delayed until around ten."

"Please tell him I'll be in then. We have to talk. It's important."

"Will do."

I rang off and dropped the cell on the passenger seat. Delayed? *Humph.* In bed with Lila, more than likely. Well, he needed to put his pants on and get to work. Things were heating up around here.

At the corner of Main and Sycamore, I lucked out and found a parking spot near Josie's Diner. Just two eggs last night and nothing this morning had left me hollow. Inside the diner, the aroma of coffee and hotcakes perfumed the air. As usual, the place was hopping. With all the booths taken, I slid onto a stool at the counter between a Sears delivery guy and a housepainter, judging from his splattered overalls.

Josie sauntered over to me with her order pad at the ready.

"A hamburger, Josie, with mayo. Well done. Hold the lettuce and tomato. And a tall cola. No ice."

"For breakfast? What's the matter with grits, a few home fries, and a couple of easy-overs? And what about some coffee?"

"No, thanks."

"Tommy Lee's got a light touch with eggs. He makes 'em good."

I shook my head. "I've been eating a lot of eggs lately."

"A burger'll mess up his morning griddle, but maybe he won't mind for just one patty."

"Thanks, Josie. I need the reinforcement."

She yelled my order over to Tommy Lee. When he yelled back, "No way," she hollered, "Just do it, T.L." Tugging a bar towel from the waistband of her apron, she took a swipe at the countertop, studying me like I was some kind of school subject. "How're things going? You look a little peaked today. And why's your hair done up in that itty-bitty bun?"

"Big hair's out."

"Sez who?"

"Everybody."

She snorted. "Not that I've heard." Done with her swiping, she bent over the counter to whisper, "Got a hot tip for you."

"Oh?"

The painter had tossed some loose change on the counter and left. The Sears guy was too busy scarfing down his grits to listen.

She kept on whispering anyway. "Word's out that Violet Norton's putting her place on the market."

I nodded. "So I heard."

"Know what else?"

"No."

Josie glanced left then right. "Rumor is the land's worth a fortune. There's diamonds on it."

"Oh for God's sake, Josie. When did you hear that?"

"A few days ago. Her nephew, Earl, comes in here regular-like. Couldn't wait to tell me."

So, Violet, the sly old vixen, had known about those stones all along. She was playing a head game with everyone, including me. Figured. Josie got busy serving donuts to a couple of regulars, and I sipped my soda for a while.

"One burger, comin' up!" Josie slid a plate along the countertop. It skidded to a stop right in front of me.

"With wrists like that, you should be in the Olympics."

"Missed my callin', I guess."

"You believe Earl's story?" I said as she

refilled my glass without being asked.

"Not so you'd notice, but I'm not surprised."

I salted my burger real good, but before taking a bite, I paused. "Why not? A claim like that's pretty unusual, wouldn't you say?"

"Not for somebody married to Henry Norton all those years. He used to go down to that diamond field in Murfreesboro every chance he got. You know, the one where for a few bucks they let folks dig around looking for gold and stuff. Gems, too. Emeralds and the like."

Josie poured herself half a cup of coffee and took a sip. "You ask me, Henry should've forgotten about that prospectin' tomfoolery and taken better care of his fields. His place got run-down pretty bad. Violet hasn't had it easy, I can tell you that. So if she wants something out of life at last, can't say as I blame her. But I dunno, almost sounds like Henry found a few gem stones and sprinkled them around his farm."

Henry, *hmm.* Maybe that was the answer.

As she spoke, I made good progress on the burger. "Not to worry about Violet, Josie. No upstanding real estate agent will touch the place until it's inspected."

She polished off her coffee. "I don't know

about that. Saxby Winthrop was in here the day Earl spouted his story, and he acted mighty interested. Said he'd go out there and take a look around."

I finished the burger, every bite, washed it down with another soda, and said goodbye to Josie. Sam should have his pants on by now.

In our company parking lot out back of the building, Sam's black Lexus sat in the "Reserved for Owner" slot. *Good.* When I stepped inside, he was pacing the outer office like he was upset or something. A tiff with Lila? A nasty thought that I put down as soon as it reared its ugly head. I wanted him to be happy, didn't I? Yes. But in my heart of hearts, I didn't believe he'd find true happiness with an uppity bitch like Lila. And that thought I refused to kill as he hurried over to me.

"Honey, I've been waiting for you and getting mighty impatient doing so, I'm afraid. You never did tell me what happened yesterday."

"No, I didn't have a chance. It was five o'clock somewhere."

One of his brows quirked up. "I almost called you last night, but I don't like to bother employees on their off hours."

Employees. Right then, my pleasure at seeing him went straight to hell. "It would have been fine if you had."

A hand on my elbow, he steered me into his office, though I could have found my way there blindfolded. "Begin at the beginning," he said, "and don't leave anything out."

So I did, telling him nearly everything, even my alias. What I didn't mention was the senator's phone call to IP. That could have been about anything, or nothing. I had my suspicions, but that's all they were, suspicions, and the man was practically Sam's father-in-law. So I just stuck to the facts as I knew them. Anyway, he listened without interrupting, staring past me at the far wall, elbows out, hands cupped behind his head.

"Okay." He sat up straight and lowered his arms when I finished. "Let's start with International Properties." He held up a finger. "Number one, Charles Ames stretched the truth. Said he was self-employed, but in reality he's working for his brother, buying properties in his name and flipping them to IP. Not illegal, but sneaky. And as you know, a good way to buy on the cheap, one parcel at a time. The owners think they're selling to separate individuals when all along one buyer with megabucks and a hidden agenda is snapping up neighboring land at below market value."

"Two." Another finger. "Saxby has apparently sold Sloane's acres, presumably to this same Mr. Ames. A fact that can easily be verified. If so, IP now owns two rocky farms adjacent to each other. Combined, that makes for a large tract that, up till recently, was fairly worthless."

Third finger. "Now another parcel on that ridge, the Norton place, is going on the market soon, and from what Josie told you, Saxby is hot on the trail. An educated guess tells me he has an interested buyer in his pocket. This same Charles Ames, maybe, fronting for IP. Not knowing for certain bothers the hell out of me. I don't want to see our neighbors screwed over by some big brother. The question is if IP's in on it, what's their game?" His blue eyes darkened. "Does it have anything to do with that poor girl's death?"

I didn't butt in or try to answer his questions. He was thinking out loud, hoping to make sense out of a puzzle with pieces missing.

"As for Violet," a twinge of humor colored his voice, "the old girl's salted her land, has she?"

"Suppose she hasn't and —"

He snorted. "Not a chance. Does she think we just came off the pig farm? Henry Norton chased the magic rainbow his whole life. Sounds like his widow's picked up where he left off."

"Until that's proven —"

"I know. Don't worry, I won't leap to judgment."

"So what are we going to do then? Sit back and let Saxby scoop up her farm for IP?"

Male pride, that's what you had to appeal to. A lesson I learned before grade school, but that's another story.

"No!" Sam slapped his desktop. "We'll have the soil tested at my expense. Once the issue's settled, we'll convince Violet to sell the place for fair market value."

He glanced at his watch. "I've got to run. I'm showing the Triangle Office Building at noon. It's been hanging fire for so long I don't want to cancel the meeting."

He shrugged a navy blazer on over his white shirt, setting off his tan to a fare-thee-well. The tan, I couldn't help but notice, hadn't faded a bit. So, how much time had he and Lila spent by that New Orleans pool, anyway?

Halfway to the door, he paused and turned

back. "Sounds like you've gained Violet's trust. So why don't you give her a call and tell her about my offer? I know you'll come across as sweet as a birthday cake." He held up a warning finger. "If she refuses you, tell her that should the property be misrepresented to buyers, we'll notify the authorities."

My jaw sagged. "You'd call the cops on Violet?"

"Not on Violet. On Saxby Winthrop."

Ha! My jaw snapped right back up where it belonged.

As he hurried off, I remembered something. Violet didn't have a telephone.

Chapter Seventeen

After that sweet birthday-cake compliment, there was no refusing Sam's request. But it did mean a trip back out to the pike. And it also meant canceling a lunch-hour appointment.

My clients, both doctors at the Eureka Falls Emergency Care Center, were interested in what some folks might call a tarted-up cracker house. Maybe it was, but without lying a bit, I can testify that sassy-looking house had everything a heart could desire: an interior of nine thousand square feet, sky-high ceilings, custom-made built-ins, and granite surfaces everywhere. Not to mention a three-car garage and an in-ground pool. For someone in my business, clients like the docs, eager to tour a Mc-Mansion like that, were as precious as, well, diamonds.

Still, I did call and rebook, all the while apologizing up one side and down the other.

For Sam was right. If we didn't act fast, Saxby would be all over the Norton farm like ants at a picnic. He needed to be stopped before he sold the place as a diamond mine or else told someone a pack of lies and let them snap up the property on the cheap, thinking they'd made the steal of a lifetime. Fabulous commissions paled in light of sneaky doings like that. At least that's what I told myself.

Then, as promised, I called Matt. His voicemail came on, with instructions to call 911 if this was an emergency. It wasn't, so I left him a message. If he had a mind to, he could find me back at the Norton place.

The golden afternoon, smelling of fresh-mown grass and sun-warmed fields, was perfect for a jaunt on a Harley. Oh well. No bad-boy wheels. With a sigh, I tossed my suit jacket on the Lincoln's backseat, lowered all the windows, and ramped up one of my favorites, Kenny Chesney belting out "Living in Fast Forward." In MHO that's classical at its best. Anyway, singing along with him — off-key, as usual, since not a soul in my family ever could carry a tune — I rode out of town more lighthearted than in days. Beautiful weather can do that for a person, make you forget life's problems, if only for a little while.

In light midday traffic, I made good time and sped past Saxby's SOLD sign with hardly a glance. Up ahead, I turned off the pike onto the rutted road leading to Violet's front yard. The rooster was nowhere in sight. Neither was Matt's cruiser, and neither were the dogs, though they sure were howling. I stepped out of the car and listened. Low, short yips then a long, drawn-out wail.

"Yip, yip, yaooooOOO."

"Yip, yip, yaooooOOO."

The hair at my nape prickled. Confident Matt would be here soon, I shrugged off the unease and hurried across the front yard to the house. The dust kicked up by my heels rose in the warm air. I sneezed. And then again.

One of the dogs, the one more brown than white, came loping around the side of the house, greeting me with another, "Yip, yip, yaooooOOO."

"What's the matter, boy?"

At the sound of my voice, he hightailed it out of sight. A second later, both dogs took up the chorus.

I climbed the porch steps and rapped on the door. No answer. Maybe Violet couldn't hear me over her noisy hounds. I rapped again. Then, in true country fashion, I let myself in. "Violet?"

My only greeting was the aroma of drying lavender and rosemary, and another herb I couldn't name.

Feeling like a snoop, I peeked around. Not much to see, just a cramped bedroom and a bathroom that belonged in a museum. No sign of Violet. Where could she be? Out wandering the woods and meadows, gathering herbs? I huffed out a breath. After canceling a showing that might have earned Ridley's a major sale, I hoped this wouldn't turn into a fruitless visit.

At least the dogs were quiet. I sat at the kitchen table for a while, a fly buzzing at the window, a clock ticking on the wall. Where was Matt, anyway? So much for police protection. The unease I'd felt earlier gradually crept over me until, unable to sit still any longer, I got up and strolled out to the porch.

If I didn't have on heels, I could've hiked up a well-worn path into the hills and maybe found her, but in my beige pumps, that wasn't a good idea. I slumped onto the porch's top step and sniffed the air. What a perfect day, May melting into June. Trees a fresh, new green, wildflowers peeking out of the grass, birds flitting from branch to branch, belting out their latest hits.

Straight ahead in the scrubby front patch, dusty tire tracks caught my eye. From the look of them, Violet had visitors recently. Who? Saxby?

One of the woe-begotten hounds, the brown one, came slinking around the house, tail dragging. I expected him to erupt into that eerie howling again, but as silent as a shadow, he came over to me and laid his head on my lap, looking up with pleading eyes.

I stroked his fur, hoping it wasn't full of fleas. "Where's your buddy? Roaming the hills with Violet?"

No answer. I didn't need one. The other hound peered around the edge of the house but came no closer. Sinking onto his haunches, he stared at me, unblinking, as if willing me to go to him.

Well, I couldn't wait all day, and with a final pat for my new friend, I lifted his head off my lap and got up from the porch. I'd toot the car horn a few times. If Violet heard it, she might think she had a visitor and come home.

The instant I got to my feet, the dog lurking by the house leaped up, tail wagging.

"You want to be petted, too?"

When I strolled over to scratch him behind the ears, he darted away, disappearing behind the house.

"Playing a game, are you?" I followed him into the rear yard.

On a clothes line strung between two trees, a couple of old gray sheets flapped in the breeze. Under them, flat on her back, lay Violet, her legs spread apart, her skirt hiked to her waist, exposing her mysterious place for all to see. Worse, far worse, in her neck, a bullet hole oozed blood into the dust.

The world, so solid a moment earlier, began a wild spinning. The light disappeared.

Oh no. I grabbed at a sheet and fell, wrapped like a mummy, into blackness.

A wet, sticky tongue lapping at my cheek woke me. Warm, doggie breath drifted over my face. How long had I been out? A minute? An hour? Afraid of what they might see, my eyes opened as slow as can be then snapped wide in shock. I had awakened next to Violet, who was staring at a sky she couldn't see, her wispy hair blowing in a breeze she couldn't feel. Reaching out a shaky hand, I touched her arm. Cold.

I struggled free of the sheet and jumped to my feet. The dogs, crouching beside her, gazed up at me, droopy eared.

"So sorry," I murmured through chattering teeth.

The cell. I had to get the cell. My heart leaping in my chest, I raced to the porch for my purse. I plunged a hand into it, but mealy fingered, couldn't find a thing. Frantic, I dumped the bag's contents onto the porch floor. Why did I tote so much stuff around anyway? I grabbed the cell, and hands trembling, tapped in 911.

Call completed, terror slammed into me. I glanced around the yard. The killer could be anywhere, behind a stand of trees, in the meadow, in back of the barn. A crow flew cawing overhead. Had he been frightened by sudden movement? Was he warning me away?

The car keys lay on the porch floor in a tangle of handbag junk. I grabbed them, left everything else where it was, and ran to the Lincoln. I locked myself in and turned on the engine. If anybody approached, even someone I knew, I'd rev the motor and race out of there. For a quick getaway, I moved the car, pointing the front end toward the lane. With my pulse pounding at my temples, I sat clutching the wheel, waiting for a siren's wail.

After a timeless blur, a cruiser — blue lights blazing, siren blaring — roared up the rise and screeched to a stop beside me. Matt shot out of the cruiser and ran over to my car. I stared at him through the closed window. He sure looked pale. Funny, I'd never seen him pale before.

"Honey, your door's locked. Open up. It's me, Matt. It's okay. It's okay. Unlock the door."

"Oh. Oh." I pressed the release.

Matt yanked open the passenger door and unbuckled my seatbelt.

"Come out and get some air. Come on," he coaxed.

I did as he asked, sucking in huge gulps of the balmy afternoon air as he walked me over to the porch and eased me onto the top step.

"You all right?"

Anything but. I nodded.

"Where is she?"

"Out back. Under the clothesline."

He opened his holster and removed the Glock. "Don't move. If anyone shows up, anyone at all, yell your head off."

When I didn't answer, he said, "Do you understand?"

I nodded. "Yell."

"That's good. I'll be back in a minute."

True to his word, he returned in no time flat, reholstered his gun, and pulled out his cell.

■ ■ ■ ■

Once again, as in a dream gone bad, I watched a forensic team — the state homicide detective, the county coroner, the ambulance medics — swarm over a crime scene, asking questions and taking pictures of every detail. When satisfied that no possible clue had been overlooked, Detective Bradshaw turned his attention to me. A middle-aged man possessed of a long-jawed face and few words, he recorded everything I said twice over. The third time, he turned off the recorder and jotted notes on a notebook as I spoke.

I tried very hard not to change my story from one telling to another. Not that I wanted to hide or twist anything. No need. Besides, I was too scared for that. But remembering everything the same way had my hands shaking by the time he flipped his notebook closed and rose from the porch steps.

"Sheriff Rameros will fill you in as to what's expected." He pocketed the notebook. "The drill will be much the same as last time." With a parting smile that I believe was meant to soothe me but failed to do so, he turned to Matt. "Got a minute, Sheriff?"

Together they walked over to Detective Bradshaw's Ford pickup and stood there talking. I leaned against the porch post and closed my eyes. What was that Frenchie saying for when you lived something all over again? Sifting through the fog in my mind, I searched for the words. Ah, déjà vu! You'd been there, done that, so no surprises were in store. Wrong. Some things were too horrible to be anything but raw each and every time.

Seeing Tallulah, beautiful young Tallulah, with a bullet hole in her chest had been a shocker. Now, finding Violet spread out on the ground with her throat torn apart, had all the makings of a brand-new nightmare. Poor soul, she —

"Honey, you can leave now."

My eyes opened, heavy-lidded. One foot on the bottom step, one hand on the post, Matt stared at me, his body held easy, his expression tight and troubled.

"Think you can drive?" he asked.

Wordless, I nodded.

"Sure? I can take you home in the cruiser. We can come back tomorrow to pick up your car."

I stood slowly, like someone trying out brand new legs. "Thanks, but no need to go out of your way." A few minutes earlier, I'd dumped everything back in my purse. While Matt watched, I fumbled around in it.

"Your keys are in the ignition," he said.

"Oh, I forgot."

"Not surprising." He took my hand as I stepped off the porch, his touch warm and reassuring. At the Lincoln, he let go to open the door.

I stumbled a little over nothing.

Matt gripped my arm. "I'll drive you."

"No, I'm fine. Honest." I waved an arm around, at the farmhouse, the barn, the quiet fields. "I just need to get away from here."

"I could insist."

I sighed. "Why? The medic said I was fine. So, outside of arresting me. . . ."

He went to speak, seemed to think better of it, and nodded. "Rather than argue, I'll agree. But I'm following you home."

I had no problem with that, and truth be told, was right glad to have him with me all the way. For I was in the grip of a powerful longing. I needed someone to hold me and tell me not to worry, that everything would be all right. Someone like Matt. Someone a body could trust, who was loyal and reliable and warm. Warm, most of all.

At my apartment building, I pulled into my reserved slot. Matt parked behind me, waiting while I tugged the key out of the ignition and plucked my handbag off the passenger seat. I went over to the cruiser and leaned into the open driver's window. "I'm beholden to you, Matt."

"Sorry I couldn't take your first call. Zach and I were involved in a traffic stop. But 911 trumped that. Glad I finally got there for you."

But glad wasn't what was painted all over his face. He looked grim, way south of worried, his jaw tight, his mouth a thin line. If Matt was worried enough to show it, then I should be too. But right now, at this moment, I couldn't handle worry. I'd had enough of it in the last few days.

In the warm afternoon, a chill I couldn't control had me shivering. Wanting to get inside before he noticed, I backed up a step, ready to say a quick goodbye. I should have known better. Nothing escaped Sheriff Rameros.

He climbed out of the cruiser. "Come on, Honey. Let's get you inside. Where's your house key?"

"Here." I handed it over.

He laughed. "What's this dangling off it? A plastic rabbit's foot?"

I nodded, feeling kind of stupid and old-timey. "It's for good luck, you know, for when I take a client to see a house."

He shrugged. "Whatever works."

What he didn't say was what I suspected he was thinking. I needed all the luck I could get. After finding two murder victims in five days, I was in danger of graduating from a person of interest to a suspect.

The shivers were raising goose bumps on my arms. I needed warming, and I needed it now.

Matt unlocked my apartment door and gave me back the key.

I stared at the rabbit's foot. "Can you come in for a while?"

A half-smile loosening his tight mouth, he glanced at his watch. "For a few minutes. I have to admit, I've often wondered what your place is like."

He followed me in, glancing around at the rose-colored living room walls, the sisal rug, and the sky-blue sofa. And across from it, my pride and joy, a forty-inch TV on its own white distressed cabinet. He even took in the pot of paperwhites on the coffee table and the picture of my momma next to it.

"Very nice. Very you."

"What does that mean?"

"More than I can say in a few minutes." His eyes were warm. So warm.

"Then stay, Matt."

153

I dropped my purse on the sofa, and before he had a chance to move away, I grabbed him, wrapping my arms around his waist, nestling my head on his chest. Hugging a man with a loaded gun was the best feeling I'd had in years. Or ever. I purred like a contented kitten. Well, semi-contented. I wanted more, much more.

I raised my head for a kiss. Sensing my need, or maybe driven by a need of his own, he covered my mouth with his. Soft at first, and then as if a taste wasn't enough, he pressed me closer, keeping my mouth on his, keeping the kiss alive.

To say I didn't enjoy it would be a lie. I loved it. Robbed of thought, of movement, of every vow I'd ever made to stand firm until Mr. Right came along, I stood in the circle of Matt's arms and drank in his warmth through every pore.

When the kiss ended, his hands moved to my shoulders and he eased back a step. Holding me at arm's length, he gazed into my eyes. "Thank you," he said, his voice low. "I've dreamed of this."

"Then stay." I smiled, looking into his eyes. "You haven't seen the rest of the apartment."

He stiffened. "This isn't a showing, Honey."

"No, course not. What I meant is, well," I attempted a laugh and moved in for another kiss, "I'm inviting you to a pajama party."

His hands slid from my shoulders. He moved back a step and frowned. "You know I'd rather be here with you than anywhere else on earth."

"Then —"

"But not like this. Not for a one-night stand. I want all of you, Honey. For good. Not for a fling." A corner of his lips quirked up. "And definitely not for therapeutic reasons."

"It's not like that!"

"It's exactly like that." As if to keep himself from touching me, he tucked his thumbs into his belt loops. "You've had a terrible day, but this isn't the way to deal with your stress. Try a little Jack. Or psychotherapy."

"A shrink? You have a cotton-pickin' nerve, Sheriff."

"Precisely. That's what makes me good at my job." He pointed a finger at my nose. "And you, Miss Ingersoll, have PTSD."

"What?"

"Post-traumatic stress disorder. Nothing to be ashamed of. You're in need of comforting right now. Not sex. And I have just the solution for you."

"Screw your solution. You can forget about my offer, too."

He nodded, the frown back on his face. "I know. But as they say, you'll be happy about it in the morning." He strode toward the door. One hand on the handle, he paused and turned back to wink. "I'll be in touch."

I snatched a pillow off the sofa and flung it at him. Missed by a mile. God, I was a rotten shot. A disgrace to my granddaddies, both of them. Never mind picking a squirrel off a dead stump, I couldn't even hit a handsome man with a pillow.

CHAPTER EIGHTEEN

A half hour later, the front door bell rang, and I nearly jumped out of my skin. Hardly fit for company, I was curled up on the blue sofa in the old chenille robe, clutching a box of tissues. The mascara had run down my cheeks, and Lord knows, my eyes and nose were probably stoplights. Not that it mattered. I just didn't want to see anybody right then. Didn't want to talk, didn't want to answer questions, didn't want to move off the sofa.

But the bell wouldn't quit ringing. I tried yelling, "Go away!" It didn't work. Whoever stood on the stoop was paying me no mind. Finally, curiosity won out. I forced myself off the sofa and padded over to look out the peephole.

Omigod. I flung the door open. "What are you doing here?"

Startled, she lurched back a step. "The sheriff sent me. Told me about Violet. Said you'd had a terrible day and needed comforting. Wasn't that sweet of him?" Mrs. Otis held up a paper bag. "Jelly donuts. I thought they might help. They always help me when I'm upset."

She waited while I blew my nose and swiped at my eyes. "You going to let me in so's I can make us some tea to go with these goodies?"

"Of course. Come in, please, though I'm afraid I'm not myself tonight." Before I could say any more, I burst out sobbing.

Mrs. Otis gently closed the door, put her purse and the bag of donuts on the coffee table then sat next to me on the sofa and held me while I wept.

My tears soaked the front of her rayon dress pretty good, but she didn't seem to mind. While I cried, she patted my back and said little things like, "There, there," and "It's all right, dearie," until I had no more tears to shed. With a shuddering breath, I sat up straight and blew my nose for the thousandth time. By now it could probably guide ships at sea.

"Shall we have some tea?" she asked.

"Sounds good." And it did. Jelly donuts made a fine meal.

Actually, I had four, and three cups of black tea. Mrs. Otis had six and four teas with cream, two spoonfuls of Dixie Crystals in each. But who was counting?

"There are a couple left for your breakfast." She twisted the bag closed. "Feel better now?"

"Much."

"Told you. Donuts do it every time."

"Thank you for being so kind, Mrs. Otis."

She reached across the kitchen table to squeeze my hand. "Oh, Honey, no need to thank me. You're the daughter I never had. It's a darned shame you had to find those dead bodies lying around." She glanced over a shoulder at my darkened bedroom. "Be careful. A killer's out there somewhere, and Lord only knows who it is." Leaning both palms on the tabletop, she groaned to her feet. "Since you're feeling better, I'll run along. You want to sleep in tomorrow morning, I'll tell Sam you're at a showing."

She'd lie for me? God, she was grand.

"No need. I'll be in at nine as usual."

"Well, if you say so. But if you're not, my offer will stand."

I walked her to the door and kissed her goodbye, watching from the entryway as she drove off. The night breeze, hinting of rain to come, toyed with the hem of my robe and cooled my flushed cheeks. Soothed and, yes, comforted, I locked up, retrieved the cell from my purse and thumbed in a message to Matt.

Sorry for meltdown. Now have PTED. Post-Traumatic Embarrassment Disorder. Mrs. O was an angel. Thank u. H.

I placed the cell on the coffee table and eased back onto the sofa. Yes, I felt better, but that didn't mean I wasn't teetering on the edge of deep, serious trouble. Fate, or some other evil force, had put me in the path of two murdered women, one young, with her whole life ahead, the other a bitter old crone. Why those two? They probably had never met or even knew each other's names. Yet I couldn't shake the feeling their deaths were related somehow. But why? Matt said there had been no sexual assault, no sign of robbery. Not much to steal on those poor acres, either. Just those few uncut stones. . . .

I stretched and yawned. Should go to bed. Tomorrow would be another long day, but the questions kept pestering me. Tired as I was, sleep wouldn't come any time soon. *Stones!*

I bolted upright. Not the flawed diamonds, the stony farms. The land. Could that be the link to the killings? If I hadn't had a manicure two days ago, Candy Apple Red, I'd have bitten my nails to the quick trying to come up with a reason why it might be. But for the life of me, I couldn't.

I slumped against the sofa cushions. Another dead end. Two lives taken and nothing else. No, wait a minute, not true. Something else had been taken. And whatever that was both women knew.

I jumped off the sofa and ran out to the kitchen for a pad and pencil. Who had something to gain or lose from their deaths?

Back on the sofa, I tented my knees and began. Name Number One, Charles Ames. He could have reached the Hermann farm before I did, killed Tallulah and left. But why? And why kill Violet? Stumped already. Okay, next name.

Chester Ames. Charles' brother and CEO of International Properties. Problem was, he hadn't been anywhere near Eureka Falls the day Tallulah died, and I doubted he'd been here today either. The police could check on his comings and goings, but what about a motive?

Leaving my thumbnail alone, I chewed on the end of the pencil. Sam had brought up a good point. In snapping up the Hermann farm and Sloane's acres, was IP acting for itself or for a secret buyer? A buyer who wanted the Norton place too? Knowing that bit of information might shed a lot of light on the case.

Who else? Violet. For a few minutes, I played with the idea she killed Tallulah and had been killed in turn. But then I drew a line through her name. Bitter though she'd been, I couldn't believe she'd have shot a young woman to death in cold blood.

Her nephew, Earl Norton? *Yes!* Like most mountain boys, he was gifted at the business end of a rifle. Heard tell, he shot rats out by the town dump on weekends for the pure pleasure of doing so. Both women had been killed with a pistol, though, not a rifle. But who was to say Earl didn't own a pistol? His motive for killing Tallulah was cloudy, but as childless Aunt Violet's next of kin, chances were good he'd inherit the farm. There might even be a will to back that up.

And then there was Saxby Winthrop. Fancying himself a ladies' man like he did, he might have invited Tallulah for a ride. If he forced what he called his "affections" on her and she fought him off, anything could have happened. While that made some sort of warped sense, killing Violet didn't. After sweet talking her into letting him sell the place, he'd want her alive until the deal went through.

I lowered my knees and put down the pen, unsatisfied with every single name I'd listed. As likely killers, they were all flawed. What right did I have to make up a list of suspects, anyway? That was police work, as Matt would be the first to point out.

Yet, I couldn't walk away and do nothing. A devil's web hung over my future, even my life, as Mrs. Otis had pointed out. Besides, for the last three years, I'd worked hard to become a respected member of the Eureka Falls community. I didn't want to be tainted by somebody's wicked brush, or, heaven forbid, have those crimes darken the good name of Ridley's Real Estate.

The thought of bringing hurt to Sam sank my heart. No giving up with that weight on my chest, so, heaving a sigh, I picked up the pad and reread the names. I didn't get too far. My eye stopped at Chester Ames. How could I have forgotten? While I waited for him in IP's reception room, he'd received a call from none other than Senator Prescott Lott, Lila's famous daddy.

Hmm. I stewed over that for a while and chewed on the pencil some. Politicians sidled up to people in high places all the time. It was just business as usual. Or was it? Violet's little scheme might have died with her, but whatever the Ames brothers had in mind was likely still going strong. Suppose, just suppose, they were fronting for Senator Lott? If so, who was he fronting for?

I shook my head. Weariness had me chasing crazy dead ends. I'd better turn out the lights and call it a day.

A hand on the switch, I paused. Supposing my crazy notion was right, would it lead to the killer?

CHAPTER NINETEEN

"Well, aren't you looking mighty fine this morning."

"Thank you, Sheriff."

He sniffed the air. "Smell nice too. What is that?"

"Versace's Yellow Diamond," I replied, my voice as prim as a preacher's wife's. Yesterday I'd been low as a snake's hips, but not today. Today I felt like a hawk riding the sky, much as I had the day I walked out on Billy Tubbs.

Matt's dark gaze flitted over me. For some reason, I was glad I'd taken extra care with my appearance.

"Always wear blue. It becomes you." He cleared his throat. "I got your text message. No need to apologize."

"Glad to hear that, since you didn't text back."

"I don't send personals. They can be traced."

"Well, for pity's sake."

He shrugged. "A habit I got into. Saves me a lot of grief."

"Very shrewd, Sheriff. I'll be sure to remember that in the future. Now, if it's ready, I'll sign my statement."

"It's ready. Ellie's a fast typist." He shuffled through some papers on his desk.

Should I mention my thoughts about Senator Lott's call to IP? Or would Matt think that was plumb crazy, more proof of PTSD?

As I stood there trying to decide, he found my statement and held it out. "Better check it for accuracy. Also, there're some new developments in these homicides."

"Oh?" I may have looked cool and collected, but my heart skipped a beat.

"State's verified the same gun killed both victims."

"There's only one killer then?"

"No proof of that, but yeah, it's a logical assumption. And there's more. Something came to light several days ago, but I wasn't free to mention it. The *Star's* gotten wind of the story, so you'll be reading about it."

I shifted from one foot to the other, waiting.

"Apparently, the late Tallulah Bixby and Senator Lott's aide, Trey Gregson, were keeping company. Broke up about six months ago. At that time, she moved out of his house in Fayetteville."

Omigod. I sank onto the chair in front of Matt's desk. "He was in town the day Tallulah died. I saw him at the bank."

"He's still here. Staying at the senator's home."

"What does that mean to the case?"

Matt shrugged. "Possibly nothing. The state police interviewed Mr. Gregson. He accounted for his whereabouts on the day the Bixby woman was killed. Senator Lott vouched for him. Swore they were in conference at the time of her death and yesterday as well. The household staff has concurred. Apparently Gregson's here to help plan the senator's upcoming campaign. So, at this point in time, looks like he's off the suspect list."

Heat rushed to my face. "Unbelievable! He and Tallulah were live-in lovers, and he's off the hook? Just like that? And I'm still on it?"

"Whoa." Matt held up a palm. "Stop right there, Honey. Keep the terms straight. You're a person of interest. Not a suspect."

What he left out was "yet."

My face wasn't about to cool down, far from it. "Tallulah died over a week ago. Why

167

wasn't her relationship with Trey Gregson made public before now?"

Matt sighed and shoved stuff around on his desktop. I wasn't fooled. Gut deep, I already knew what he'd say.

"We were ordered to limit what we released to the media."

"The senator?"

He nodded, probably sorry to admit it, but too honest to pretend otherwise. "None other."

"That's outrageous."

"Some people would agree, but it's a fairly common practice. The public isn't always let in on every detail of a crime. In the senator's defense, he's protecting a valued aide. A man he swears is innocent of wrong-doing."

"Oh he does, does he? You and Detective Bradshaw and the state police have only scratched the surface. If Tallulah's affair with Gregson was over, why was she riding around town in that big ol' Caddy? Returning it to him? Ha! I doubt that. Stalking him, maybe." I stabbed the air with one of my candy-red nails. "Need I remind you of what I said in my report? I was at IP the day the senator called Chester Ames. You said there was nothing illegal about that and you're right. But don't try to tell me the senator's not mixed up in all this somehow. There's a dead 'possum in the woodwork, and its name is Lott. Problem is, I can't prove it." Too smoking mad to sit there any longer, I went to rise out of my chair.

"Honey Ingersoll, you put your little round rear end right back on that seat."

"You can't talk to me that way."

"You bet your sweet ass I can."

Matt leaped out of the swiveler to hustle around the desk and sit, holstered gun and all, on the edge, his knees just inches from mine.

"Why the big switch in seating arrangements, Sheriff? You trying to scare me?"

"If that's what it takes," he said, his jaw like steel, his voice as smooth as buttermilk. "Now listen to me and listen good. I know you've been through a lot lately, but, and this is a big but, don't go jumping to conclusions. Trust the system. More is being done to get at the truth than you're aware of, which is —"

"A crock. Let me remind *you* of something. You're not a person of interest," I waved my arms around, "or whatever the term is. I am. It's easy for you to be calm and professional over all this. It's a lot tougher for me."

He looked at his hands, staying silent for

a long moment. Finally, "You're mistaken, Honey. When you're involved, I'm involved." He stood suddenly. "You're free to leave."

I did, but the soaring feeling I'd awakened with collapsed all around me. Matt was my friend. I hated arguing with him.

In the outer office, I read the statement, signed it, and handed it to Ellie. As I stomped out to the Lincoln, I glanced at my watch. Nine. I called Mrs. Otis.

"Please tell Sam I'm showing that Mc-Mansion on Tyler Lane. Be in afterward."

"Happy to, Honey."

"That's legit, Mrs. O. You won't be fibbing."

"Well, just so's you know, when pressed, I can fib with the best of 'em."

I laughed for the first time in days and signed off. When I drove up to the McMansion, my clients, the two urgent-care physicians, were waiting, wearing green scrubs and great big smiles.

Though part of my brain told me not to waste my time — Sam would never see me as I wanted him to — I still placed the doctors' deposit check on his desk like a love gift.

He looked up, smiling. "You did it. Excellent."

170

"Cletus has preapproved them for a loan."

"How could he not? They're an asset to the town." He flung down his pen. "I have good news too. The Triangle Building sale went through."

"Well, praise be. We're on a roll."

"Yeah, I'll be glad to see that boarded-up old building open and thriving. It'll be great for Main Street. They're planning a coffee shop on the first floor and offices upstairs."

I smiled, more at his pleasure than his news. "Sounds good."

"Yeah, no question about that." He sneaked a peek at his watch. "Glad you caught me before I left."

"You're leaving?"

"That conference in Little Rock, remember?" I was about to admit I'd forgotten, when he said, "There's more." His mouth broke into a grin, the facial equivalent of a happy dance.

Uh-oh. The only other time I'd seen him looking so thrilled was when he announced his engagement.

"Lila and I set a wedding date. The third Saturday in December. Right after the senator declares he's running for president."

I managed to blurt out, "That's a lot of exciting news all at once."

He nodded and picked up his pen. "Lila

says a Christmas wedding'll be romantic. I know one thing. As a married man, I'll have to work harder to keep those sales coming in."

He speared me with a single glance. Left unsaid, "You'll need to work harder too."

I wobbled back to my cubicle and shut the door behind me. Before the third Saturday in December rolled around, I had a heavy decision to make.

CHAPTER TWENTY

The next day, Saturday, I had three showings. Two of them, I had a feeling, would
amount to nothing. The third probably
wouldn't end in a sale any time soon, either,
though a young couple expecting a baby —
like yesterday, from the look of things —
were very taken with a two-bedroom cottage on a quiet street of neat lookalikes.
Problem was mortgage approval. If First
Federal recommended they turn to HUD
for financing, approval could take weeks.
Such was the game I'd staked my future on.
No good moaning about it. It was what it
was.

At dusk, back in the apartment, I noticed
the red message button on my house phone
blinking like a crazy eye. When I pressed it,
Amelia's voice floated over the line, humming with excitement. "Call me the minute
you get in. I have the best news!"

Well, that would get any girl's juices flowing.

"Guess what?" she said, picking up on the first ring. "Joe's momma offered to babysit tonight."

"I can't believe it." Usually babysitting the boys wasn't a high priority for Mrs. Swope.

"I know. I'm bowled over. So, if you're free, what do you say we party?"

I kicked off my heels. "I don't know. It's been a long day."

"Oh, come on. I hardly ever get out. And admit it, you haven't been anywhere fun in ages."

I sighed. "Right on both counts. What did you have in mind?"

"The roadhouse."

"You mean the Hog Wild?"

"It's the only one in town with live music. And that's what we both need, a rollicking good time. Come on. It'll help you get over what's been happening lately."

When I didn't answer, she said, "Do it for me. Please, Honey. I can't walk in there alone, but the two of us together would be different."

How could I spoil Amelia's rare evening out? "Okay, you win. Pick you up when . . . nine, ten?"

"Not ten. If I'm still here that late, Grandma Swope's liable to leave for home."

"Nine then. We'll get there before the place heats up, but that's okay."

"Any place without diapers will seem hot to me."

I showered quickly, squeezed into skinny-legged jeans, and pulled on a pair of tooled leather cowboy boots, my favorite high school graduation present. For a top, a holdover from my Billy Tubbs days, a midnight blue camisole studded with sequins and tiny mirrors that caught the light. From the bottom of my jewelry box, I dug out some half-forgotten shoulder-scraping earrings, midnight blue like the camisole and great with my eyes. I hadn't been to the Hog Wild in years and doubted I'd know anybody there. So, figuring I might as well forget about looking conservative and businesslike for one night, I backcombed, sprayed, and teased my hair into BIG.

It had been so long since I fixed my hair like that, I'd kind of forgotten how good it looked, the front all teased and piled up, the back hanging down wavy, past my shoulders. Too bad those magazines I studied didn't feature such dos. I'd sure looked for them but never found a one. Anyway, to keep everything in place, I sprayed up a storm cloud and then went to work on my eyes, layering on mascara, shadow, and liner, stopping just short of raccoon. Went light on the lip gloss, though. I'd let the eyes do the talking.

Good to go and feeling foxy, I packed my blue sequined wristlet with driver's license, car keys, and cash. Roadhouse ready, I killed the lights.

Music, loud, thumping and country came pouring out into the parking lot.

"Hey, it's crowded already," Amelia said.

I slowly cruised a lot jammed with a mishmash of pickups, massive boy-toy bikes, and a jumble of old Fords and Chevys spattered with back-road mud.

I hoped I wouldn't have to park out on the pike. The Linc didn't have a single ding, and I didn't want to come out later and find some midnight cowboy had caved in a fender.

I'd about given up when Amelia said, "There's a spot. Over there, next to the Jag."

The lights strung around the Hog Wild roof didn't quite reach this far, but I pulled into the empty space anyway, next to the one and only XJ in the entire lot. Way over here, we'd be out of the line of fire, so to speak.

Amelia hopped out of the car like a teenager. In black jeans and a lacy white top, sheer sleeves billowing to her wrists, and rich hair cascading down her back, she looked like the queen of the junior prom. No one would believe she had two little imps at home.

The hulk at the door let us in without ID'ing us. Amelia gave me an eye roll. We laughed and strutted on in. Four good ol' boys with fake Stetsons on their heads and electric guitars slung across their chests had lashed into "Gimme Three Steps." Everybody in the place was talking and laughing and munching on food, everything but listening. The boys in the band didn't seem to care. Just kept strumming those strings and banging their boots on the platform that passed for a stage.

"That's the warm-up group," Amelia shouted over the din. "Talk about howling dogs. They need to get back to their garage and practice some more."

A girl in a peasant blouse and denim shorts so skimpy the cheeks of her butt practically mooned the crowd led the way to a tiny table at stage right. Multicolored klieg lights cast a rainbow all over us.

"Anything less lit up?" Amelia asked.

The girl popped her gum. "Yeah, but take

this one, wouldya? The manager saw you come in, and he likes cute girls seated up front."

"You talking about the bouncer?" I asked.

"Yes, ma'am. He wears a lotta hats."

Another eye roll from Amelia as we pulled out the chairs and sat.

"What can I getcha?"

"Two Bud Lights. In bottles." After Miss Moonie left, Amelia leaned across the table so she wouldn't have to shout so loud. "You don't want to drink out of glasses in here."

I arched a brow. "An insider's tip from the darling mother of two who never gets out?"

She smiled, sort of. "When Joe and I were dating, we used to come here a lot. It feels good to be back. Without him." Her tone left no doubt she meant it.

As I sat sipping my beer, I glanced around the crowded room. It was like revisiting an old home you hadn't seen in years. I took in everything. The knotty-pine walls studded with photos of country stars, the wagon wheel fixtures overhead, the bar with its shiny varnished top, and the rowdy, dating couples at the other tables.

Amelia waited until my trip down memory lane was over then inhaled a deep breath of the beer-laced air. "I have a confession to make. Promise you won't get mad when I tell you."

"How can I promise before I know what it is?"

"Promise anyway."

"Amelia!"

"We're going to have company tonight."

"Here? Who?"

"Cletus Dwyer."

Without question, my jaw dropped. "Egads." I patted my stiff hair. "Think he'll recognize me?"

"What's that supposed to mean?"

"Oh, just wondering is all."

Our beers came. I took a swig then thumped the bottle down fast. "Hey, wait a sec. Cletus was at your house the other night when I called, and now he's coming here tonight. You two dating?"

She shrugged and took a sip of her beer. "I don't know. He's stopped by a couple of times, but I can't figure out why he'd be interested in me. All my baggage and everything."

"Because you're beautiful in every way. The boys are darling too. Especially when they're all sugared up."

"This isn't a joking matter, Honey. I like Cletus." She swung her attention back to the band, though they didn't deserve it.

"Really like him."

Oh my. Then and there, I made up my mind not to say a word about his sleeve garters. Or that I'd thought he was kind of sweet on me.

"How did he find out we'd be here tonight?"

"He phoned earlier, wanted to bring over a bottle of wine and some treats for the boys. When I told him I was coming to the roadhouse with you, he asked if he could join us. Sorry to spring a surprise, but I couldn't say no."

" 'Course not. You did the right thing. I'm glad he's coming," I said, not really meaning it.

Anyway, we polished off our beers. On an empty stomach, even light lager created a nice buzz. When Miss Moonie strolled by, her tray empty, Amelia raised two fingers in the air. While we waited for our second round, should I go to the ladies' room, wash off the makeup, and brush down my hair? No ma'am. Cletus was coming to see Amelia, not me. Besides, I kind of liked my hair this way. And I didn't understand why blue eye shadow was such a no-no to all those big fashion experts in New York City.

We were nearly through our second beers when I spotted him. He was standing by the bar with . . . no . . . yes! Matt Rameros and a petite, curly-haired vision who barely came up to Matt's shoulders. If that was his date, I sniffed, he must be feeling like a giant about now.

Leaning across the table, I shouted above the band's foot stomping. "Cletus is here. Over by the bar." I was about to wave and catch his attention when he half turned to greet someone. *Well, I'll be dipped.* None other than Senator Lott's aide, Trey Gregson, as serious and stern-faced as I recalled. What on earth was he doing here?

As Gregson went over to shake Matt's hand, Cletus glanced around the crowded room. He spotted our table, waved, and raised a finger in the air.

"He'll be over in a minute."

Visibly tense, Amelia gripped her beer bottle as if some yahoo was about to rip it out of her hands. All this tension because of Cletus? Well, different strokes.

"Ladies!"

"You made it." Amelia's voice went all fluttery. "Do join us." Even under the kliegs, her rainbow face flushed a bright pink.

He borrowed a chair from a nearby table and sat, knees banging into ours. "Sure is a lively spot. Haven't been here much since my college days. Nothing's changed, I see."

"Nope," I replied, "except for a few new faces hanging on the walls. That's how the regulars like it, I guess. Maybe newcomers do too, like the senator's aide over there."

"I was also rather surprised to see him. Said he's scouting out local bands. When the senator kicks off his campaign, he wants some music to liven things up." Cletus shook his head. "I'm no judge, but that sure doesn't sound like music to me."

"You're right. It doesn't. Not at all," Amelia said.

"You know your music, Miss Amelia?"

"A little." Her cheeks were pinker than ever.

"Maybe you can teach me about it some time."

"I'd surely love to," she said.

Well, I'd be darned. This was chemistry in action. And two weeks ago to the very night, at the Eureka Falls Inn, Cletus told me I was a perfect woman. Perfect. That was what he said. While I hadn't believed a single word, it sure made for easy listening. Now, tonight, if I wasn't mistaken — and I've got Grandma Ingersoll's sixth sense for this kind of thing — he was romancing Amelia.

Not that I blamed him. Not a single bit. With her lacy sleeves flowing over her arms, her flushed cheeks and her hair easing into little, bitty curls around her face, she was beyond beautiful, not to mention the sweetest person in the whole wide world.

Just about then, Miss Moonie plunked down three cold ones. Where had they come from? I didn't worry about it and took a hefty swig. So did Cletus, staring at Amelia over his upturned bottle. After he got through drinking her in, he swiveled his glance over to me. "You look lovely tonight too, Honey. I'm a lucky man to be sitting here between two such beauties." His eyes narrowed. "Though I must say, you do look different this evening."

"It's the rainbow," I said, conscious of the beers guiding my tongue.

"Not just that. There's something else."

"Well, you're just the same darling Cletus you've always been. You never change. You know what, just for fun, why don't we change you too just a li'l ol' bit." The beers had definitely taken over. I could hear them talking. When had I eaten last, anyway? Breakfast. Those two leftover donuts. I set my bottle down and didn't give him a chance to refuse. "Allow me." I reached up and undid the knot in his lilac tie.

"Now, Miss Honey, that's enough." He

laid his hands over mine, but I shook them off.

"Don't 'Miss Honey' me, you great big sweetie." Ignoring Amelia's frown, I grabbed one end of the tie and slid it out from under his collar like a limp snake. Once I'd whipped it off, I tossed it on the table right on top of the wet beer rings. "Now for your buttons." Before he could figure out how to stop me, I undid the top one and then the next. "My, my, you certainly have chest hair, Cletus, you sexy ol' dog you." I put a hand on his arm and ran it up above his elbow. "Now for the best part. Your sleeve garters."

"Honey . . ." Amelia warned.

"It's all right," Cletus said. "She's just having a little fun at my expense. I think she needs it."

"Zackly." I launched out of my seat, and bending over him, slipped off one garter then the other and dropped them over the little glass oil lamp in the center of our table. Ignoring the gel that felt icky against my fingers, I ruffled up his carefully combed hair.

"Your part's gone all to hell, Cletus, but that's the whole idea. Now, if you'd kindly take off your cufflinks."

At that, he stared at me, as stunned as if I'd asked him to take off his pants.

"Go ahead. Go ahead. Put them in your pocket or something and roll up your sleeves."

Amelia leaped to her feet. "Let's go to the ladies' room."

"No." I folded my arms. "I don't have to pee."

"Omigod. She's had a terrible week," Amelia said from somewhere far away. "Maybe coming out tonight wasn't such a good idea."

" 'Course it was," I retorted in a voice I didn't recognize.

"Let's go."

"No. I'm not leaving this sex machine alone." I waved my arms around. "There are man-hunting women all over the place. Anything might happen to him. You want that on your conscience?"

Amelia didn't flinch. "Either you come to the ladies' room this instant, or I'll ask Cletus to take me home."

My chin wobbled. "You'd leave me here alone?"

"No. Under the care and supervision of the bouncer."

She meant business. I'd only seen that determined set to her jaw once before, the day I drove her to the Yarborough County Court House for her divorce. There was no arguing with that jaw, so I polished off what was left of my drink and blew out a beery breath. "Very well. You win."

"I don't believe this is a winning situation." Amelia clamped her teeth together and led me to a door against the back wall with the cutest little cowgirl you ever did see painted on it.

The ladies' room was empty.

"Guess nobody else has to pee either." I pointed to the empty stalls.

Hands on hips, Amelia leaned against a wash basin. "What's wrong? And don't tell me 'nothing.' I know you're upset about those two murders, as you have every right to be. But more than that is eating at you. I'm your friend, Honey. You can trust me. So, for God's sake, whatever's the matter, tell me. Let it out. Let it all out."

I stared past her at a mirror that threw back the image of high-piled blonde hair and big blue, owly eyes — well, some kind of animally eyes. They kept opening and closing, seeing two of everything, then everything they saw began to churn. The sight made me sick of a sudden, and stomach heaving, I dashed for one of the empty stalls. Good thing. Like an exploding volcano, up came the lager lights, spewing out of my mouth into the toilet bowl, just barely missing my tooled boots.

When the retching ended, I stumbled over to the bank of wash basins. Amelia wiped my face with damp paper towels and waited, arms crossed on her chest, while I washed my hands and rinsed my mouth. Then, both hands leaning on the sink rim, I risked a peek in the mirror. My piled-up hair had tilted to one side.

"Well?" Amelia's foot was tapping.

"Sam's getting married in December, and there's nothing I can do to stop it."

CHAPTER TWENTY-ONE

If I expected Sam's news to blow Amelia away like a dust bunny, I was mistaken.

Her hazel eyes brimmed with sympathy. "He's not the only pup in the litter. I know that for a fact, so learn from me, Honey. I had to have Joe Swope. Nobody else would do. And look what he put me through."

"But —"

She swatted my protest away with a flick of her hand. "I know, I know. Sam isn't Joe, far from it. But he isn't worth making yourself miserable over either. No man is. Not a single one of 'em. That's why, if I ever marry again, it won't be for passion. It doesn't last. What you need, Honey, is someone who will care for you. With a man like that, a woman can be happy her whole life long."

She meant well, I knew that, so to the music of a flushing toilet, I hugged her. "Have Cletus take you home, okay? I think

I'll leave as soon as that beer's out of my system."

She nodded and gave me a farewell hug in return. "Call you in the morning." She laughed. "Not too early."

I did pee after all. Then, using paper towels from the dispenser, I washed off every speck of makeup and raked a comb through my hair, letting it fall straight and natural as usual.

When I unscrewed the foot-long earrings, the girl touching up her face at the next sink glanced over. "Whatever did you do that for? I love those earrings."

I held them out. "Here. They're yours."

Her eyes gleamed. "You mean it?"

"Yup."

"Oh gee, thanks. I'll put them on right now."

At least I'd made one person happy tonight. Terrific. On the minus side, I'd hurt a valuable relationship with the Eureka Falls Savings & Loan and nearly wrecked my friendship with Amelia.

I sat in an empty stall for a while, clearing my head and my bladder, then, sorry but sober, I squared my shoulders and walked out into a roadhouse electric with energy. A different band had taken over the stage and had the place rocking. Sounded like they could bring a political rally to fever pitch with no trouble at all.

To the pounding rhythm of "Shake It for Me, Girl," I inched through the crowd, trying not to make eyeball contact with anyone. I just wanted to go home, snuggle under my comforter, and tune out the world.

No such luck. As I sidled past the bar, a low, cultured voice said, "Well, Honey Ingersoll, as I live and breathe."

Shit. In a simple red-linen sheath dress that was wrong for the roadhouse and right for every other reason on earth, stood none other than Lila Lott.

Putting her to the test, I held out a hand. "Miss Lott."

She flunked. Without taking my hand or inviting me to call her Lila, she turned to Trey Gregson at her elbow. "You remember Honey, don't you, Trey? She works for Sam."

He half bowed and nodded. "Come here often?"

"My first visit in five years. You?"

Lila laughed, a fluty, bell-like trill. I itched to slap her.

"Trey and I only dropped in to judge the band for Daddy."

"Oh? Not for your wedding?" Some ornery demon spoke those words, not an angel

190

the likes of li'l ol' Miss Honey Ingersoll.

She let her gaze trail over me, kind of slow-like. I swear she didn't miss a single mirror glittering on my camisole. "But I've heard enough, so I'll be off." She tilted her chin at the stage. "Book them, Trey," she ordered, and with a cool nod for me, she sauntered toward the front entrance.

"Guess I better look for the manager," he said with a half-smile, his gaze following Lila's slim red back as she wove her way through the crowd.

In the middle of all those jeans and plaid-shirted locals, she was like a bright-feathered bird or a tropical flower, out of place and ripe for plucking. And then it happened. A big, bearded guy jumped up from his chair and blocked her path. She tried dodging past him, but no dice. The big guy looked to be beered up and about as unmovable as a full-grown oak tree.

From where we stood, we couldn't hear what he was saying, but we didn't have to. Whatever he was selling, Lila clearly wasn't buying.

"Be back." Trey moved through the crowd as fast as a snake through grass and hurried over to Lila. They exchanged a few words; then, draping a hand over her shoulders, he pulled her close.

Big Guy flung a chair out of the way. It hit the floor with a bang that echoed over the music. Two men at the same table leaped to their feet and tried to pull him back. He was having none of it and whacked them away with his fists.

I glanced around. Where was that bouncer?

Busy working a tap, the bartender hadn't noticed the ruckus.

I ran over to him. "You've got trouble in here. Get some help fast."

Startled, he let the beer overflow the glass, served it up to a waiting Miss Moonie and yanked his cell phone out of a pocket.

Big Guy was shouting now. Trey had shoved Lila behind him. With that bully ready to wipe him out, he scanned the room, eyes feverish, searching for help.

Like a hero in a cowboy movie, the good guy arrived in the nick of time. With no bugles, no spurs, not even a horse, Matt Rameros stepped between the two men.

Half the body weight of the bully and half a foot shorter, he stood, legs apart, hands on hips. He was out of uniform, so if he was packing, I couldn't tell. Couldn't hear what he said either, but stomach clenched, I watched every move, waiting for a dustup that never happened. Whatever he said was magic. Within minutes, someone righted the fallen chair and the bully slumped into it, droopy as a pricked balloon.

Trey, holding Lila by the arm, hurried her out the front door.

Now that the horses were all safe in the corral, the bouncer came running up to Matt. Wouldn't you know?

Longing for a breath of fresh air, I'd about reached the exit when Matt's, "Honey, wait up a minute," stopped me in my tracks.

While he held the door open, he gave me a thorough eye search. "You look like hell. What's the matter?"

"It's a long story."

"You came in with Amelia Swope. Why you leaving without her?"

My turn for hands on hips. "Since when is my business your business?"

"I could say since the day you reported a Caddy stolen. But I'd be wrong. Our history's longer than that."

"Go back to your date, Matt. Enjoy the rest of the evening. I'm going home."

"I'll walk you to your car."

I strolled outside. "You don't need to."

"Let me be the judge of what's needed."

"Aren't you supposed to be taking care of your date?"

A slow smile lit his face. Starting with the

corners of his lips, it spread until it reached his eyes. "She's in good hands."

That smile starting to rile me, I changed the subject. "First time I've seen you in civvies. You look nice." He did. Handsome, actually. "You should wear white shirts all the time."

"The town council might have something to say about that."

"Off duty, I meant."

"A compliment?"

"Yup."

As he took my arm, I inhaled a deep breath of the clean, crisp midnight air. It was spring water clear. No beer. No burgers. Just Mother Nature at her best. Whether I wanted to admit it or not, I felt safe having Matt by my side. The fight he'd stopped had been a reminder that danger stalked the streets of Eureka Falls, and I'd best not forget it.

"How did you get that bully to back down so fast, you out of uniform and all?"

"Little Moose McGill? He's been a frequent guest in our town jail. So it was easy enough. I borrowed a line from Clint Eastwood."

"Which is?"

"Go ahead, make my day."

"Meaning?"

"He's out on parole. One more arrest, he heads for state prison. A long stretch and he knows it."

"Oh." I couldn't help but sigh. "What a day, what a week. . . . What a life. I might as well throw that in."

"Sounds like you need to get home." Matt still had his hand on my arm. "Where's your car?"

"On the edge of the lot, near the fence. Next to a Jaguar XJ."

"That should be easy to spot."

We picked our way over the rutted, gravelly ground, a slice of moon lighting our footsteps.

"There it is," I said, "three cars over."

A few feet behind us, someone brought a pickup to roaring life and backed out of a slot. Headlights flaring, he shifted into drive, lurched forward, and swerved around us. As the truck drove off, its high beams lit up the row of parked cars.

Omigod. I grabbed Matt's arm and came to a sudden stop. In the backseat of the Jag, oblivious to the world around them, Lila Lott and Trey Gregson were locked in each other's arms, deep in the mother of all passionate kisses.

CHAPTER TWENTY-TWO

"Walk on by," Matt said.

We did, arm in arm. At the Lincoln, I unlocked the driver's side door and got in, wincing at the flash of ceiling light.

"They're so caught up in there, I don't think they noticed us," Matt said.

I nodded, but anxious to peel away, I didn't bother to mention a girlie tidbit. In the dark, they might not have recognized Matt, but when the truck's headlights flashed past, the mirrors on my camisole lit up like a fourth of July sparkler. One quick glimpse was all Lila would have needed.

"Be careful. Lock up tight when you get home."

"Will do."

"I'll stick around for a while. See where they go. Make sure they don't follow you."

"What about your date? She must be waiting for you inside." *Why am I harping on that?*

In the sliver of moonlight, I caught a

glimpse of a white grin. "Like I mentioned, she's in good hands," he said then paused. "I'll explain another time, if you're interested."

"I surely am, Sheriff. I want to know all about her."

That was no word of a lie, either. I did want to know who he was seeing, but most of all I wanted to know why Lila Lott would bother making love to any other man in this whole wide world when she had Sam Ridley crazy for her.

It was a rainy Sunday, the kind of Sunday that didn't cause you to feel guilty for lazing around the house in a robe and bare feet, reading the paper, putting clothes in the washer, taking finger food out of the fridge. The kind of Sunday when you screwed up the courage to phone your friends and apologize before they called to see if you were back to normal — whatever that was.

The kind of Sunday you spent wondering, what now? Should I tell myself what I'd seen in the parking lot didn't mean a thing? Lila was just showing her gratitude to Trey? I tried that thought on for size, but it didn't fit. Yet, I'd never be able to go up to Sam, lay a hand on his arm and say, "Darlin', your beloved is a two-timing bitch." Watching the light die in his eyes would kill me too.

Chances are he wouldn't believe me anyway. Then I'd have to drag in Matt to tell what he'd seen and after that . . . oh God Almighty . . . there'd be no staying at Ridley's Real Estate. True, when wedding bells chimed, I'd hit the highway, but Christmas wasn't rolling around anytime soon. And I wasn't ready to roll yet, either.

But if I didn't warn Sam in some way, he was bound to marry Lila, put his whole life in her hands, and as sure as I was slopping around in my ratty chenille robe, she'd destroy him.

Try as I might, no shiny new answer flooded my mind, only the same old, same old — wait and see, he wasn't married yet. Somewhat soothed by that notion and by the rain softly falling against the windows, I whiled away the day, waking to a Monday bright with sunshine and filled with possibility. Something would happen. I knew it right down to the tips of my toes.

Something did, but not what I expected.

With the weather channel calling for warmer than normal temperatures, I searched in the back of my closet for last summer's favorite outfit. Not quite corporate, not quite party, the pink-flowered skirt and snug pink top suited my mood for something light and breezy. I was tempted to add my prettiest necklace, the one made out of big pink shells from the Gulf of Mexico, but I figured it was a bit much for work. Instead, trying not to sigh, I screwed pearl studs in my lobes and settled for some pastel-pink lip gloss. A straw tote, the ivory pumps, and I was good to go.

Eight a.m. and Josie's was jumping. The sausage and hotcakes aroma spilling out onto Main Street lured in anybody who had the price of a greasy good breakfast.

I yanked open the door, hoping for once I'd find an empty booth. Ah. . . . on the end, down near the far wall.

"Well, well, well. Aren't we looking mighty fine this mornin'."

The sugar voice halted me midstride, though I should have ignored it and stomped on by.

But I didn't for some reason. "Morning, Saxby."

He eyeballed me in that leering way he'd perfected and I hated. "Miss Honey, there's one thing about you that's undeniable. You sure can move your real estate."

The pig. I should have known better than to stop.

He waved a hand at the bench opposite

him. "Don't rush off. Sit and have breakfast with me."

"Now why would I want to do that, Mr. Winthrop?"

"Because you never know what interestin' news I might be persuaded to impart."

He had me, the blabbermouth. If I endured his company for a spell, maybe I could pick up a little useful information. I shrugged. "All right. Why not?" I slid onto the empty bench.

Josie came over, one eyebrow raised.

"Put my order on his tab," I said.

At that, her brow came down and the corners of her lips went up.

"I'll have a burger patty, fries, sliced green tomatoes, raisin toast dry, and a large black coffee. Oh, and one more thing. A cinnamon Danish to go." That'd be for Mrs. Otis. She'd find her treat all the sweeter knowing Saxby paid for it.

"A burger. I give up." Without writing a thing on her pad, Josie took off to give Tommy Lee the bad news.

I swung my attention back to Saxby. "If you put a hand on mine, try to play footsie, or brush my arm with a single finger, you'll get scalding coffee. In your lap."

He reared back against the booth.

"That's not nice. What with me payin' and all."

"Exactly. Just so you'll know. Also, when you leave, give Josie a big tip."

"Always do. Don't tell me you forgot."

"I don't mean one of your little-bitty tips." I smiled a saccharine smile. "I'm talking about money."

"Oh, Honey, you're hard. Very hard."

If that was my cue to refer to him, he was bound to eternal disappointment. "So now that I'm sitting here, what do you have to impart?"

He took a sip of his sugar-laced coffee. *Four packets of Dixie Crystals.* "Will you pardon me if I gloat a tiny bit?"

"I'm not sure that's possible, but you can try."

"I sold Sloane's acres right out from under your boss' nose. My client wouldn't even consider letting Ridley's handle the sale."

My coffee came. Josie prided herself on always serving super-hot java, so I'd let it set for a while to cool. "We've both had a sale on Pea Pike, so if anybody's tallying, we're even. Of course, the Norton farm is still available." I foolishly tried a sip of coffee. Lava. "So far, you haven't told me anything you can gloat about."

He ripped open another sugar packet and

dumped it in his mug.

How can he drink that stuff?

"Here's where the gloatin' part comes in."

"I'm all ears."

His gaze fell to my chest. "Not quite."

"Don't be tiresome. You have something to say, say it."

"I've got a client hot to trot on the very Norton property you just mentioned. Said she wanted to consummate," he grinned, "the deal today."

I so want to smack him.

He glanced at his watch. "She's due to meet me here shortly. Comin' in special, all the way from Fayetteville. With a check for the full amount. So add it up. You and Sam got one sale out on that pike. I got two."

"Is Earl Norton claiming the farm's a diamond field? If so, I'm on my way to the sheriff's office."

"Don't get your knickers in a twist over nothin'. Earl's Uncle Henry found some little diamonds down in Murfreesboro years ago. Had a diamond scam in mind but never had the guts to give it a try. Violet was about to, though. Poor ol' gal. Tough way to go." He actually looked upset.

"Why you softie, you."

He gave me a sly smile. "Don't go jump-in' to conclusions, missy."

Josie came on over with a plate of fried eggs and grits in one hand and a coffee carafe in the other. She plunked the eggs in front of Saxby and topped off his mug.

"Your burger'll be out in a minute, Honey, but I've got to tell you something. Tommy Lee's all riled up again. Next time you come in, could you order hotcakes or something?"

"I promise."

She nodded and took off.

"So far, the gloating doesn't amount to much, Saxby."

Egg dripped off his fork. "You want more, well hear this. Somebody else contacted me about another no-account piece out there on the pike. The one at the top of the ridge. It don't even hold scrub grass most of the year, so I'm tellin' you, Honey, Pea Pike's hot, and Winthrop Realty's got it all sewed up." He stirred his coffee, banging the spoon against the mug. "Too bad you left me for Sam Ridley. But I'm a forgivin' man." He stopped fiddling with the spoon for a moment. "I'd consider taking you back."

I nodded as if thinking about his offer. "You know what I'd consider?"

He shook his head, but a light leapt into his eyes.

"Spilling coffee on your crotch."

"A woman scorned."

"Let's get one thing straight, Sax. I'm the scorner. You're the scornee."

"Here's your breakfast," Josie cut off his retort, "or whatever it is you call it."

I dug in, too hungry to just get up and march off. Besides, eating gave me a chance to keep quiet and think. Whoever was buying up that land on Pea Pike did seem to like Winthrop's more than Ridley's.

I shot a quick glance at Saxby. He was scarfing down his grits. Not a pretty sight.

Somehow, I didn't think he'd figured out there might be an underlying reason for his recent sales. Or that those sales might be connected to the two murders.

But those weren't reasons to dismiss him as a rival. Far from it. He'd had great success in his own wily, back-slapping, dirt-scuffing way. By being a good ol' boy whose family helped found Eureka Falls, whose great-granddaddy fought in the War Between the States, whose momma bestowed blue ribbons each year on the best rose growers in the garden club. . . . The list went on.

Coffee halfway to his lips, he peered out our window onto Main Street. "Well, bless my stars." He thumped down his mug.

"That must be my Fayetteville client now. Right on time too. Said she'd be wearing a black pantsuit with a gardenia in her lapel." He squinted through the glass. "That look like a gardenia to you?"

CHAPTER TWENTY-THREE

Tall and willow-slim, except for her well-filled jacket, the blonde strode to Josie's door and stepped inside. She stood by the cash register for a moment and glanced around, no doubt searching for Saxby. I wondered how he'd pictured himself to her. Balding, overweight, oily. Not likely.

Anyway, he slammed down his fork, jumped up as fast as his belly allowed, and hustled over to her. She looked familiar, the hair, the smile, the way she moved her hands. As they approached, an alarm bell bonged in my head. She was the receptionist from IP. The one who gushed into the phone the day Senator Lott called.

My, my. I swallowed the last bite of burger, put on my shades, and flung my purse over a shoulder. Grabbing the doggy bag with Mrs. Otis' Danish, I got up from the booth. No need to sit and chat. This girl was what my daddy would call a shill. Someone I'd call a messenger for the big boys. Sent to do a simple task, she'd have no information to impart.

Still, I didn't fancy being recognized, so without giving Saxby a chance to introduce us, I said, "Thanks for breakfast, Sax. Sorry, have to run," and dashed for the door.

Mrs. Otis was thrilled with her Danish, but I wasn't thrilled that Sam wouldn't be back from the conference until late afternoon. I had so much to tell him, but on the other hand, so much I couldn't tell.

Still, there wasn't time to fret about it. This would be a busy day. Every Sunday, Ridley's placed full-page ads in the *Star,* so on Mondays our phones rang for hours. Mrs. Otis, with her talent for sorting out good leads from bad, forwarded only the most promising to Sam or me. Today I'd have to handle them all. Oh well, business was business.

I'd hardly settled behind my desk when the phone lit up. "Honey Ingersoll speaking. How may I help you?"

"I assure you, we'll find a way."

At the smooth voice oozing through the line, I stiffened in my chair and forgot all about swiveling.

"This is Trey Gregson," he said. "I'm interested in buying a condo here in town.

207

Thought of you right away, Honey."

"Oh, that's so nice to hear. But wouldn't you like to deal directly with Mr. Ridley? He'll be back sometime this afternoon."

"No, I expressly asked for you. The other evening you struck me as someone I'd enjoy doing business with."

"Well, that's downright flattering, I must say. I'm sure we can work something out, Mr. Gregson."

"Trey."

"Tell me, ah, Trey, what do you have in mind?"

"Essentially a bachelor pad, for when I'm in town. The senator's been most hospitable, but it's time I had a place of my own here. Nothing too pricey and it needn't be large. A main room, some kind of efficiency kitchen. A deluxe bathroom would be nice. One bedroom will do."

I'll bet.

"Garage?"

"Yes, thanks for reminding me. I hate leaving my car out in all kinds of weather."

"Understandable." *Wouldn't want that backseat to get wet.*

"The senator and I are returning to DC in a few days, so I'd like to get on this as soon as possible. Today if you can manage it."

"Well, I surely can. Just give me a little bit of time to check Multiple Listings." I glanced at my watch. Nine o'clock. "How about right after lunch?"

"I never eat lunch."

"Neither do I, as a matter of fact. Twelve then. Can you meet me here at the office?"

"I'll be there."

The phone went dead. I hung up and rode the swivel chair like my granny used to ride her rocker whenever something heavy weighed on her mind. Trey's call coming in so soon after Saturday night couldn't be a coincidence, could it? Wanting a private place to crash when he was in town made sense. But why search for one today, practically the first minute we'd been open since his backseat tryst? Besides, even if he did want a condo, guaranteed he had another reason for calling. And I surely did want to learn what that might be.

After asking Mrs. Otis to hold all calls, I closed my cubicle door. Being cooped up usually made me feel like a bug in a box, but today I couldn't let a prissy thing like that stop me. By ten I had a printout of three possibilities and by eleven the owners' okays for afternoon walk-throughs.

At eleven thirty, I refreshed my makeup then set the GPS in the Lincoln. I slipped in a classical music disc too. Something called Handel's *Water Music.* The little tinkling sounds did kind of remind me of something running down the walls, but that was about all I could say for it. I'd rather hear Mariah stomping out a tune, but what kind of impression would that make on the senator's elegant aide? *Humph.*

Back inside, her Danish long gone, Mrs. Otis was munching on a ham and cheese sandwich. She swallowed. "I have five hot leads lined up."

"Sounds good. Why don't you give them to Sam when he comes in?"

I placed a sheet of paper on her desk. "These are the addresses of condos I'm showing this afternoon. I'll be with the senator's aide, Mr. Trey Gregson. If I don't come back or call you by five, I want you to contact Sheriff Rameros. Tell him to come looking for me and give him these addresses. That's his cell phone number on the bottom."

Mid-chew, she looked up, worry lines furrowing her brow. "What are you saying, Honey?"

"Being cautious is all. Not to worry."

She snorted and seemed about to retort when Trey walked in ten minutes early.

A ready smile sprang to his lips as he hurried over to take my hand. "Thanks for meeting me on such short notice."

"Why it's my pleasure."

"And mine," he replied, his smile still in place.

Despite his pockmarked skin, he had an easy, polished air about him. Not hard to see why he might be a famous politician's right-hand man. And in striped blue and white shirt, tailored tan pants, and tasseled loafers, he was one of the best dressed clients I'd ever had.

Hoping he wouldn't see through it, I decided to put an old realty game plan of Saxby's into play. You start with the least saleable property on your list and stress whatever good points it had. "Ahead of the viewing, talk it up," Saxby had said. "Then. when you walk in, keep your mouth shut and let the place do the talking. Make sure the next one in the same price range shows a little better. Save the best for last. After going through a couple of dogs, it'll look like a palace in comparison." Though I never took a shine to head games like that, today, dealing with Lila's lover, I didn't feel like abiding by the Girl Scout oath of honor.

Bottom line, Saxby's sneaky trick did work. When we got to number three, Trey's eyes flared open, a surefire sign of client interest. On the edge of town, farther out than the first two, this condo had all the bells and whistles on his list: a high-ceilinged great room, a galley kitchen with new stainless appliances, a tiled bath featuring a corner Jacuzzi big enough for two, and a single bedroom with plenty of space for a king-size bed. Best of all, on the top floor of the Eureka Arms, the condo offered a sweeping view of the surrounding hills, all decked out in their early summer finery.

"I like it." He nodded. "I like it a lot, but do you mind if I get a second opinion?" He glanced at his watch. "It's one thirty. You have time?"

"Of course."

He strolled into the kitchen with his cell and stood talking as he stared out the window. I couldn't hear who he was talking to, but my heartbeat picked up anyway, kind of like it does, I expect, when a grizzly's coming after you. He hung up, and after fifteen minutes of chitchat that I struggled to keep light and carefree, in came Lila. In riding pants, a crisp white shirt, boots to the knee, and her shiny black hair held back from her face with a velvety ribbon, she was, as always, a sight to behold.

No wonder Sam had fallen in love with her, and from the way Trey rushed to open the door at the chimes' first ring, he had too.

She greeted me with a thin smile and a nod. Wasting no time on small talk, she strutted through the empty rooms, her boot heels clicking on the hardwood floors. Her tour quickly over, she returned to the main room, frowning as if she hadn't seen a thing to her liking. "Well, I suppose it will do, Trey. But I don't see the necessity for it. You know you're welcome to stay on with Daddy and me. Just as you always have. In fact, Daddy would prefer it."

"Perhaps so." His voice was chilly. "But your father understands my need for privacy."

She looked past him, directly at me, her eyes dark and lustrous. Was there nothing about this woman that wasn't downright beautiful? I heaved a mental sigh.

"Are you aware, Honey, that my father, Senator Lott —"

"I know who your daddy is."

Her frown deepened. Being interrupted must be a new experience for her.

"Yes, most people do." She cleared her throat. "But what most people don't know is Father's planning a run for the presidency. Are you aware of that?"

Ah, the real reason she had joined us

today. Damage control. So she had recognized me in the parking lot and was afraid I'd recognized her. Now she wanted me silent about what I might have seen. Not surprising. Screwing around with Daddy's top aide, a man whose ex-girlfriend had recently been murdered, would make headlines. Toss in Lila's engagement to another man and the media would go wild.

Underneath her cool, smooth skin, she must be scared stiff. She'd have to be to stoop to a faked-up meeting like this, even though she was acting mighty uppity about it. Anyway, real estate sure hadn't brought her here. As she arched an eyebrow, waiting for my reply, a to-hell-with-the-condo attitude practically seeped out of her pores.

"Yes, I heard tell the senator has his eye on the White House,"

"You 'heard tell' correctly," she said with a sneer. "He'll be announcing in August, during the Senate's recess."

"Interesting, Miss Lott. But why are you telling me this now?" *Let's get our cards on the table here.*

"No particular reason."
Liar, liar, pants on fire.

"Except I don't allow anything to disturb Daddy. He likes having Trey close by, so I'd prefer he stay with us when he's in town.

And though I hate to have Sam's firm lose a sale, I really wish to discourage this purchase." With a catch in her voice, she added, "Daddy's everything to me. I don't want anything or anyone to upset him. Ever."

"That's mighty sweet of you." I cleared my throat, though I didn't need to. "But I save my worrying for Ridley's Real Estate, and for Mr. Ridley himself."

"I have Sam's interests in mind too, but you need to understand something, Honey." She crossed the room, coming so close, the angry flush blooming on her cheekbones couldn't be missed. "Someday soon, my father will be president of the United States. He'll take his place in history. That's the important factor here. In comparison to that, nobody else's needs matter. Not mine, not Sam's, not Trey's.

"Before the election, every aspect of Daddy's life will be examined under a microscope. The public thrives on half-truths, misconceptions. Lies even. What will surely be brought up is Trey's relationship with that unfortunate girl who was killed."

"Tallulah Bixby."

"See what I mean? Everyone knows."

"In this, I'm not everyone. I found her body."

"Oh. Right. We're sorry about what happened to her." Lila paused. "For several reasons. The press will drag their relationship out into the sun and make hay with it. At this point, there's nothing to be done about that. But any further upsets of any kind are to be avoided at all costs. We can't give the press more ammunition to use against us. We can't risk anything that might derail Daddy's campaign."

I glanced across the room. As Lila launched into her willingness to fight for Daddy, Trey left the battlefield in her hands and turned away to stare out the window. This had all been a setup. Compared to it, my sneaky sales plan had been pitiful. I'd been used. Trey Gregson wasn't the slightest bit interested in buying a condo.

Red hot mad and boiling over with it, I stared into Lila's perfect, movie-star face. "Since Daddy's political career is so fucking important, all concerned parties need to behave themselves. At all times. In all places. Don't you agree, Miss Lott?"

She gasped. For a second there, I thought she would hit me. Glad she hadn't brought her riding crop along, I stared her down, daring her to kick up a fuss, to out and out threaten me. But she didn't. I had to hand it to her. She was too smart for such doings.

All's she said was, "I believe we understand each other, Honey. I don't want Daddy upset, and you don't want Sam upset. It's as simple as that. Maybe we should shake on it."

I made no attempt to take her outstretched hand. For a long moment, it hovered in the air between us before she let it fall to her side.

Her voice soft, she said, "I heard you grew up in a trailer. It shows."

Boots clicking, she strode toward the condo door. "Coming, Trey?"

"Not yet, Lila. You run along. I'll see you at the house as soon as Honey and I finish our business."

We still had business to finish? Don't tell me Trey was going to up and feud with the boss' daughter?

Yessiree.

"The asking price is fine," he said as soon as we were alone. "Let's not dicker. I don't have the time."

Using the kitchen counter as a tabletop, I filled out a sales agreement while he wrote a deposit check.

"I'll see Cletus Dwyer in the morning about a mortgage," he said.

"I'm sure you won't have a problem."

He sent me a half-smile. "Not with Cletus." His gaze drifted back to the window. "I love the place. It's just what I had in mind."

So he'd been interested in buying a condo all along. I'd misjudged him and felt a little guilty about it and more than a little surprised.

"The view *is* gorgeous," I said. "It reminds me of the one from the Hermann farmhouse."

That was when he gave me another jolt. "It does, doesn't it? The same rolling hills, the same southern exposure."

What? When had Trey been on the Hermann farm? I stared at him, gape-mouthed. Could it possibly have been the day Tallulah was killed?

CHAPTER TWENTY-FOUR

For what it might be worth, the police needed to know Trey had likely paid a visit to the Hermann farm. I'd call Matt as soon as I got back to Ridley's. As for Lila and Trey and whatever their relationship might be, my lips were sealed. Sam was a mighty clever man. If his fiancée wasn't worthy of his trust, he'd find that out, wouldn't he? Yes, sooner or later, and I hoped to God it wouldn't be later, as in too late.

"I'm back," I said to Mrs. Otis as soon as I stepped in the office. "No problem."

"Not so sure about that, Honey. The sheriff's in Sam's office with that detective from Fayetteville. They're waiting for you."

For the second time that afternoon, my heart began a wild racing. And rightly so, as things turned out.

They both stood when I walked in. Neither one smiled.

"Honey, Detective Bradshaw has a few

questions for you," Matt said. "Why don't you have a seat?"

I did. Good thing. My knees had gone all wobbly.

"Those diamonds you found on the Norton property . . ." the detective began.

"Yes?"

"What did you do with them?"

"I gave them to Violet Norton." I shifted in my seat, trying to find a comfortable spot. "Look, I've already gone on record with that."

He held up a hand, palm out for silence.

"I'm aware of your statement. The heir to the Norton estate . . ."

What a highfalutin word for that scruffy hilltop.

". . . claims he can't find the stones."

"That's strange. I put them in Violet's hands."

Matt and Detective Bradshaw exchanged a glance. Not good.

My chin came up. "I'm not a liar, Detective." True most of the time and especially about serious doings like this.

"Honey," Matt said, "Detective Bradshaw is just trying to protect you. The problem is, you found the bodies of two murder victims. Now, even in something relatively minor, you need to be free of any hint of blame. Do you understand?"

I nodded, feeling lightheaded. "What you're telling me is folks will say if I could steal, I could kill. Is that it?"

"That's exactly what we don't want said." Matt stopped all of a sudden as if he hated to go on. "Violet's nephew, Earl Norton, is planning to sue you for theft."

"That's downright silly. Why would I tell the police about the diamonds and then do something so stupid?"

"We believe you, Miss Ingersoll," Detective Bradshaw said, "but it's your word against his. We want to keep him from pursuing this lawsuit idea. He won't win the case, in any event. Miz Norton could have thrown those stones into the creek for all we know, or done any of a thousand things with them. Or her killer could have. But a lawsuit would drag your name through the county courts. We know you don't want that. Neither do we. So if you have anything to tell us, now is the time before this thing escalates."

"You've already been told everything." I stood, my knees as firm as rocks. "Am I under arrest?"

"Of course not," Matt said.

"We're only trying to help, Miss Ingersoll."

"I understand. Now, if you gentlemen will excuse me, I have work to do."

"Don't take that atti—"

I strode out of Sam's office and over to Mrs. Otis, back ramrod straight. "When Sam comes in, please tell him I sold a condo in the Eureka Arms. Here's the paperwork." I stepped away from her desk. "I'll see you tomorrow."

"Where you off to?"

"The Norton farm. There's a problem out there."

"I'll say. Poor Violet."

"No, not that. Well, yes that, but something else has gone wrong."

"And you're going out there alone?" She gestured over a shoulder. "You should ask one of the policemen to go with you."

"No. I have to prove something to them, or I'll be accused of theft. Big time theft. Diamonds."

"Well, for land's sake." Mrs. Otis reached into her lower desk drawer for her purse and heaved to her feet. "I have no idea what you're yammering on about, but whatever it is, you're not going out to that farm alone. I'm going with you."

"But it's not five yet. The office —"

"Honey Ingersoll, you shut your mouth."

This was far from a laughing moment, but

I busted out laughing anyway. "I can't believe you said that."

"Believe. Now, let's get the cops out of here and close up shop."

Lord, she was wonderful.

After locking up, we hurried out to the Lincoln and headed for the pike. So Earl had searched Violet's house, had he? Well, I'd stake my next sales commission on the fact he hadn't looked in the most logical place of all. A place a man wouldn't dream of searching.

As we drove along, I gradually cooled down, and a little reality set in. If I hadn't been so furious leaving the office, I might have asked Matt to come with us. Probably should have. But I'd been too damn mad to think straight. Besides, when folks said a murderer always returned to the scene of the crime, they were just repeating an ol' granny's tale. Everybody knew that.

At the top of the rise, wisps of smoke trailed out of the farmhouse chimney. A pickup sat in the front yard. I parked behind it and turned to Mrs. Otis, who was belted into the passenger seat and as calm as if we were on a church outing. "I'm going in alone."

"No, you're not." She fumbled for her seatbelt buckle.

"Alone. If I'm not back out in ten minutes, call 911. You have your cell handy?"

She wasn't happy, but she nodded, and taking her phone from her purse, she set it on her lap.

I kissed her cheek, feeling guilty as sin for involving her in all this. "You'll be fine, Mrs. O." I hoped to heaven that was true.

"It's not me I'm worried about," she said tartly, waving me on. "Go ahead, do whatever darn fool thing you came out here to do, so's we can get on home."

I locked the car and carefully made my way over the lumpy ground. High heels did great things for legs but not much for feet.

Before I reached the front porch, the farmhouse door creaked open. Tucking his hands into his overall bib, Earl Norton stood blocking the doorway.

"My, my. This sure is a surprise. You got some reason comin' out here?" His eyes narrowed as he gave me a whole body scan. "Reckon there's no need of askin'. You must've heard I went to the sheriff about those diamonds you took."

I sighed. This wasn't going to be easy. "I didn't take Violet's diamonds. I found them and gave them to her."

"Yeah? Where're they at, then?"

"If you'll let me in, I might be able to find them."

He stepped aside. "Sure, come on in."

"You alone?"

A grin split his face. "Yes, ma'am."

He wouldn't try anything, would he? Small, weaselly Earl Norton? I took a deep breath and stepped up onto the porch. "I can't stay but a minute. Someone's waiting on me in the car."

"No need to rush off. Let 'em wait." He followed me inside and shut the door.

With Earl on my heels, I headed for the kitchen. A wood fire burned in the old-timey stove, most likely getting ready to heat up Earl's supper. Over by the far wall, next to the Scottish sideboard, hung the peg row I remembered. Violet's frayed brown sweater hung from one peg and next to it the apron she wore the day I brought back the diamonds. My hope was that Earl, like most men, would tear a house apart but not think to check out a woman's apron pocket.

I marched across the rickety floor, and plucking the apron off the peg, felt the pocket. Sure enough, the little cloth sack sat right in there. I removed it and dumped the diamonds into my palm.

I held them out.

"Here they are. Safe and sound."

He snatched them up, and after rolling them around in his palm, dropped them into his overalls pocket.

"Be sure to tell the sheriff you found the diamonds," I said, "because I surely will."

I'd about reached the outer door when a hard, callused hand grabbed my arm. "I'm not tellin' him nothin'. Not unless you co-operate."

I looked at his grin and shuddered. "I have to get back to work, Earl. Sam's expecting me."

"And I 'spect some of what he's gettin'."

"You're wrong there. He's my boss, that's it."

"Yeah? Ol' Saxby Winthrop was your boss too, and he tells a mighty different tale."

"Get your hand off me, Earl."

His grip tightened. "You want to go to jail for stealin'? You will if you don't get off your high horse."

"Blackmail? You're going to blackmail me, you little wimp?"

"I'll show you who's little."

My heart was jumping in my chest like a live animal. I needed to smack Earl with something hard, but all I had was my purse. Loaded as it was, that ought to do. "How can we get it together, Earl, if you don't let go of me first?"

Taking that as an invitation, he released me. Freed of his grip, I raised my right arm, and using the same smash to the head I'd used on Billy Tubbs, I let him have it right between those leering eyes.

"Ooowww!"

I ran for the door, swinging it open so hard it banged against the outer wall.

Earl recovered fast and raced me to my car. I had the lead but also the high heels. A split second ahead of him, I slid behind the wheel and jammed down the locks. He grabbed the door handle.

"Too late, Earl!" I yelled.

His face livid, he pounded on the window. Mrs. Otis, not to be outdone, pounded as hard on the inside glass. Between the two of them, they'd break it if I didn't get out of there. I turned on the engine, ready to do an Indy 500 down the rise when a car came surging onto the scruffy turf, screeching to a stop in back of me. A quick glance through the rearview mirror and my heart slowed to a sweet, steady beat.

Sam got out of his car and slammed the door. "Get away from her, Earl."

"Hey, this is my property. You can't tell me what to do."

Sam sauntered up to him, slow and easy, like he was on a country stroll. An arm's length away, he stopped, saying nothing, staring straight ahead. I think he was staring at the red spot between Earl's eyes, right where a bullet usually landed in those TV crime shows. Right where I'd smashed him with my purse.

Well, as for Earl, he couldn't stand the silence. Before long he was scuffing at the dirt with a toe of his shit-kickers. "Aw, you don't have to take on that way, Sam. Nothin's goin' down."

"Good." Sam's voice was as cold as a gulp of ice water.

I lowered my window and leaned out. "Sam, have Earl show you the diamonds."

"The what?"

"Just ask him. They're in his overalls pocket. I saw him put them there."

Though not knowing what this was about, Sam upped his chin at Earl anyway. "You heard the lady. Show me what you got."

"No problem. She's fussin' about nuthin'."

Earl reached into his overalls for the stones and held them out to Sam. Then, dropping them back in his pocket, he jerked his head in my direction. "Satisfied now?"

"Yes. Thanks for being so honest."

"Always have been. Always will be. Now, you got any more reason to talk to me?"

Sam nodded. "You lay a hand on Honey again, you won't live to regret it."

"Oh, yeah? You fixin' to kill me, that it?" Earl pointed a skinny arm at the rut road. "Get off my land. Both of you."

"*Your* land? Heard tell you sold it, Earl."

"You heard right. I'll be outta here soon enough, but I want you outta here now."

"No problem. We're leaving."

Mrs. Otis lowered her window. "Shame all over you, Earl Norton. Violet must be turning in her grave about now."

Sam ducked his head in the open window. "Follow me out to the pike. Park by the highway. We need to talk."

Nerve endings frayed but otherwise in control, I drove down the rise. Sam had parked a few hundred feet ahead on the edge of the pike. I pulled up behind him and walked over to his car.

Jaw set, lips pressed together, he said, "Get in."

He sat quietly, hands on knees, looking straight ahead for a moment before turning his gaze full on me. One more second without a word and I swear I would have. . . .

"I have a question for you," he said. "What in hell possessed you to come back out here, and with Mrs. Otis, of all people, in tow?"

"The diamonds."

He raised a hand and made little circles in the air with it. "I don't understand. Enlighten me."

"Didn't Matt Rameros explain?"

"No, I haven't spoken to Matt in days."

"How did you know where I was?"

"Mrs. Otis had the presence of mind to leave a note on my desk. The desk in the office that I found closed and locked in the middle of the afternoon."

Oh.

"Well, go on. Let's hear it." His voice was cold, so cold, and his eyes. . . .

"Earl accused me of stealing those uncut stones. He was threatening to sue. So I had to find them."

"Did it not occur to you to ask me to go with you? Or the sheriff?" His eyes were spitting fire. "You know Earl Norton's shady reputation around town. A beautiful girl like you putting yourself in harm's way, coming out here to deal with that creep. . . . His aunt was murdered here. Who knows? Maybe he was involved. I don't get it, Honey. You're intelligent as well as beautiful. A dumb move like this doesn't add up."

That he was beyond vexed was painfully clear, but all I really heard was "beautiful." *Imagine.* And "intelligent." Then he said something I couldn't ignore.

"Earl would have lied, you know. Kept on pretending you were a thief."

Oh Lord, that was right. How could I not have figured that out ahead of time? Embarrassed, I tried to slump into the cushions, not easy when you were perched on the finest Italian leather.

All the starch washed out of me. I sat there like a scolded child, hardly daring to move. Finally, I did risk looking up from my hands and across the seat at him. "Thank you, Sam. I'm beholden to you."

He leaned over to pat my hand, but he didn't smile.

"We've discussed this subject before," he said, "but understand, this is the last time. From here on in you only handle listings in town. Got that?"

I nodded, not trusting myself to speak.

"Good. Because that's an order."

CHAPTER TWENTY-FIVE

What Sam left unsaid was that I'd better follow his order to the letter or he'd fire me. Though he didn't know it, my days at Ridley's Real Estate were numbered anyway. That pat on the hand had made up my mind once and for all. I wasn't the kind of girl a man could pat like a puppy and then get in his car and drive away. Next thing you knew, he'd be patting me on the top of the head.

If I'd been wishy-washy about leaving Eureka Falls, I no longer was. No question, I'd hightail it out of here by the time Sam married Lila. Not just because I couldn't stand to lose him, but for another reason. He'd saved me today, but I couldn't save him. Not without trashing his dream and his love. Something I couldn't bring myself to do.

Since I was leaving anyway, I should have grabbed him while I had the chance, thrown my arms around him and kissed the blue right out of those eyes. Stunned them purple. Made that mouth soften up and open wide, made. . . .

I banged the wheel. *Damn.* I'd been too wimpy to do a single one of those things. Earlier, I hadn't even had the guts to tell Lila to quit two-timing Sam, hadn't made Saxby admit IP was up to no good, hadn't even asked Trey why all of a sudden he had to have his own Eureka Falls pad. None of that was strictly my business, but still, why hadn't I? What did I have to lose? Nothing, now that I'd made up my mind to leave. On the other hand, by pushing back, I might get to the bottom of whatever the hell was going on around here. Maybe even get myself off the Arkansas State Police radar screen. Who knew? I might even find out who killed those two women.

As Sam's rear lights turned into red dots on the horizon, I put the Linc in gear. Doing ten over the speed limit all the way back to town, I drove Mrs. Otis to the office to pick up her car then headed directly to Winthrop Realty's parking lot, hoping Saxby hadn't left for the day.

Good, he hasn't.

His Cadillac — real estate rule number one: impress the clients with major wheels

— occupied pride of place in the sacred slot signed, RESERVED FOR PRESIDENT. Another man with leadership ideas.

I eased into one of the customer parking spaces and marched up to the rear entrance. At least I wouldn't have to break in this time.

Mindy of the long black hair and the long white legs sat at a computer filing her nails. She glanced up when I yanked the door open, surprise flaring in her eyes. Away from the Inn's flattering candlelight, she looked older than I remembered. A good thing. Saxby didn't need to toy with somebody's kid sister.

"I'm here to see your boss." Without waiting for permission, I barged past her and strutted right in to Saxby's private office.

At the sight of me, he half rose out of his chair. "What are you doing here?" He slumped back on his fanny. "The enemy camp, so to speak."

"Thanking you for breakfast." I sat in the leatherette chair facing his desk. "Also looking for some answers, for old times' sake."

At a soft rap on the door, he barked, "Come in."

I glanced over a shoulder.

One hand on the door, Mindy poked her head in. "She slipped past me without so much as a by-your-leave."

"It's all right. Go back to your desk."

The door closed on silent hinges.

"You have her well trained."

Sighing, he cradled his belly in his hands. " 'Fraid so. No challenge there. Too bad, a man likes a challenge."

I leaned forward. "Good. Here's one for you. Who's buying up all that property off Pea Pike?"

His eyes flared wide, well, as wide as his puffy cheeks would allow. "You know I can't say."

"Yes, you can. If you choose to. Let's face it, Saxby. You've already let the horse out of the barn. I know International Properties is in on it. What I want to know is why. What's their game?"

For an answer, he opened a lower desk drawer and hauled out a bottle of Jack Daniels and two shot glasses. "It's almost closin' time. Care to join me?"

"No thanks."

He poured himself a stiff one, raised his glass in a silent salute and down went the Jack.

"That the same bottle I remember?"

"Very funny. That's what I always liked about you, Honey, the challenge."

He poured another and cocked an eyebrow.

I shook my head. Good bourbon, and bad, always mellowed him. I remembered that only too well. So I waited, engaging him in small talk, flirting, flattering, biding my time, in hopes that he would spill what he knew between drink number two and drink number three. After that, he'd turn nasty, and his mouth would get mean. *I raised you out of the gutter, Missy, and don't you go forgettin' it.*

"The problem, Saxby, is that families who paid taxes on that land for years are making mighty little on those sales, and that's wrong. Very wrong. Cobbled together, worthless farmland can be worth a fortune. So, say some conglomerate is coming in with big plans. They have almost half a mile of open land to build on. Isn't that right?"

His eyes got smaller and narrower. The bourbon or me? He slammed the empty shot glass on his desktop.

"Pumpin' me for information, are you? While I'm philosophically opposed to such doin's, you may be in luck." He leaned back, a man at ease, just doing a little light swiveling. "I sold me another parcel up there on that ridge. The one I told you about this mornin'. So tote 'em up. Three for me and one for you and that current boss of yours. Yeah, IP is the buyer of the whole damn shebang." He brought the chair to a halt. "Now hear me good. Nobody's getting screwed." He tried for a smile but failed. "That land's not worth a plug nickel. Can't hardly grow an ear of corn on it. I sold my three parcels for what the market would bear. Fair and square. And the sellers were grateful to unload them. You heard me, missy, grateful. No conspiracy theories. Just sales."

He poured a third. About to raise it to his lips, he paused. "You tryin' to make trouble, Miss Honey? Do me out of my hard-won prize? Well, don't bother. My momma didn't raise no fools."

Hoping my momma hadn't either, but not at all sure about that, I left him swiveling and drinking away. So, from the lion's mouth, I'd heard what I suspected all along, though the knowing didn't make me feel a single bit better.

On my way past Mindy, I stopped at her computer station.

"He's going to need a ride home," I told her.

"I can drive," she said with a sniff.

" 'Course you can." I rummaged in my tote for a business card. "Me too. Been on that drive, but I got off." I dropped a card beside her keyboard. "Take care of yourself, 'cause if you don't, nobody else will. Should you ever need help, feel free to contact me. Any time."

What I didn't mention was she had a six-month window of opportunity to take me up on my offer.

"I'm beholden to you," she called as I reached the rear door.

I waved and hurried outside.

Phew, what a day. I'd made a sale, squelched a lawsuit, almost got raped, and had nearly been fired. Enough. I needed to shop for groceries then go home, toss on my chenille robe, and collapse with a cold one.

In the morning I had a little social call to make. Depending on how fruitful it turned out, a second call might also be in order. Whatever it took, until I got some solid answers, I'd follow every lead, every question, no matter who I offended, no matter whose toes I stepped on. That was one great thing about burning your bridges. You had nothing to lose.

Or did you?

Chapter Twenty-Six

The apartment house I lived in was a fair to middling place. The janitor kept the grass cut in summer, the snow shoveled in winter, and put the trash out for pickup as regular as sunrise. Its units rented mostly by working singles and a few middle-aged couples I seldom laid eyes on, the building was quiet as a graveyard, which suited me just fine.

Best of all, it was affordable. As a bonus, my first-floor apartment boasted a bedroom patio that faced a small stand of evergreens, a perfect spot for morning coffee on days I didn't have to hurry off to work.

I parked out front in my assigned slot, grabbed the groceries from the backseat, and keyed my way in. Dusk's soft, gray veil had settled over the rooms, so I snapped on the living room lights and carried my bundles out to the kitchen. That was when I felt it. The warm, humid air of summer, strong enough to riffle the pages of the morning

Star left out on the kitchen table. Where could that draft be coming from? Before going to work, I'd turned on the AC and closed the windows.

Oh, no, I hadn't. The bedroom sliders were open. I dropped the groceries and my purse on a countertop and went to close the sliders. One foot in the bedroom was as far as I got. Quick as a lightning flash, before I could scream or turn around, something heavy struck a blow to my head and the world disappeared.

Dusk had deepened when I came to, awakened by the throbbing on my scalp. Chill, damp air flooded in through the sliders. I shivered and opened an eye. Why was I on the bedroom floor, my cheek pressed to the carpeting? *Oh.*

Someone moaned. That couldn't be me, could it? I raised my head an inch or so and glanced around. Everywhere I looked, to the left, to the right, clothes and underwear littered the room. How strange. A rainy gust of air set my teeth chattering. I had to move. Get up. Call for help.

On hands and knees, I hovered until the room stopped spinning then crawled across the carpet to the side of the bed. With no strength to pull myself onto the mattress and reach across for the house phone, I laid my head on the comforter and waited a while. After a time, my eyes opened, but the room kept on spinning.

On my knees, I inched over to the night-stand and fumbled for the phone, in my panic knocking the receiver off the cradle. *Oh, God,* had it rolled under the mattress? My fingers groped around in a circle. *There.* I grasped the phone and punched in 911.

Matt turned up first. He found me on the floor beside the bed. I remember blinking as the lights flared on. He knelt beside me, taking one of my hands in his, rubbing it, murmuring words I couldn't seem to under-stand. Then, in no time at all, he leaped to his feet, shouting, "In here. She's in here!"

A faint pink colored the sky when I woke in a strange room. A hospital room. A blanket covered the sheet on my narrow bed. Warm and safe, I was about to drop back to sleep when I spotted Matt slumped in an arm-chair. Legs wide apart, eyes closed, he looked dead to the world. What on earth was he doing here? I must have stirred, for his eyes snapped open.

He jumped up and hurried over to me. "You're awake."

I nodded and regretted it. "Where am I?"

"Yarborough County Hospital. How are you feeling?"

"The way I must look."

"You look fine as always. A little pale maybe."

"How long have you been here?"

He hesitated.

"All night?"

"Yeah. In case you got scared or needed something, or . . . hell, I just wanted to be near you."

"I didn't see it coming, Matt." My voice was all trembly.

"No. Looks like you caught the creep by surprise." His jaw tensed. "But don't worry. We'll find who did it."

Careful to avoid the bump on my forehead, he leaned over to give me a hug, and his comforting didn't stop there. Before I knew it, he had slipped off his shoes and slid under the blanket beside me. Taking me in his arms, he cuddled me against him. His solid strength felt so wonderful, my whole body curved into his, and I would have breathed a sigh of content but for one thing, "I thought you didn't like one-night stands?"

"I don't. It's morning."

"Oh. You packing?"

He laughed and pulled me closer. "Go to

sleep, Honey."

And I did.

He must have too, or else he lay still as a stone, for the next thing I knew, a nurse came bustling into the room. "My, my," she said, "look at you two."

"Just keeping the patient warm." Matt eased out from under the covers.

"So you'll know in future, sir, we keep blankets for that purpose."

"Won't happen again, ma'am." Matt slid on his loafers. "Crisis is over."

"Would you mind stepping out for a few minutes?" The nurse's tone was as full of starch as her green scrubs.

He winked at me. "Not at all. I'll be right outside."

When she finished taking my blood pressure and other vitals, she checked the bump on my head. "You have a concussion, but you responded well to your overnight wake-ups. So you should be released today. Normally we wouldn't have kept you overnight, but according to your chart, the police officer who found you insisted. Said you lived alone and would be at risk. Offered to pay for your stay. Wasn't that considerate of him?" She helped me to the bathroom. "You don't find many cops like that. By the way, who's your boyfriend? He's real cute."

"I guess you've never gotten a speeding ticket." I closed the bathroom door on the question springing to her lips. "I'll be fine alone."

A pasty-looking image stared at me in the bathroom mirror. I rinsed my face, scrubbed my teeth with a toothbrush I found in a small basket of grooming supplies, and raked a hand through my hair, careful not to touch the throbbing spot above my left ear.

Finished, I let the nurse guide me back to bed, though I didn't need to be helped.

She arranged the covers. "Want your boyfriend to come back in?"

I nodded. *Uh-oh.* I'd have to remember not to do that for a while.

Wide awake now, I could see how tired and weary-eyed Matt was. "You have a bad night?"

"Not one of my best, but it could have been a lot worse."

"Thanks, Matt, for everything. I owe you."

He grinned. "That's a subject for another day. For now," he pulled a chair over to the side of the bed, "if you're up to it, I'd like to talk about what happened."

"I'm up to it, but I don't have much to tell."

"Whatever you can recall."

After I went over the ugly little scene, he asked, "What was the rest of your day like yesterday? Tell me everything from early morning until the time of the assault."

When my story ended, he said, "That's it? Nothing more?"

"Only a question. Think whoever killed Tallulah and Violet wanted to kill me?"

He shrugged. "First of all, we haven't established that the same person killed both women. Though it's highly likely. Second, if the intent was to kill you, you wouldn't be here now. The signs point to a scare tactic. You've been asking questions, probing wounds. Somebody doesn't like that. I'm reading the assault as a warning to cool it. Also, we can't discount the possibility of a random break-in."

"You don't believe that, though, do you?"

"No. My cop's gut says otherwise. Your clothes scattered all over the room sent a message. 'You mess up my life, I'll mess up yours.' If I had to guess, I'd say someone wants you to stop asking questions about Pea Pike."

"Then there *is* a connection between those sneaky real estate deals and the murders."

He shook his head. "That's a conclusion

you can't jump to. So, take the warning seriously and let the police do their work."

"But they're not making any progress."

"You don't know that. A certain amount
of secrecy is the name of the procedural
beast. Also," he paused, "I've been in touch
with Mrs. Otis. We agreed that you should
stay at her place for a while."

I bolted upright. A bad move. It sent my
head reeling. I eased back against the pillows, vexed with the way I felt, with life in
general, and with Matt Rameros in particular. "Shouldn't I have been asked first?"

"No, you shouldn't. I didn't want to risk
your refusal."

"You didn't? Since when —"

He threw his hands in the air, palms out.
"Whoa, girl. It's temporary. Only until your
landlord can install an alarm system in your
apartment. Mrs. Otis is pretty excited." The
suspicion of a smile quirked up his lips.
"She's putting you in her pink bedroom,
the one with all her granddaughter's teddy
bears."

"Not funny. I think this is —"

"The best possible plan. Also —"

"Another 'also'?"

"This one you'll like. Your boss agrees you
can't go home until that alarm system's in
place. To sweeten the deal, he's giving Mrs.

Otis a bonus for having you."

"So now I'm a charity case."

"So now you're an object of loving concern."

Well, that did sound a sight better. Besides, it made horse sense, and I was lucky to have such kindly people looking out for me. No point in acting as if my momma hadn't taught me any manners. I held out a hand. "It's a deal. Also, thank you." He rewarded me with a lopsided grin. "Thank you very much."

Circumstances being what they were, I was forced to wrap myself in one of Mrs. Otis' robes and lay low for a couple of days reading, watching TV and napping on her doily-covered furniture. When not at the office, she likely crocheted up a storm, for her house was festooned with her handiwork. The sweetheart. Each evening, after working all day, she came home with a box of pastries for dessert and started right in preparing a hefty dinner for the two of us. She was a great cook, a firm believer that butter, cream, and pork fat were part and parcel of any decent meal.

I could die happy eating her greens alone. She fixed them with a ham hock bought special for that purpose and a dab of lard, flavored them up with salt, and kept them on the fire till they were cooked through and went all limp. I hadn't had anything as good as them . . . those greens since Momma passed. Nowadays all the restaurants gave you was little bitty salads made out of lettuce and tomato and served up raw. The only way I could ever get one down was to slather on the ranch dressing, and what kind of vegetable was that? No, give me a mess of well-cooked greens any day. But as much as I loved them, and Mrs. Otis, I had to heal fast and get out of there before I blimped up beyond all recognition.

Still, the pampering warmed my heart, so I tried to relax and enjoy it, though my mind was refusing to cooperate. I had to get back to normal, back to work, back to searching for answers to the questions that wouldn't go away.

Two days later, with Grandma Swope pressed into babysitting the boys, Amelia, accompanied by Deputy Ellie, went into my apartment. As far as they could tell, nothing was missing. Amelia hung up my clothes and folded my underthings in the bureau drawers then packed a bag with toiletries and a few basic outfits. Her assignment over, Ellie went back to the station, and

Amelia brought my things over to Mrs. O's. I wasted no time switching into black pants and a fresh T-shirt. Right away I felt like a different woman.

"Can you stay for a while," I asked, "have some tea?"

"Yes, Joe's mom won't mind if I do. She's been very helpful lately." A shadow passed over Amelia's face.

"You're not happy about that? Isn't it a relief to have a little help once in a while?"

"Yeeees." Long, drawn out, sounding like a no.

"What's the matter?" And then I knew. "Joe?"

She nodded. "His momma wants us to get back together. Says the boys need a father. That's true. I know that's true, but," she clenched her hands so tight the knuckles turned bone white, "he found out I went to the roadhouse with you."

"How?"

She shrugged. "Any one of a half-dozen guys could have told him. He didn't like it." She shuddered. "Not one bit. Said he was going to see you about it too."

"Oh he did, did he?" I placed a hand over her white knuckles. "He hit you?"

"No. Threatened is all. Told me if I went out drinking and carousing again, he'd have the boys taken away from me. Claim I was an unfit mother."

I snorted my disgust. "That's crazy. He has a record and he's threatening you?"

"He won't make good on it. He never makes good on anything, but it's worrisome all the same. I feel him all around me, all the time, even when he's not there."

"You need to tell the police," I said.

That was when she hit me with a surprise.

"Don't fret, Honey. I'm not listening to Joe. He may be the father of the boys, but he's no daddy to them. He never will be." Her chin came up. "We're finished. Either I make a new life for my sons, or I might as well up and die. And I'm not ready for dying." She smiled. "Not with Saturday night to get ready for."

"Oh?" I put down the butter cookie I was about to bite into.

She took a sip of tea. "Yup. I need a dress. Something simple but nice. Any chance you feel up to going shopping with me? I haven't bought a dress in so long, I don't know where to go or what to look for."

I bit the cookie in half. Mrs. Otis was right. Butter made a big difference.

"You going someplace special?"

She carefully placed Mrs. Otis' dainty, flowered teacup in its saucer. "Yes, ma'am.

Mr. Cletus Dwyer invited me for dinner at the Inn on Saturday evening. And you know something?" She glanced over at me with shiny eyes.

"You're going!"

"Yes, I surely am."

We fell into each other's arms, whooping with delight. Her smile, like morning sun coming over Pea Pike, lit up the kitchen.

I jumped off my chair without thinking, and for the first time in two days, the room didn't tilt. "Let's go while you have a sitter. You drive." I bustled around, putting away the rest of the cookies, rinsing the cups, and hurrying into the pink-teddy-bear room for my purse. All the while moving faster than I had since before the break-in. "First stop, Belinda's Boutique. Her prices are good and she usually has a few plainer things mixed in with the sequined stuff. Do you have a color in mind?"

Long-legged, full-bosomed, and with a waist as narrow as a teenage girl's, Amelia looked lovely in every dress she tried on. I took a fancy to a yellow one with beaded orchids on the skirt, but she rightly decided on a sleeveless cotton in a soft shade of peach that brought out the auburn highlights in her hair.

251

"What about shoes?" I asked as we left Belinda's.

She came to a panicked halt on the sidewalk. "All I have are sneakers and flip-flops."

"Let's go to Shepherd's Department Store. They have a good selection."

"But I can't afford new shoes."

"My treat." I drew her over to the car. "Let me do this. For all you've done for me."

"Well, I guess Cletus wouldn't care for my sneakers too much."

Amelia had never worn spikes, so rather than wobble around all Saturday evening, she chose a pair of low-heeled ivory sandals that would go well with the dress.

Though my head pounded, I wasn't ready to give up. We had one more stop to make. The Clip Joint. Luckily the manicurist had an opening, and over my protests, Amelia sat down and enjoyed the first mani-pedi of her life.

That she would be beautiful on Saturday evening there was no doubt. And with a little nudge from the gods, maybe her life would turn out to be beautiful too.

I hoped so and rode back to Mrs. Otis' dog-tired but happy. I'd have a nap after Amelia left for home, enjoy one of Mrs.

Otis' lumberjack dinners, and, relying on the notion that if I could shop I could work, I'd pay a few calls around town tomorrow. Though pooped, I could hardly wait for that morning sun to shine.

CHAPTER TWENTY-SEVEN

Morning stop number one: the Eureka Falls First Federal Savings & Loan.

For the only time I could recall, Cletus Dwyer didn't break out into a gigantic smile when I walked in. He did hurry over, though, to take my hands.

"Why, Miss Honey, I'm so pleased to see you. I heard what happened." Lowering his tone to a hush, he peered into my eyes. "No wonder you're looking a mite poorly today."

So much for mascara, shadow, and liner applied with a trowel.

"No call to fuss over me, Cletus. I'm doing just fine this morning and hoping you can spare a few minutes for some intimate conversation."

He glanced at his watch as if not quite sure.

Hmm. This was a brand-new Cletus. Never before had he been so distant so . . . ah . . . Amelia.

Without putting his hand on my elbow or anywhere else, he escorted me into his office and offered me a seat. Leaving the door open, he sat facing me across his desk.

I got up and shut the door. "What I have to say is private. Hope you don't mind."

He frowned as if he minded a great deal, but other than drumming his fingertips on his still unstained blotter — some things never changed — he didn't object.

"You might like to know that I had the loveliest day yesterday. Amelia Swope and I went shopping. A girls' day out, so to speak."

The drumming stopped.

"She told me you two have a date tomorrow evening. I was so pleased to hear it, Cletus. Y'all will have a marvelous time together."

He cleared his throat. "You mean that?"

"Of course I do, darlin'. Cross my heart and hope to die." I sounded like Scarlett O'Hara, but I was hoping a touch of the deep South might help my mission. It always seemed to work for Scarlett.

In plain fact, it helped right away. He rose out of his chair to lean on the front of his desk and peer down into my baggy eyes. "I have something to confess to you, Honey. With your assurance that it will never leave this room."

I looked at him from under my lashes. "I closed the door, didn't I?"

He smiled, though a bit wanly. "You are one of the most beautiful girls I've ever had the pleasure to meet."

"Oh, you don't have to —"

He held up a finger for silence. "But you don't need me. You have your career and your independence. Despite your recent, ah, accident, you can take care of yourself. But Miss Amelia now, she needs me. So do her little ones. And you know something? That's what I want. To be needed." He shifted his weight from one leg to the other. "I'm placing my life in your hands here. Should a word of what I just revealed leave this room, I'd likely be laughed out of town."

"My lips are sealed. I'd never betray your trust."

He nodded. "I know, that's why I'm confiding in you. So, I might as well tell you the rest of it. My parents passed when I was a child. After that, my granddaddy raised me in his own house, just the two of us and the help. But he's gone now, too, and these days the house is quiet as a tomb. I want to liven it up with a family, a noisy, happy family, and I'm thinking I've found me one.

And if my luck holds out, who knows? Maybe with time, it'll grow bigger and stronger."

"Of that there is no doubt, Cletus. No doubt at all."

This time the smile reached all the way up to his eyes. I was touched that he had chosen to tell me of his feelings and happy that his intentions toward Amelia were so high-minded. He was right, too; I didn't need him. What I needed was information. And my sweaty palms were asking if he'd be as open about imparting that as he'd been about his personal life. Only one way to find out.

I wiped my hands on my thighs. "You've been so honest and open, I just know you'll answer a question for me, which is really the reason for this visit today."

He laughed, relieved, my female instinct told me, that on one level nothing between us had changed. "You can have a mortgage on any piece of property in town."

Using my magnolia voice, I said, "Well, I surely thank you for that. But I have something else in mind. Something that's been bothering me to no end."

"That right?" He appeared both perplexed and guarded.

Staring him straight in the eyes, I didn't

mince words. "Cletus, whatever's going on out at Pea Pike?"

Startled, he stood suddenly. "I have no idea."

"Then allow me to put it this way. According to Saxby Winthrop, IP has bought up all those farms. That's mighty curious, don't you agree?"

He studied his nails as if they were facts and figures. "I had nothing to do with those transactions. The farms were all sold for cash on the barrelhead."

"After opening your very heart to me a moment ago, you refuse me now?"

He looked up from his fingernails. "What I've been told was in strictest confidence. I can't divulge the reason."

"Oh, yes you can."

"With all due respect, you're not the police. And in case you're wondering, I haven't discussed those sales with them either. There was no reason to."

"Oh, is that so?" My tone dripped ice. "Two women were killed out on that ridge." I reached up to my scalp. "And I've been assaulted. Even the sheriff thinks there may be a connection, but you see no reason to tell what you know?"

"Nothing nefarious is going on. I can assure you of that, or I would have gone to the authorities."

"No big words, please. Just the facts." When he didn't answer, I took a guess, not such a wild one, either. "Senator Lott's involved, isn't he?"

Hesitation sprang into Cletus's eyes.

"I knew it!"

He threw up his hands, palms out. "I haven't said a word."

"Your face gave you away."

I hunched forward so he could whisper if he wanted to. Instead, he strode to his office door and flung it open. "Goodbye, Honey."

I rose, lightheaded for the first time that day. "Very well then, since you refuse to answer me, I'm going directly to the *Star.* I'll tell them everything I know and everything I suspect. They'll eat it up and plaster it all over the front page. The paper'll be sold out in no time."

Cletus closed the door. "You're threatening me."

"To help capture a killer. You want to prevent that?"

He snorted, a very un-Cletus-like sound. "I doubt you'll capture the killer. Besides, I'm fearful of getting you mixed up in a situation that —"

"I'm already up to my hips in it, and I'm

scared, Cletus." I sent him a pleading look from under my lids. "Next thing you know, they'll have me on the suspect list."

He heaved a sigh. "For a sweet-looking blonde, you sure cut a hard bargain."

Trying to look like Melanie gazing at Ashley, I smiled at the compliment and paid no mind to the barb.

"Take a seat." Cletus pointed to the chair I'd just left.

Pulse thrumming, I did as he asked. He sank into his own chair as if what he was about to say was too weighty to relay standing.

"The master plan is to build a world-class gambling casino up on that ridge. A five-hundred-room hotel with all the bells and whistles, French chefs in the dining rooms, an eighteen-hole Greg Norman golf course, three swimming pools, a spa, a ballroom . . . the works."

Shock caused my breath to catch in my throat. This was worse than a big-box store sucking the life out of every ma and pa business in town. Worse than anything else I could conjure up, except for the ugliness of strip mining. Though fearing the answer, I asked anyway. "Will this world-class casino offer slot machines, blackjack tables, stud poker, craps?"

He inclined his head. "All of the above and more. Happy now?"

I shook my head and regretted it. "No. Far from it. A casino's no more than a license to print money. For the backers. Not the bettors. I know firsthand what gambling can do to a family. My daddy was a gambling man. His habit came first. My momma and me, well, we trailed far behind his dream of big winnings. Always the next stake, the next game, the next roll of the dice."

"Every enterprise has its dangers."

"Not this kind. I've lived it. I know."

How could I forget? *Yeah, I took it, Honey. What good's money hid under your bed? Aw, don't carry on like that, sweet thing. Next time Daddy won't lose it.*

"Daddy didn't have a big fancy casino to urge him on, either, just a pack of playing cards and a set of dice." Rooted to my chair, I lacked the energy to get up and leave after all.

"Don't take it so hard, Honey," Cletus said. "Not every person who walks into a casino is addicted to gambling. Think of the plus side. All the jobs it'll create, the prosperity it'll bring to town. Why, a casino will put Eureka Falls on the map. We'll be a tourist attraction. According to Trey

Gregson, there's so much natural beauty hereabouts, all we need is an economic boot in the pants."

Of course. Trey was in on this too. He'd had a hidden reason all along for buying that condo. I tuned out the rest of Cletus' sales pitch and sat there, numb. From the way things stood, the future of Pea Pike had been sewn up tight, but what about its past? The murders still hadn't been solved. Nor had my name been cleared.

Then something Cletus said snapped me back into the moment. "Think of what this means to the business you're in. So many people will be clamoring for housing, Ridley's Real Estate won't be able to keep up with the demand."

Sam. Had he known about this right along and not said a word? Or had he been shut out too? Surely he hadn't known a thing, or he would have told the landowners not to let their farms go for so little. Oh, how I wanted to believe that of him, but he was engaged to the senator's daughter, for Pete's sake, practically family. Strange that he wouldn't have been privy to the whole deal, been drawn into the club. Then why hadn't Ridley's sold all four parcels?

Because somebody doesn't want us to get involved.

Even so, wouldn't Lila have told her realtor fiancé about the biggest real estate deal to ever hit town? Unthinkable that she wouldn't. Unless, of course, the senator hadn't told her about it, was protecting her in some way.

"Cletus," I abruptly cut off his happy talk. "What's in this for the senator?"

"I don't . . ." he stopped midsentence. "I don't know. Not for sure. But Eureka Falls is his hometown. Maybe he wants to help it grow."

"Horse feathers. He's hiding something."

"What politico isn't?"

True. We all, politicians or not, had our secrets. Our shames, our hidden desires. The promise of vast wealth could lead a man, even a rich man, down a dark path. But what if the senator wasn't lusting after money? What then? What else did he need bad enough to become a silent partner in a sleazy business like gambling?

Think. Think. If not money, what else? There had to be something.

Silence.

Like the blow to my head, the thought struck with the force of a lightning bolt. I sat quietly in my chair, hardly daring to move, but doing mental high fives. What the senator needed was silence. IP and their backers had something on him. Something that if it came to light would destroy his career.

Slightly unsteady, I rose to my feet, glad I'd worn flats and left the stilettos in the closet. I had to get out of there and go talk to Sam. Find out if I was working for a liar. Or not.

Chapter Twenty-Eight

Paying no mind to how I looked, not caring a bit if I was peaked, baggy-eyed, or needed a shampoo, I stormed into Sam's office. "Did you know?"

Startled, he swept his shoeless feet off his desk, taking a pile of papers along with them. "Know what?"

"About Pea Pike. The casino." I stood in his doorway, panting with effort, telling myself the room wasn't tilting, I wasn't dizzy, and Lord help me, I wasn't going to pass out. "Did you?"

"What's this all about, Honey? You come in here yelling like a hog caller, looking like you're ready to pass out and —"

"Yes or no? Did you or didn't you?" I needed to sit before I fell down, but I didn't dare let go of the doorjamb. "Tell me, Sam, please."

He got up from behind his desk and padded over to me in his stocking feet. Wrapping an arm around my shoulders, he helped me to a chair. "You're pale. Should you be out and about so soon?"

"There's nothing wrong with me. No, that isn't true. Something is bothering me. So, for the love of God, Sam, answer my question."

I must have been shouting. Mrs. Otis walked in, silently closed Sam's office door, and left us without a word.

While I sat watching his every move, Sam paced around, running his fingers through his hair, checking his chin for stubble and finally stomping to a halt in front of me. "Look. I swore I wouldn't tell this to anyone."

Another man sworn to secrecy.

"But you're not just anyone. So here it is." He repeated almost word for word what Cletus had revealed.

My heart nearly stopped. "So you did know."

At the blame in my voice, his eyes widened. I'd never spoken to him in that tone before, never wanted to again, didn't want to now. With my pulse pumping like a chicken's with an ax over its head, I waited for his answer.

"Yeah, I know about it. I found out last night."

My pulse slowed. "You've only known since then?"

"Trey Gregson told me over dinner. What's this all about?"

"That's what I want to know."

Bending down, he set both hands on the arms of my chair and stared ahead at me, not at the wall or the woodwork, the closed door, or anything else. Straight at me. "Now I have a question for you."

A proposal? Ha!

"Why is this upsetting you so much?"

"I have to spell it out for you?" For the first time since we'd met, I wanted to slap him.

"Yeah, do that, spell it out."

"Because I hate gambling in all its forms. Because our neighbors were robbed of their just rewards, and because two women were killed on what is now casino land." I drew in a breath. "All over a secret plot." At his frown I said, "Yes, a plot, to build a gambling empire that nobody around here wants or needs."

"Well, well, everything's all summed up according to the Book of Honey." He lifted off the chair arms and turned away from me, but I wasn't finished.

"If this is such a highfalutin deal, why the secrecy? Why weren't you told about it earlier? If you're not insulted by that, I'm insulted for you. You're practically a member of the senator's family, and you didn't know what was going on until last night?"

No reply.

"That *is* true, isn't it?"

Halfway back to his desk, he spun around. "If you're calling me a liar, watch what you're saying. You're overstepping your place here."

"Oh, is that right? I'm out of place, am I? You want to fire me for that, then fire me. But for God's sake, ask yourself why you, Lila's intended and a Realtor . . . a Realtor . . . didn't know about the biggest real estate deal that's ever hit town."

A thundercloud, he strode back to me and pointed a finger at my nose. "One, stay out of my personal life. Two, I'm giving you a week off to rest and recuperate. I don't want you back in this office until you're well again."

"That's not necessary. I'm riled up, not sick."

"Bullshit. You look like hell, and you're acting like a crazy woman. Go home and rest. That's an order."

An order? Another man ordering me around? A hand on each hip, I squared off. "Am I fired?"

"Not yet."

"Good, because I quit."

CHAPTER TWENTY-NINE

So just like that, I burned my bridges, every damn one. No need now to wait until Sam's wedding bells rang. I was out of Ridley's and out of Eureka Falls like yesterday. My knees wobbling, my head floating in some kind of fuzzy cloud, I marched out of his office, slamming the door so hard all the partitions shook.

Over by the front window, Mrs. Otis reared back in her seat. "I could hear you hollerin' in there right through the walls. You up and quit your job?"

"Yes."

"I can't believe it."

I stomped into my cubicle without replying, adding bad manners to my stupidity and temper.

Dazed, I looked around at what I needed to gather up and take with me when I stormed out once and for all. Framed photographs of my momma and Amelia's boys, my state realtor's license, my favorite coffee mug, emergency cosmetics stashed in the lower desk drawer, the accumulation of three years. But the idea of collecting everything and toting it out to the car was just too much. I'd only take my iPad and purse and come back for the rest after-hours. It would be less painful that way.

For a heavy woman, Mrs. Otis was light on her feet and suddenly there she was in my cubicle doorway, her forehead creased, her mouth a tight line. "No need to tell me what's wrong, but whatever it is, I thought you'd like to know the security company just called. The alarm system's all set in your apartment. Not that you have to leave my place or anything."

The poor dear, my shouting scene had upset her.

"Thanks, love." I wanted to leap up and hug her, but in that moment, I couldn't find the energy. I had to save it to stand, get out of the building, and into my car.

She laid a piece of paper on my desk. "Their phone number. Call when you get home, and they'll activate the alarm." She hovered, twisting her hands together. "If you'd like me to go with you, maybe Sam will —"

"No, no, but thanks anyway. I'll call you

over the weekend and come get my things."

"No hurry for that. But do call. I'll be worrying about you."

I nodded, hoping Sam would stride out of his office and beg me to stay on. But his door didn't budge. So it was a done deal. Well, maybe that was for the best. Casino or no casino, I couldn't continue on like this much longer, always aching for something or someone I could never have.

Palms flat on the desktop, I pulled myself up and dropped the iPad in my purse. Then, slinging the bag over a shoulder, I gave Mrs. Otis a goodbye hug.

At the apartment, I left the front door open, and cell phone in hand, checked out each room, ready to tap in 911 at the first sign of trouble. I peered behind the doors, in the closets, under the bed, and tried all the windows, including the bedroom sliders. Only then did I lock the door and call the security company. They told me to press in my five-digit code and the system would come alive. My home would be as safe as a fortress.

Safe and sorry, I kicked off my shoes and stretched out on the living room sofa. On a Friday afternoon. The time to call clients and set up appointments for weekend showings. But instead of putting my mind to my job and doing what I was paid to do, I'd taken matters into my own hands. Gained a heap of information I could do nothing with. In the bargain, I'd messed up my life more than I would have thought possible the day Tallulah Bixby strutted in on those flashy silver shoes.

I blew out a sigh that practically lifted the sofa off the floor. What a joke I'd been. Honey Ingersoll on the hunt for a killer. I had no training, no detective skills, no right to meddle. Only a deep need to stop a bully from hurting others, or worse, from stealing their lives. I'd rolled onto my side, ready to curl into a ball of misery, when my glance fell on a stack of newspapers neatly piled on the coffee table. The alarm people must have brought them in. How thoughtful. That's when it leaped out at me, Tallulah Bixby's photograph on the front page of the *Star*. A teenage shot from the look of it, maybe her high school graduation picture. Underneath, a headline in great big capital letters, FUNERAL PLANS AN-NOUNCED FOR SHOOTING VICTIM.

I grabbed the paper off the coffee table. The funeral service was scheduled for two p.m. tomorrow in the Fayetteville Baptist Church.

Though I'd hardly known Tallulah, I wanted to be there, to express my sorrow to her momma, and yes, to see who else cared enough to pay their last respects. No telling who I might run into or what I could learn. I lowered the paper to my knees. Getting there meant driving two hours each way with this lump on my head. Even if I was up to it, what would Matt say about that? I could hear him now. *Stay out of it. Stay home. Let the police do their work.*

A strand of hair fell across my face, tickling my nose, a strand of limp, unwashed hair. That did it. The instant I touched it, the thought of not messing with the case melted like fog on a sunny day. Enough with playing the victim. What was that U of A motto anyway? *Never Yield.* And damn it, I wouldn't. Starting right now. Of course I was up to the drive. Or if not, I'd find somebody to drive me. Pay them if I had to. Either way, I'd be at that funeral. What I'd do with the rest of my life, I couldn't tackle right now. Like Scarlett, I'd save that problem for tomorrow.

I leaped off the sofa with more energy than I'd had in days. Now for a shower and a shampoo. The ER nurse had told me the wound should heal fast. That was Monday; this was Friday, practically a whole week

274

later. I'd chance it, for whether I liked it or not, there was gambling in my blood.

In my U of A T-shirt and cutoffs, hair dry and shiny, face scrubbed clean, I felt like a brand-new woman. In hardly no time at all.

Now to eat something. I opened the fridge, took one look inside and slammed it shut. Well, nothing wrong with a can of soup and dry toast.

I had my little feast simmering when the chimes rang. *Sam. Can it be Sam? Oh God.* I hurried to the front door. One glance out the peephole and my hopes sagged to my bare feet.

I yanked open the door.

"Your alarm?" he said.

"Oh, gosh, I forgot to turn it off just now."

He dropped the bags he was carrying on the living room floor, pulled out his cell, and called the alarm company. "Sheriff Rameros here. At the Ingersoll address. All's well." A few more words and he hung up.

I stood there, hands on hips. "How do they know it's you?"

"We're in frequent communication. They know my voice. Still, I wouldn't be surprised if they come by to check."

"So, why are you here?"

"A couple of reasons. You going to invite me in?"

"You are in."

"That's not what I mean."

I waved an arm at the living room. "Make yourself at home."

He picked up the bags. "You like Chinese?"

"Love it."

"Good, I brought dinner." He grinned. "And breakfast."

"In your dreams."

"How did you know?" He strode into the kitchen as if he owned the place.

Seeing him in shorts was a first, and I followed him through the apartment, admiring his hairy, tree-trunk calves. "You off duty or something?"

He glanced back and caught me scoping out his legs. "Your powers of observation —"

"Are pretty good. No badge. It's a giveaway every time."

He reached into one of the bags and pulled out a bottle of wine. "Pinot Grigio?"

A good cold beer would have been more to my liking, but he looked so hopeful. "Perfect."

Another reach produced "a couple of brewskies for me," and a bottle opener. He uncorked the wine and poured me a glass.

I sipped it. "Yum, wonderful."

He smiled, and we clinked, bottle to glass.

In the living room, I took the club chair and let Matt have the sofa to himself. He arched an eyebrow as he sat but didn't comment. Not about that, anyway. "I have some good news for you."

"Oh?"

"We've arrested your assailant."

That brought me to the edge of my seat. "Who was it?"

"Joe Swope."

"Amelia's ex? Oh no!"

"Yeah, his prints were all over your bedroom door. To your knowledge, has he ever been in here?"

"Never. And the whole place was freshly painted before I moved in."

"I'll talk to the landlord. Make sure Joe didn't work for him."

One ankle resting on a knee, he took a sip of his beer. "You notice anything missing?"

"I haven't checked, but I don't think so. The TV's still here. There was no money around or jewelry to speak of, so, no."

He picked at the paper label on his bottle for a second. "Joe Swope have any reason to target you?"

"Maybe."

The foot he'd been balancing on his knee hit the floor. "Why?"

"Remember that night at the roadhouse? When Joe heard Amelia and I had gone there, he threw a fit. Threatened her. Told her he'd see me about it too."

"Oh he did, did he? In harassing his ex-wife, he violated the restraining order. Cause for arrest right there."

"Arrest him again and I'm afraid he'll blame Amelia for that too."

Matt set his beer on the coffee table. "Yeah, domestic violence cases are some of the worst."

"I know." Though I'd never told anyone.

No, Billy, please.

Whaddya you mean you don't want to do it again? What else are you good for?

"Is there any chance Joe will be let go tonight or tomorrow?"

"If he's smart enough to get an attorney, yeah. Otherwise, he's in until court convenes on Monday and bail can be set. Why? You afraid he'll come back here tonight?"

"No, not here. I think he only wanted to scare me. Amelia's the one he wants to control."

Matt stood and slid his cell out of a pocket. "I'll call the station. See what I can do. If a lawyer wants to release him on bail, my hands are pretty much tied." He smiled. "But let's give it a try. It's amazing sometimes what one good ol' boy will do for another."

He spoke into his cell for a few minutes, the lines in his forehead deepening by the second.

"You're not going to like this." He slipped the phone back into his pocket. "Joe's out."

"When?"

"Twenty minutes ago." Matt stood. "Save the Chinese. I'm going to check on Amelia and the kids."

"Don't leave without me." I ran into the kitchen, flung the bag of Szechuan or whatever it was into the fridge, grabbed my purse out of the bedroom, and toed on a pair of flip-flops.

Matt's wheels waited out in front, a spanking new Dodge Ram pickup, all polished maroon and shiny hubcaps.

"Pretty cool." I climbed into the passenger seat. "For cruising when you're not in the cruiser?"

A white-toothed smile. "You could say that. I went all out. It's a Ram 2500, the latest Turbo Diesel, Mega Cab model. A boy's gotta have his toys." He put her in gear and pulled away from the curb. "You have your phone?"

"Of course."

"Call Amelia. Warn her not to open her

doors until we get there."

A hand in my purse, I hesitated. Joe Swope had no car. Even if his cousin gave him a ride, he couldn't get from the jail to Amelia's house in less than a half hour. And no way would an attorney drop him off there.

Still, she needed to be warned. "All right, but it's a darn shame this had to happen just now."

"Is there ever a good time?"

"You don't understand. She has a date tomorrow night."

"A date? What's that got to do with it?" He stared across at me as if I'd taken leave of my senses.

"She's met someone and has a chance to get her life out of the Dumpster. Head it down a whole new path. But if Joe's dead set on causing trouble, she'll likely refuse to go out and leave the boys with a sitter. And that would be awful. She and Cletus have so much in —"

"Cletus Dwyer?"

"The same."

"Well, I'll be darned. That's a surprise." He smiled but scanned the scene carefully as he drove. "Just to be safe, make the call. Ask if everything's all right. If she says no, tell her help's on the way."

As I fumbled in my purse for the cell, Matt's hands tightened on the wheel. "No need to call. There he is."

Up ahead, a few blocks from Amelia's house, Joe Swope was stomping along, head back, hands swinging at his sides, cowboy style. His swagger caused a surge in my blood. The nerve of him, strutting along like the biggest rat in the pack, hell-bent for Amelia's cottage. And when he got there, then what? Beat her up again? Frighten his sons?

Like I was frightened. *You sassin' me, gal? Ain't you learned yet? Well, this oughta show ya.*

Matt slowed down. "He hasn't spotted us. We'll stay behind him, see if he gets close enough to violate the restraining order."

As we crawled along, I stared at Joe's frayed work pants, his faded plaid shirt, the lank hair riding his collar, and my heart softened. A little. I was staring at a man with nothing except his fists and a once-handsome face now marked with bitterness.

With stops and starts along the way, we trailed Joe for three blocks.

"Okay, close enough." Matt slammed on the brakes, bringing the truck to a halt by the side of the road. "Stay in the cab." Then he leaped out and yelled, "Joe Swope."

Joe froze for a second before turning around. "Yeah?"

I rolled down the window so as not to miss a thing.

"Wait up," Matt said. "I want to talk to you."

"Who the hell are you?"

Matt strolled over to him, a casual, at ease kind of move. He kept on until Joe backed away, one step at a time, his eyes darting left and right.

"Recognize me now?" Matt's voice came across reasonable, even-toned.

"Yeah, so what?" Joe half turned to go.

"Hold it there, buddy," Matt said.

"Bug off."

"You're violating the restraining order. You're under arrest."

"Says you."

"That's correct." Matt stood his ground, feet apart, arms at his side.

Joe sneered. "I'm an innocent man. Haven't done a damn thing wrong. And you're going to arrest me? Don't make me laugh."

"This street's off limits for you, Joe. Why are you here?"

Matt never got an answer, for with the speed of a ferret, or of some other weaselly creature, Joe darted into the middle of the road and began running in the direction he had come from, back toward Matt's truck. Almost without thinking, I unlocked the cab's passenger side door and grabbed the handle. As Joe was about to run past, I flung the door wide open, smacking him in the face, knocking him off his pins.

Matt was all over him in an instant, forcing his arms behind his back, yanking him upright beside the truck. "Call 911," he said to me. "Tell them we've made an arrest. The prisoner's injured. Send medical help."

Blood was pouring out of Joe's nice straight nose. It was the prettiest thing about him, and I might have wrecked it.

He swiveled his bloody face over a shoulder to glare at me, spewing the cab with droplets. "Look what you did, bitch."

I shrugged, every ounce of sympathy for him gone for good. The B word will do that every time.

"All I did was follow the sheriff's orders. Like he told me to, I stayed in the cab."

Chapter Thirty

Later, we polished off the Szechuan and shared the rest of the wine.

"Something's come up, Matt. Something you should know."

Ready to drop the empty cartons in the trash can, he tensed, the way a body will when bad news is about to strike. Somehow, though, I had trouble getting the words out, making them official. He dropped in the cartons and snapped the trash can shut. Then, arms folded, he waited.

"I'm leaving," I told him.

He nodded. Even so, he looked like he hadn't understood a thing I said.

"Did you hear me?"

"What do you mean 'leaving'? Exactly."

"I quit my job today."

The crease on his forehead disappeared. "Glad to hear it. You needed to get out of there. All that frustration wasn't good for you."

Heat rushed into my face. "And you know what is good for me? Who are you, my shrink? You don't know anything."

His voice was icy cold. "I know more than you realize, but enlighten me anyway. You've quit your job, and now what? You're leaving town?"

"That's my plan."

"Why?"

"You have to ask? I can't stay here now."

"Why the hell not?"

"Because. . . ." All my words dried up.

"Well?"

"I'm leaving because —"

"You're a coward."

"No. I'm not."

"Then stay. Face your demons. Face the fact that Sam Ridley's not yours."

"There's more to it than that."

"Like what?"

"Pea Pike's being turned into a gambling casino."

He shrugged. "So?"

"So? That's it? That's all you have to say? Do you understand what a casino will do to Eureka Falls?"

"I have a dim idea." He strode toward me. "Right now, that's not what's bothering me. You are. You have been since I first set eyes on you. Remember that day? You were straddling your boyfriend's bike when we stopped him."

"You were there when Billy Tubbs got arrested?"

"I was the rookie cop."

"I don't remember that."

"I do. And I remember when you hooked up with Saxby Winthrop."

I glanced at my fingernails. By some miracle, my manicure was still looking fine. How could that be, when everything else was such a mess?

"I waited Saxby out. It wasn't easy. It wasn't easy at all, but I knew that bloated cat couldn't hold you." He stood over me, looking down. "When you left him, I thought maybe I had a chance at last, but then you went to work for Sam. At the shine in your eyes every time you looked his way, I almost gave up. But not quite. Not quite."

Matt reached out and pulled me to my feet. "Do you know what 'not quite' means?"

I stared at him, not sure of how to answer, or whether to at all.

"It means I'll never give up on you, Honey Ingersoll. Never."

I found my voice. "I'm not worth it, Matt. Forget about me."

"Never. I'll never forget you. That would

be impossible. You're everything anyone could ever want. You're sassy and witty and smart. You're loyal to a fault."

I shook my head. "I'm trailer trash."

"Men turn to look at you when you walk down the street." He touched his forehead to mine. "And I'm one of them. Don't leave, Honey. You have a life waiting for you here."

My throat too dry to speak, I listened. I had done nothing to earn Matt's feelings for me, nothing at all. But as I stood there in the circle of his arms, what he was offering wasn't anything that could be earned. It was a gift.

"Please." His voice was soft in my ear, his lips close to mine.

I didn't know if he was asking me to stay or asking to kiss me. I nodded anyway. His arms tightened, and his mouth came down on mine. About then I stopped thinking and gave in to the moment, ignoring all my vows and all my promises to myself. In my neediness, I wanted to be kissed. I wanted him to make love to me.

His hands slid under my T-shirt. His voice was hoarse. "Take this off."

Mesmerized, awakened, I was about to do as he asked when a question popped up out of the blue. "Hey," I moved back a little in his embrace, "I thought you don't like one-night stands."

"I don't." He raised the top over my shoulders and flung it aside.

CHAPTER THIRTY-ONE

Starbuck's French Roast perfumed the morning-after air as I settled across the kitchen table from Matt.

Freshly showered, his black hair shining wet, his jaw stubbly, he smiled and reached for my hand. "Thank you." His glance was as warm as his voice.

"No need to thank me, Matt. We gifted each other last night." I slid my hand out from under his. "So why don't we use the good sense the Lord gave us and let it go at that?"

His smiled dimmed. Though I was sorry to see that, what happened between us hadn't changed my mind or sent me down a brand-new path. No question, the sex had been first-rate. But not a game changer. I had no future here in Eureka Falls, and the sooner I did something about it the better.

"I've been thinking of what you told me, you know, about planning to leave and all."

He put down his coffee mug.

Uh-oh. "Yes?"

"Want to hear an alternate solution?" He didn't wait for a reply. "Stay and go into business for yourself. Open your own realty office."

"But how? I have no money, no nothing."

He leaned forward, elbows on the table. "Listen for a minute. You know the real estate business inside out. The prime areas, what the local market will bear. You're licensed, and you have a following. Why not? What's to stop you?"

Taken aback by his suggestion, I stared at him, tongue-tied. From time to time, I'd gnawed on the same idea, but I hadn't wanted to leave Sam. Still didn't, not really, not way down deep where I lived, but that wasn't something I'd ever say out loud.

"Money would be a problem," I finally said.

"How much would it take? Office rent, a couple of computers, a printer, telephone, electric."

I threw up my hands. "Stop right there, Matt. I don't want to go into business in Eureka Falls. I want to get out of here."

His blackberry eyes lost their shine. "Nothing has happened to change your mind?"

Shaking my head, I put down the corn muffin I was about to bite into, and stood.

"No need to hurry off," he said. "You've made your point. Sit back down and finish your breakfast."

"That isn't it. I have to get dressed. I'm going out."

"My cue to leave? Not a problem." He checked his watch. "Ten thirty. I need to hit the road anyway. I'm meeting Detective Bradshaw later."

"About the case?"

"You could say that." He took a gulp of his coffee.

I'd hurt him, and that felt terrible. He and Amelia were the two best friends I'd ever had, and after last night, Matt was also my lover, whether I wanted to admit it or not. I owed him one. The truth, then.

"I really do need to get ready. I'm going to Tallulah Bixby's funeral."

He glanced up fast. "Me too. I'm meeting Bradshaw there. Why are you going? You didn't know the victim."

"Neither did you."

"No, but it's part of my job. And I'm not recovering from a concussion." He studied me for a long moment.

"Do I pass muster?"

"Fayetteville's quite a drive from here. I'm

291

not sure you're up to it."

"I'll manage."

He put his coffee mug in the sink and stood there with his back to me, shoulders slumped, hands spread wide on the countertop. "Anyone ever tell you that you're a very independent-minded woman?"

I laughed. "Yes, just yesterday, in fact."

"Well, whoever it was knew what he was talking about." He spun around. "I'm going home to shave and get dressed. I'll be back in time to pick you up."

"No, that's not —"

"Be here. Don't force me to put out an APB on you."

"You wouldn't!"

"Wanna bet?" He strode toward the front door. "One hour." He slammed the door shut.

An hour later, I waited outside my building, wearing the same outfit I'd worn the night Cletus invited me to dinner at the Inn, my black silk dress, fake pearls, and heels. Sixty minutes to the second, up came the Ram and out jumped Matt. Too bad he was going to a funeral. In a navy-blue suit, white shirt, and striped tie, he looked like a man on his way to be married.

I buried that idea fast and dangled my car keys. "The Lincoln?"

"Under the circumstances, it would be more fitting. We need to stop for gas?"

"I always keep the tank topped off."

He laughed and took the keys. "Why do I believe you?"

Basking in the scent of his aftershave and the sight of his big, capable hands on the wheel, I relaxed on the drive to Fayetteville. The countryside, soft with summer, almost fooled me into believing this was an afternoon's outing, not a police mission.

Matt didn't talk much on the ride. Eyes straight ahead, he focused on the road.

No music, no NPR, we drove quiet as dust most of the way until, finally, I cracked. "What all do you expect to find today?"

He gave me one of those non-answers. "I'll know it when I see it."

Another probe. "You looking for anybody in particular?"

Without glancing away from the road. "Nope. You?"

Sam. Would he be there? I didn't think so. If for some reason he showed up, what would I say to him? Or do? Torn between hoping to see him and hoping not to, I felt my relaxed mood drain away like water running down a gulley.

No time to wallow in self-pity, though, for the sexy-voiced GPS lady cooed that we were closing in on the First Baptist Church of Fayetteville. A few hundred feet ahead sat a squared-off yellow brick building with pointed windows shining in the sunlight and a bell tower reaching for heaven. No funeral bell tolled, though, for which I was mighty grateful. That would have made an already sad afternoon even sadder. Besides, the hearse and two black limousines parked in front were reminders enough of why we were there.

In the parking lot, Matt pulled into one of the last empty spaces. We mounted a short flight of stairs and entered the crowded church through a side door.

From the back of the church, where the usher seated us, I could see a casket blanketed with lilies resting in the center aisle. I couldn't tell who was sitting up front in the first few pews, though. More than likely Tallulah's nearest and dearest. Was Trey Gregson among them? Or not? And what of Senator Lott? He had been a frequent visitor to Trey's home, so surely he'd known Tallulah well. For that matter, Lila might have known her too.

Frustrated, I glanced over at Matt. His feathers unruffled, he sat calmly beside me, nodding once to Detective Bradshaw across the aisle. The organ swelled into "The Old

Rugged Cross," and when the hymn ended and the pastor stepped up to the pulpit, a hush fell over the congregation. The next hour passed in a blur of music and sorrow. As the service continued, the temperature rose in the packed church and the aroma of flowers and perfumes became downright dizzying. I caught Matt glancing at me more than once and squeezed his hand.

"I'm fine," I whispered, wanting it to be true, determined to make it so.

We had come here to learn something about Tallulah's death, and beyond all reason, I believed we would. What that something might be, I didn't know, but as a wise ol' mountain woman would surely do, I clung to my certainty.

When the organ burst into the recessional, the congregation surged to its feet. Slowly, like they were steering a barge down a narrow river, the pallbearers moved the casket down the aisle. Walking behind it, two men gripped the arms of a middle-aged woman nearly doubled over in grief. Without their aid, she couldn't have taken a single step. That had to be Tallulah's momma, poor thing. Following her, tissues in hand, eyes red from weeping, were two young women so like Tallulah I guessed they were her sisters. Then the rest of the mourners filed past in an orderly fashion, but no Trey, no senator, no Lila, no Sam. Hmm.

After a wrenching graveside farewell — Tallulah's momma tried to fling herself onto the lowered casket — a solemn-faced funeral director invited everyone back to the Bixby home for a fellowship repast.

Matt looked at me and cocked an eyebrow. "You up for that?"

" 'Course I am." If we were going to learn anything helpful today, the Bixby house was where it would be.

The sapphire-blue Caddy, as bright and glittery as when Tallulah drove it into Eureka Falls, sat in the driveway of a modest frame house on a leafy street thronged with cars.

Clearly we weren't the only ones wanting to pay our last respects. Matt parked halfway down the block, and we walked back to the house. Chatting guests spilled out onto the front porch, and from there, onto the lawn, their occasional spurts of laughter turning a sad event into something like a party.

Matt peered through the crowd and nodded at Detective Bradshaw but made no attempt to approach him. So they would act the role of two mourners then, not two cops looking for clues to a killer.

The party atmosphere outside turned

somber inside, where Tallulah's momma and her daughters sat in the parlor, taking turns wiping their eyes and greeting their guests.

I stood in the corner of the room for a while, listening to the steady thread of condolences. "So sorry . . . such a beautiful girl . . . what a shame. I'm suffering for your loss, Mamie. She's with the Lord now."

When the line thinned out, I paid my respects too, laying my stranger's comfort, for what it was worth, at Mrs. Bixby's feet. Though she didn't know me from Adam, she thanked me as sweetly as a body possibly could, and in turn, my heart went out to her. Something had to come out of this today. It *had* to.

I glanced around the small, crowded room, but didn't see Matt. In the dining room, the church ladies had provided an awesome array of food. Ham and casseroles, salads and finger sandwiches, tall tiered cakes, cookies, and fudge brownies. After chatting with a few folks and praising the pastor's sermon, I helped myself to some lemonade from a cut-glass punch bowl.

In the warm, overcrowded room, a pulse throbbed at my temples. The concussion acting up? Oh Lord, I hoped not. Needing a breath of fresh air and a cool breeze, I hurried through the kitchen without stopping to chat and stepped outside into a quiet back garden.

Unless Matt was having more luck than I was, so far the day had yielded nothing of value, nothing that would help solve the crimes. So my ol' mountain-woman hunch had been wrong. The trip had been a kindly gesture to a heartbroken family, nothing more.

Cool drink in hand, I strolled across the tidy lawn. Toward the back of the garden, nestled in a shady arbor draped with wisteria, I spotted a wooden bench. *Perfect.*

In the leafy shade, half hidden by the vines, I sank onto the bench, sipping lemonade, watching bees buzz in and out of the flowers. From the house came a drift of voices. Glad to be alone for a spell, I'd rest a while and then go find Matt. See if maybe he'd heard something.

I was about ready to doze off when the odor of cigarette smoke came wafting across the lawn, snapping me awake. Cigarette smoke and voices. Angry voices.

"I told you he wouldn't show up. He never cared about Tallulah. All he did was use her. The old windbag."

"It'll kill Momma if she ever finds out."

"How's she going to? You going to tell her?

Am I?" The woman snorted.

Hardly daring to breathe, I sat motionless, listening. More smoky cigarette odor.

"How could she fall for such an old man? I never understood it."

Old man? Trey isn't old. Far from it.

"He must have promised her the moon."

"Yeah. Everything but marriage."

"Imagine having that snooty Lila of his as a stepdaughter."

What?

A disgusted bark of a laugh. "They were the same age."

"That's what the senator liked, I guess."

The senator?

"Shh. No names. You never know who's listening."

I froze, clutching the empty glass so tight it nearly shattered in my hand.

"I need another drink. And I don't mean lemonade. Where did you hide that flask?"

"In the big flowerpot by the back door."

A sob rent the air. "Oh, dear Lord, we've lost our baby sister. Tallulah isn't coming back. She won't ever be with us again. Not ever."

"Come on, Clara. You've had your smoke. Let's go inside. Momma will be wondering. We can have a drink after this is over."

"It'll never be over, never."

"Come on. Momma's waiting on us."

I didn't dare risk a peek, but a few minutes later, the screen door slammed shut, and once again I was alone with the wisteria.

And with the goods on a secret sugar daddy.

CHAPTER THIRTY-TWO

Matt . . . I had to find Matt. But I couldn't seem to move and sat there a while, clutching my empty glass, my mind whirling with what I'd just overheard. Senator Lott had been Tallulah Bixby's lover, not Trey Gregson. But Tallulah had lived at Trey's house. They had been a pair, an item, a couple. Except, they never had been. That meant Tallulah had lived with Trey for the convenience of her real lover, Senator Prescott Lott. There was a fancy French saying for such doings, but for the life of me, I couldn't bring it to mind.

Too excited to sit still any longer, I jumped off the bench, and in case Tallulah's sisters were in the kitchen, I tiptoed past the back door and hurried around to the front of the house. Matt was leaning on the porch rail, talking with several men, but he broke away as soon as he saw me.

"Where have you been? I've been worried

about you."

I tugged on his hand. "I'll tell you in the car. Let's go."

"No fond farewell to Mrs. Bixby first?"

I shook my head. "No, I don't want to go back inside. Let's just go." I grabbed his hand as we hurried toward the car. "Did you learn anything?"

"Yes." He chuckled. "Sylvie Cooper's known for making the best white mountain cake in all of Arkansas. And Maddie Ryan's chicken salad's based on a hundred-year-old family recipe. How about you?"

It wasn't easy, but I kept mum until we were seated in the Lincoln with the air-conditioning blasting away, and then I blurted out my story.

He listened without interrupting. "That's a sleazy tale for sure, but what they did wasn't illegal."

"But —"

"I'm not through. It bears looking into. I'll contact the —"

"Word of this gets out, it could destroy the senator's career."

A wry, half-smile lifted Matt's lips. "Possibly, but it seems to me the American public doesn't examine a candidate's private life the way it used to, it —"

"This isn't just about the senator's love

life. His girlfriend has been murdered."

"Are you always like this?" Matt turned the key in the ignition.

"Like what?"

"I'm having the devil of a time finishing a thought."

"Sorry."

"If this story is true —"

"If? Senator Lott was living a lie and so was Trey. They used Tallulah, led her on, treated her like she was someone to be ashamed of. Someone to hide away like, like dirty laundry."

I remembered, oh, I remembered, *No, I can't bring you to meet my momma. She'd up and die if she ever found out about you.*

"However —"

"And now the poor girl is dead."

"See what I mean?" Matt seemed halfway fit to be tied.

"My lips are sealed. Spout off all you want."

"Let's assume what you're saying is correct, but consider —"

"Suppose Tallulah came to Eureka Falls that day to threaten the senator. Marry her or she'd go to the media, spill her guts, let the public know all about that phony little love nest. That's —"

"Enough to get a girl killed."

"You took them . . . *those* words right out of my mouth."

"High time." He shot me a fast glance across the front seat. "Here's something else to think about. Both victims were killed with the same weapon, so more than likely by the same person. Yet they came from different worlds. Didn't know each other. Didn't know the same people."

"Then what was Tallulah doing on Pea Pike that day? There had to be a reason."

"In murder cases, there's always a reason. Either she was forced there by her killer, or enticed there."

A Walmart rig the size of a city block roared past. I stared at its rear lights as they turned into red bull's-eyes in the distance.

"But why did she come to town in the first place? If it was to see the senator, and I believe it was, what can we do about it?"

"*We* aren't going to do anything. That's for the state police to deal with. As soon as I drop you off, I'm calling Bradshaw. No doubt he'll want to talk to you, so be available for the next few days. In the meantime, don't mention this to anyone. And I mean anyone. Got that?"

"No problem. Not with being available, either. I'll be around. For a while, anyway. I'm out of a job, remember."

"I seriously doubt it."

"What's that supposed to mean?"

"I predict you have a call from Sam Ridley in your future. Monday morning at the latest." Eyeballing me across the front seat, he tried for a smile. "How's that make you feel?"

CHAPTER THIRTY-THREE

When Matt parked in front of my building, I was sure that after last night we'd have one of those awkward walk-to-the-door, come-in-or-not moments. But I needn't have worried none.

He unlocked my door and handed me the keys. "I owe you a tankful of gas."

"I don't figure it that way at all. You saved me a long drive."

"High test premium. I insist." He smiled a quick, white flash. "The car's great. Purred like a kitten the whole way." The smile fled. "That was good work today, Honey. Expect to hear from Bradshaw sometime soon." He sent me a two-fingered salute, shrugged off his jacket, and hopped into the Ram. All without the tiniest hint that he wanted to come in and stay a while.

Hmm.

When the Ram disappeared around the corner, I went inside, reset the alarm, and locked the door. I picked up my mail from the foyer floor. Bills. I tossed them and my purse on the coffee table. As I was about to kick off the heels, the front doorbell chimed.

Matt with a change of mind?

A one-eyed glance out the peephole was all it took to send my heart into overdrive. Matt's prediction had been off by a couple of days. It was Sam, in the flesh. I leaned against the door for a spell, struggling to catch my breath. The chimes rang again. And again. He wasn't going away. He really wanted to see me.

All right then. Though I had a suspicion my lipstick was worn off and my hair needed brushing, I didn't waste time fretting but straightened up real good, took a deep breath, and flung the door wide.

Startled by the sudden movement, Sam nearly slipped off the front stair. "I saw your car and knew you were home. I tried calling earlier, several times in fact, but you didn't answer." He cleared his throat. "So I came by."

He tried to reach me all afternoon.

He held out a green paper sheath filled with long-stemmed yellow roses. "For you. With an apology."

I pressed the roses to my face and sniffed but couldn't detect a scent.

"May I come in?"

"Oh, yes, of course." My pulse drumming in my ears, I turned and led the way into the living room.

He glanced around. "Nice," was all he said. That was enough. What he thought about the apartment didn't matter a hoot. He wasn't here for an appraisal, at least not that kind.

I set the flowers on the coffee table next to the bills. "They're beautiful. Thank you." I waved a hand at the club chair. "You're welcome to take a seat."

He shook his head. "I can't stay. I just came by to tell you how sorry I am about our dust-up yesterday. Bottom line, I can't accept your resignation. Ridley's needs you." He paused. "I need you."

"For sales?" I tried to keep the bitterness out of my voice, but some of it leaked through.

He flushed, so I knew he'd understood my meaning. "No, not for sales alone. We're friends, Honey, colleagues."

He went to run a hand through his hair but stopped in time. Though handsomer than ever, in a tan summer suit with a blue shirt that brought out the color of his eyes to a fare-thee-well, he hadn't donned that fancy outfit for me. He was probably on his way to meet Lila.

"I've been thinking about what you said. In fact, I've thought of little else. Trey's joining Lila and me for dinner tonight, and I intend to ask him how long he's been in on this casino business. I'll ask him about the senator's role in it as well. Lila won't know anything, of course. She's never let in on the senator's projects. He protects her from all that."

The day had been long, the heels high. I sank onto the sofa and gazed up at him. I wouldn't break my promise to Matt, but not saying anything about what I'd learned that afternoon was hard, very hard. For in my bones, I knew Trey would lie and Lila would back up whatever he said.

Still, Sam had business smarts. He should be able to spot a lie when it smacked him in the face. On the other hand, he was a man in love and would tend to believe anything his beloved might say.

My head throbbed. And my feet.

"Well?" Sam paused, waiting for an answer to a question I hadn't heard.

I blew out a breath. There was only one question, would I or wouldn't I? Yes, I'd go back to Ridley's, at least for the time being. But not for Sam alone, and not for the money, though Lord knows I needed it. I'd go back for Tallulah's sake. Sam Ridley was the closest connection I had to Senator Lott and Trey Gregson. After today, I was downright certain one of them, or maybe both, had murdered that poor girl.

Who might have harmed poor ol' Violet, though, I hadn't a clue. The only one who stood to profit from her death was her creepy nephew Earl, and Matt claimed he'd been working in the lumberyard at the time she was killed. But about Tallulah, I did know something. The men she had believed in and trusted had used and abused her. If I couldn't feel sorrow over that, I was as good as dead too. And right now, I was too damn mad to die.

"So?" An arched eyebrow, a worried forehead.

"It warms my heart that you want me back, Sam. I'm sorry for what happened, too." *This isn't easy.* "Not that I'm regretful about what I said, but the way I said it was far from mannerly."

At my words, his shoulders eased, and he flashed a big Sam smile. "It's a go then?"

"Yes, it is."

"Excellent. My offer still stands. Take some time off. I'll handle your calls and see you a week from Monday."

I was about to tell him of an idea I had

for a special promotion. A weekly email blast, each one featuring a different property. We could give it a name that would be easy for folks to recollect . . . Deal of the Week or some such. But before I could mention it, he checked his watch, anxious to leave.

"Stay where you are, Honey. Relax, get some rest. I'll let myself out." He pointed a finger at my nose. "See you next week." Then he strode toward the foyer and departed, closing the door behind him without the slightest thump.

I sat there for a while, staring at the flowers he had brought, telling myself he didn't know that yellow was for friends, red was for lovers. On the other hand, maybe he did. With a sigh, I got up and tossed the yellow friendship roses into the trash.

CHAPTER THIRTY-FOUR

In cutoffs and a T-shirt, with my hair scrunched into a ponytail — and in case Detective Bradshaw called, the cell in my shorts pocket — I got to Josie's early Sunday morning. This time, no burger and fries. I'd have sausage and grits and make Tommy Lee's day.

As usual, the place was hopping. After eating, I'd do some grocery shopping, for the first time in living memory, then drop in on Amelia. We had a lot to talk about. Among other things, I didn't have good news from the zoning board, so the daycare idea was out. She'd likely have to go to Plan B, waitressing nights, not a magic remedy for her money problems, not by a long shot.

"Well, if it ain't Daisy Mae," Josie drawled when I walked in. Without waiting to be asked, she poured me a black coffee. "What happened to the suit?"

"I have a week off." For once, I added

cream and two sugars, turning the brew into a kissing cousin of one of those latte drinks.

Josie leaned over the counter. "Just so you'll know, I think T.L. will quit if you don't order off the breakfast menu."

"Grits, sausage, hotcakes, and two eggs, over easy. How's that?"

"At last. High time, too."

In her orange and brown uniform, a handkerchief with a crocheted edge spilling out of a breast pocket, Josie never changed. She was always cheery, ready with a joke, and quick on her feet. I didn't know how she kept up the pace, working in the diner seven days a week, month in and month out.

"When are *you* taking some time off, Josie?"

"When the public stops eatin', that's when. Besides, what would I do if I wasn't workin'? Go nuts, that's what. I like it here, meeting folks, pressing the flesh, you know what I mean?"

"You're a born politician. Why don't you run for Congress?" I waved my arms around the diner. "You'd have the votes of everybody who ever ate in here."

She snorted. "Congress? Dogcatcher more likely."

"Well, that's a start."

"Good morning," he said quietly in my ear.

Startled, I sloshed coffee onto the countertop.

"Detective Bradshaw. What a surprise."

While I sopped up the spill with paper napkins, he eased onto the stool next to mine. "Just drove in from Fayetteville."

"The sheriff get in touch with you?"

He nodded. "It's early yet, so I thought I'd eat and then give you a call. I see now that won't be necessary." Steam rising off the mug Josie'd put in front of him, he took a careful sip. "We need to talk, but not in here. Can you meet me at the station after breakfast?"

Imagine saying no to a question like that?

Matt, in full uniform, awaited us in his office. He eyeballed my legs, quickly looking away, but not before a grin escaped him. The cutoffs suddenly felt too short, my legs too long for a police interview. But it was a tad late to be worrying about that, so after Detective Bradshaw turned on his tape recorder, I put my mind to retelling what I'd heard the Bixby girls say. When I finished, he shut off the recorder and thanked me for my testimony.

"Will it help with the investigation?" I

really wanted to know.

"Yes and no. Though you say you didn't actually see who was speaking, your story supports what we were told."

I gasped. "You *knew* about Tallulah and the senator?"

He shifted in his seat behind Matt's desk. "We knew only what the Bixby girls said. So, in answer to your question, you've verified their story, but I'm afraid it offers us nothing new. Nothing we can use in a court of law."

I turned to Matt, who was seated beside me on a plastic chair he'd pulled in from the outer room. "When I told you about this yesterday, you already knew?"

A cautionary flicker crept into his eyes. Didn't look like he wanted to answer. "That's about the size of it."

We stared at each other in silence, until too vexed to keep quiet, I blurted out, "Good grief, isn't there a man in the world I can trust?"

Matt's jaw firmed up, but he didn't wing an angry retort back at me.

"Miss Ingersoll," the detective's lips formed a thin line, "the fact that Sheriff Rameros didn't reveal what he knew is proof he *can* be trusted."

The man was dead right. "My apologies,

Sheriff."

"It's okay, Honey."

Bradshaw made a show of clearing his throat. "While what you overheard wasn't about an illegal activity, it does help confirm Senator Lott and Trey Gregson as persons of interest in Miss Bixby's death."

I sat up straight. "Because it provides a motive?"

He nodded. One nod only.

It wasn't enough. I wanted more. "What of the Ames brothers and IP? They're fronting for the casino investors, and the senator's in it as well. Using his political clout to get clearances, county support, easements. You name it. And he isn't doing it for free. He's being paid off, if not in money, in campaign aid." I moved to the edge of my chair. "You must've heard the rumor circulating around town. He has his eye on the White House."

Bradshaw nodded. "Most everybody in the state knows."

"Somehow, some way, Tallulah Bixby had him running scared. I'd stake my life on it."

"Please be assured no possible suspect or piece of evidence is being overlooked."

"Can I ask you a question?"

"Certainly, but I may not answer it." Bradshaw's face cracked into what, for him, passed as a smile.

"How can we trap them?"

"We can't. Both men have denied the Bixby girls' allegations. As long as they do, our hands are tied. Let me remind you again, they have committed no crime."

"As far as you know."

"Precisely."

I wasn't ready to give up. "There must be some way to squeeze the truth out of them. What about lie detector tests?"

"We tried that," Matt interrupted him. "Submitting to one is strictly voluntary. Both men scoffed at the idea."

So more had been going on behind the scenes than I'd been let in on. Though I knew I was being unreasonable, I was a bit miffed, all the same. Matt sure had held out on me. He stared at me now, looking as if he understood how I felt, waiting for some kind of snarly remark, but I was too low to say a thing.

Bradshaw favored me with another non-smile. "Not to worry, Miss Ingersoll. We haven't given up yet. Not by a long shot."

Maybe not, but I didn't see what else I could do or even where the case would go from here with no leads, no proof, no nothing.

Discouraged that my big breakthrough

hadn't so much as scratched the surface, I left the station with Matt's eyes burning holes in my calves, or so I imagined. That was one of my problems. I imagined too much.

Once outside, I headed for the grocery store to stock up on girl food. TV dinners, deli soup, skim milk, strawberries, diet soda, fluffy stuff that wouldn't put on a pound or cause me to rush to the supper table either. I sure did miss Mrs. Otis' meals, but when hunger pangs struck with force, I could always rely on Josie's.

Back home, I put away my supplies and drove over to Amelia's. No need to worry about Joe today. He was a guest at Yarborough County Jail, thank God.

Four little sandals sat by Amelia's front door. From the look of them, the boys must have had a wonderful time in a mud puddle somewhere.

Joey yanked open the door on the first ring. "Hi, Auntie Honey." He eyed the bakery bag I held. "Did you bring us some treats?"

"I answer no questions before I get a hug."

He threw his chubby little arms around my legs and squeezed me tight. "There! So what did you bring?"

"Joey?"

At the scold in his mother's voice, Joey peered at me with an impish grin. "It's not polite to ask for things."

"That's right," Amelia agreed, coming to the door with Jimmy in her arms.

One glance at her, and I could tell last night had gone well. She was all aglow, almost a girl again. I gave her a hug and handed her the bag. "For the boys," I whispered.

"Treats?" Joey asked.

"Yes," Amelia said, "for after your naps."

"I don't want a nap."

"Don't want one," Jimmy echoed.

"Come along now, Joey. Aunt Honey will tuck you in. If you go to sleep, she'll leave the treats for you. Otherwise, she'll have to take them back home."

"Oh, all right." Resigned to his fate, he padded on bare feet toward his bedroom.

"Bathroom first, remember?"

"I guess so, but you can't come in, Auntie Honey. I'm a big boy now."

"Okay. I'll wait here in the hallway for you."

A few minutes later, he came out rubbing his eyes and climbed into his bed with a grateful sigh. I covered him with his cowboy blanket, kissed his warm, soft cheek and tiptoed out of the room.

Amelia met me on the porch swing with iced teas.

"So," I half turned to grin at her, "how did it go last night?"

"Fine." She colored and took a cooling sip. "We all had a wonderful time."

"We *all*?"

"The four of us."

"You took the boys?"

"Yes. Cletus invited them."

"Oh." For her sake, my heart sank a little. So she hadn't had a candlelit, romantic evening after all.

"Cletus insisted they come, even though I told him they had never been to a proper restaurant before and might act up." She smiled. "But they didn't. They were perfect gentlemen. Sat in their booster chairs, said 'please' and 'thank you.' Joey first, of course." She laughed. "I think they were overwhelmed by the experience. So out of their element they didn't dare misbehave."

"Well, that sounds . . . interesting."

"Uh-huh. Cletus was just wonderful with them, telling them stories, answering their questions, letting them order what they wanted, chicken fingers and chocolate milk. Then ice cream sundaes for dessert."

I arched an eyebrow. "Any dessert for you?"

"No, I don't . . . oh, very funny." She sipped some more, staring straight ahead past the hanging basket of Boston fern out onto the front lawn. Finally, she gave me a big-eyed, big-toothed grin. "The answer is yes."

I whooped.

"And that's all I have to say on the subject."

"That's enough." I swallowed a gulp of tea and felt better for it. Sometimes things do work out well after all. Too bad I had to be the spoiler, but there was no help for it.

"After your lovely evening and all, I hate to barge in with bad news, but I called the county about the zoning rules."

"Yes?"

"In-house businesses are not allowed in your neighborhood. So, I'm afraid the day-care idea won't fly."

"Oh." Suddenly she seemed fascinated with the inch or so of tea left in her glass. "Maybe I won't need to go into business after all."

"Meaning?"

"I can't tell you right now, Honey, but I know you'll be happy for me when I do."

Cletus.

We sat quiet for a while, taking pleasure in the warm afternoon and the peaceful naptime. Then Amelia brought up the elephant in the room, Joe Swope. "Matt Rameros came by to tell me what Joe did and how you stopped him. I want to thank you for that, Honey, and say how sorry I am he assaulted you." Tears filmed her eyes. "Sounds like now we'll all be safe from him for a long time to come." Her chin came up. "Life's going to be different for the boys. I'm determined to make it so."

"From the silence, I guess they're sound asleep."

She nodded. "Between the excitement last night and our outing this morning, they're all tuckered out."

"What happened this morning?"

A cardinal, a ruby-red jewel, lit on the fern.

"They begged to go wading in the creek. So I took them up to the Norton place for an hour or so. We ran into some of our neighbors there, hiking around, picking wildflowers, enjoying the view. Put me in mind of Violet. She spent many a day roaming Pea Pike, looking for herbals. She'd cover a lot of ground, wandering from her place to the Sloanes and the Hermanns and back again."

Omigod. I nearly dropped my iced tea on the porch floor. Of course. Why hadn't I seen it sooner? The day Tallulah was killed, Violet could have been roaming around the pike. If so, she might have run into the killer.

I forced myself to sip the tea. She couldn't have witnessed the murder or she'd have been killed on the spot. Without knowing anything evil had happened, she had simply disappeared into the woods. The killer had recognized her and gunned her down a few days later.

Why not right away? Didn't want to chase her through the woods, wanted to get away fast for fear of being seen by someone else. Knew Violet lived alone and wasn't likely to talk to anyone. Came back a few days later and silenced her once and for all. Just in case. And what if that same person had killed Tallulah, who was the lover of Senator Lott, who was a driving force behind the whole casino enterprise?

The pieces of the puzzle were beginning to fit together. I huffed out a breath. Now I had to get the police, especially Matt Rameros, to agree. And I had a heavy suspicion that wouldn't be easy.

CHAPTER THIRTY-FIVE

Promising to get together again soon, I left Amelia before the boys woke up. I needed time to think things over. For even without any proof as backup, I was pretty darned sure Violet had seen something or someone that led to her death.

I knew of only one person who might help in finding that someone. Earl Norton. This time I heaved a sigh so heavy it fogged up the car windshield. The day he chased me across Violet's yard, we hadn't exactly parted friends. I'd probably have to grovel to get him to say hello, never mind anything else. My hand brushed against my thigh. Right! Shorts were cool and hot at the same time. As my daddy was fond of saying, nothing bet, nothing gained.

For all the do-it-yourselfers around town, the lumberyard where Earl worked was open on weekends. With a little luck, he'd be on the job today.

I pulled onto the dusty lot of Lumber Stop and parked between a couple of well-used pickups. I'd only taken a step or two when a wolf whistle split the air.

Leaning out of the cab of his truck, his John Deere cap on backwards, a guy hollered, "Great laigs, gal."

The shorts. I waved without replying and kept on moving.

Inside the automatic sliding doors, a bored, gum-chewing cashier stood behind the register.

"Earl Norton on today?" I asked, peering at her uniform name tag. Darlene.

She shifted her wad to the other cheek. "Who wants to know?"

"A friend of his, Darlene. Honey Ingersoll." A stretch, but I needed something that would flush him out into the open.

"Can't help you, Honey. He works in back, and customers aren't allowed out there. Too dangerous what with the ripsaws and all."

"You know when he'll be off?"

She popped her gum. "I gotta ring this one up."

A man pushing a dolly loaded with plywood approached her station.

After he checked through, I went up to her again. "Any way you can find out if Earl can see me for a few minutes?"

"Yeah, I can phone out back. He might be coming up on a break."

She made the call. "Somebody here wants to talk to you, Earl. Says her name is Honey. Yeah, that's what she said, Honey." Her chin came up at me. "Can you wait a half hour? That's when he gets his break."

"Yes, I can. Tell him I won't leave. I'll be setting right here by your register."

She gave him the message and hung up. "You go for his type?"

"Absolutely. Can't get enough."

A bubble burst all over her cheeks. "Well, praise the Lord."

"Yup. Earl's my kind of guy."

I sat on a scratchy plank bench to wait. Above it a sign with a picture of a hammer and a saw read, "You Can Make Me. Directions Free at Customer Service."

A few funny glances came winging my way, but I paid them no mind. My mind was on what I'd say to Earl. And on what he'd say to me.

He showed up in twenty-five minutes flat, the brim on his John Deere shielding his nape, his coveralls sprinkled with sawdust.

Showtime. I leaped up. "Earl! Well, if it isn't good to see you." Beaming big ones, I took his hand and led him to the bench.

"Never expected to see you again. Thought Darlene over there had the name wrong. So, what brung you?"

"I, ah, I've been feeling bad about what happened out at Violet's." I lowered my gaze, hoping that made me look kind of soft and sexy. "So I didn't want to let any more time go by without making amends. I, ah, I'm here to —"

"To suck up to me."

I glanced away from my fingers into two gleaming, weasel eyes and forced a nod. "Yes," my voice a kitten's.

"Wal, since it's you, I figure it's okay."

"Oh good. That's a big load off my mind. You still go out there? To the farm?"

"Yeah, huntin' rabbits. But not for long. The new owners are plannin' on bulldozin' the top of the ridge soon. What all for, I dunno. Said I've got till the end of next week to empty out the house." He plucked off the John Deere to scratch at his scalp with a fingernail. "I won't bother, though. I got the diamonds. And a check for the land. As for that ol' stuff of Violet's, I don't want any of it. My girlfriend don't neither."

He stopped, coughing over what he plainly saw as a slip-up, quickly covering it with, "Don't go worrying your head about my gal. I got plenty to go around." He winked.

327

"Know what I mean?"

"A man like you? Of course I do." I raised my right hand then dropped it, palm down. "You sure you don't want anything of Violet's."

"Yeah, I got no use for it."

"In that case, I'd be pleased to buy the Welsh dresser from you."

"That big old thing she kept her preserves in?"

I nodded. "I like antiques and would love to have it. Name your price."

"Hell, you can have it for free."

I shook my head. "I'd rather pay you."

He grinned, giving me a good look at his Halloween teeth. "You got yourself a deal, and I got just the payment in mind."

Gross.

"That sound good to you?" He looked hopeful.

"Sure does. Suppose I rent a truck and meet you out there some night this week?"

"How about Friday? My girlfriend works Friday nights. She don't need to know nothin' about it."

"Fine with me." I gave out one of those long, soulful sighs. "Yes, I'd surely enjoy having something that belonged to your aunt. Kind of a memento, you know? She was such a sweetie."

"Violet?" That one word and his mouth fell open. My whopper had stunned the starch right out of him.

"Yes, Violet. Roaming around those hills like she did, searching for herbs and roots, wanting to do good for people, help them ease their aches and pains."

"I guess." He sounded kind of reluctant like.

"People used to come across her in those fields all the time. And you know something, Earl?"

"What?" His eyes squinty with suspicion.

"The day the Bixby woman was killed, Tallulah by name, I wonder if Violet saw who done it? I mean did it."

"Doubt that."

"She might have run into somebody that day, you know, while she was searching for herbs."

"She wasn't a great one for talkin', but that particular day does stick in the mind, don't it? I 'member her saying she was tired of seein' folks around them parts who had no business being out there."

My pulse quickened. "Think she knew them . . . those folks?"

"Didn't say. Could have." He checked his watch. "Break's about up." Quick as a flash, he laid a hand on my left thigh. "See you

329

Friday night."

"Looking forward to it. Seven?"

"I'll be there. Waitin'."

But I won't.

He squeezed my leg then stood and swaggered off. I sat on the bench a while longer, idly watching Darlene do her thing and wondering what use I could make of Earl's tellings. He might have lied, of course, but I didn't think so. Saying nothing would have been easier. Not that he said much, just enough to perk up my curiosity. The day of Tallulah's murder, I'd lay odds Violet had seen someone on Pea Pike who didn't belong there. The question was, who could it have been?

Finally, head throbbing, I got up from the bench and sent Darlene a farewell wave. I had to get home and wash my left thigh.

CHAPTER THIRTY-SIX

The next couple of days, I holed up in my apartment doing girlie stuff, cleaning out my clothes closet, taking care of laundry, flipping through back issues of *Town and Country.* I still did that every so often, to keep my eye trained on the uppity look Lila Lott had no doubt nailed by the time she was twelve, the look Sam admired and that Billy Tubbs and his like would never understand. To be honest, I didn't understand it very well myself. Though I did know about wearing black to funerals and suits to work. And I'd caught on that, for reasons known only to the Lord and the glossy-type magazines, pearl earrings were more acceptable than rhinestone danglers, but darned if I could figure out why.

I also spent quite a bit of time on my computer, fiddling with ideas for a Deal of the Week flyer. The graphics had to be eye-catching, so I tried different colors and letters till I found a red and yellow combo that was pleasing. I'd already picked the first week's deal. A 1930s bungalow with a front porch — that being almost a requirement around these parts — original Craftsman-style moldings, a wood-burning fireplace, two bedrooms, and a big, if outdated, kitchen. I ended the flyer with a teaser.

****PRICED TO SELL****
Call Ridley's Realty at 555-6888

By keeping the colors the same but switching out the sale property each week, we'd have an ongoing ad folks would easily recollect. Pleased, I printed out a copy to show Sam. In December, when I left Eureka Falls for good, I'd take a sample along with me. Use it as a bargaining chip for a new realty job. But that was months away, and while still working for Ridley's, I wanted to earn my money fair and square. Also do everything possible to help nab the murderer. Though, when you came right down to it, what could I do except wait on the police?

That was what I thought anyway. Until Wednesday evening, when fidgety in front of the TV, I had a great idea. Like one of Darlene's bubbles, it suddenly popped up and out into the open.

I'd wear a wire. Do a real-life police-approved entrapment.

Yes, yes, and yes!

To celebrate, I padded to the fridge for a cold beer. Hey, wait a minute. Before I could twist open the cap, like Darlene's bubble, my idea collapsed all over me. Entrap who?

I set the bottle back in the fridge and meandered out to the living room. What good was my idea without a commonsensical target? I turned off the TV so I could think, and I kept getting the same thought. Whoever killed Tallulah to keep her silent had then silenced Violet because she'd been in the wrong place at the wrong time. She'd seen the killer. Whether she knew it or not didn't matter. She was a threat in an ol' brown sweater.

Hmm. Well, Charles Ames was one possibility. No way of telling — innocent-looking wire-rimmed glasses and all — if he'd gotten to the Hermann farm before me, did the dirty, and then returned. But why? Even after sitting in silence for a while, I couldn't come up with a motive. Besides, the police had found nothing linking him to the crime. Or crimes. He was a long shot at best. A long shot? Oh God.

I put a pillow under my head and

stretched out. My toes needed a pedicure. Maybe tomorrow.

Then there was Earl Norton, always ready to jump every woman he came across. He would have been mighty attracted to Tallulah of the silver stilettos. Suppose he'd found her stranded by the side of the road, picked her up, and forced her out to the farm for his own private reasons? Then killed his aunt because she'd seen him there that day. No, I shook my head. Didn't make sense. Earl lived out on the pike; nothing unusual about him being around any day, any time. But supposing he killed Violet to get his hands on her farm? Not impossible, but somehow I doubted it. I sensed a larger hand in all of this, a schemer, not just a guy hung up on sex.

Speaking of sex, what about Saxby Winthrop? He'd have enjoyed Tallulah. But trap her into going out to an old abandoned farmhouse? Not likely. And from the way he adored his momma, I didn't think he'd murder another ol' woman. Even if Violet had seen him, he had a ready-made excuse for being out there. He was inspecting a property up for sale. Besides, he might be a sleaze, but he didn't strike me as a killer. Never raised a hand to me either, just his. . . . Well, some things were best forgotten.

That left only two other possibilities that I knew of, or that Matt had ever mentioned. The two men the police had called persons of interest, Senator Lott and Trey Gregson. Actually, they had the most to gain by Tallulah's death. Her silence. And then Violet's.

Problem was, I hadn't met the senator. I'd seen him around town on occasion, but the likes of me never got close enough to shake his hand, never mind exchanging folksy words. He usually kept to his horse ranch behind its locked gate. Had to have a security system. Probably a bodyguard. A great man like that.

I definitely needed a pedicure. Pale pink this time, soft and summery.

So only one person remained on my list of possibles. Trey. And Trey was a man I could get to.

Time for that beer.

In the morning, all wound up, I called Matt at the station. We hadn't spoken since last Sunday, when I dissed him in front of Detective Bradshaw. I suspected he'd been avoiding me as a result, and who could blame him? So I wasn't too surprised when Deputy Zach said the sheriff wasn't available but he'd make certain he received my message.

This was the first time that had happened, and I rang off a tad disappointed. On the other hand, Matt took his work seriously. He wouldn't refuse a call unless he really was tied up with something.

Anyway, keeping my cell handy, I drove to the Clip Joint for that pink pedicure. Afterwards, I was halfway home, trying to figure out what to do with the long day stretching ahead, when close behind me, a siren screamed for attention.

I glanced out the rearview mirror into flashing blue lights. A police car rode my tail, so I pulled over to the curb and stopped. The cruiser wailed to a halt, the driver's side door swung open, and Matt stepped out. As he came striding toward me, I lowered my window.

"License and registration, please." No smile. No greeting. No warmth.

"You've got to be kidding."

"Your license and registration, ma'am."

"Oh, for Pete's sake. Is this some kind of game? I'm sorry for what I said on Sunday, but I did apologize."

"If you don't comply, I'll have to ask you to exit the vehicle."

"I can't freakin' believe this." I rummaged

through my purse for the billfold. After a brief scramble, I found it, yanked out the license, and handed it to him.

"Registration?"

"Just a New York minute, Officer." I unlocked my seatbelt, stretched across the front seat, and opened the glove compartment. "Here it is."

"Thank you, ma'am. I'll be right back with your documents."

Through the mirror, I watched him stride toward the cruiser. My, he did look fine in those snug uniform pants. While he examined my docs or whatever, I sat there squirming, wondering how to get past this coldness and onto my wire entrapment plan. As Daddy was known to say, the odds sucked.

Without wasting much time, Matt marched back, documents in hand, and peered into my side window. "Here's your license and registration, Miss Ingersoll."

"Are they in order, Officer?"

"Yes, ma'am." He handed me another slip of paper. "This is for you as well."

My mouth gaped open. "Don't tell me that's a ticket? What did I do wrong?"

"Your left rear brake light is out. I suggest you have it repaired as soon as possible so you won't be stopped again."

"Yes, sir. Sorry, sir."

"Have a good day, ma'am."

He strode back toward the cruiser, but this time, I didn't bother to admire his tush. Instead, I stared at the large, square handwriting on the slip of paper.

Tony's Bistro. Tonight at seven. Be there.

The nerve of him. As I looked up, he went sailing by in the cruiser, grinning from ear to ear. I gave him the finger. Too bad he zipped by too fast to see it.

Well, I had absolutely no intention of eating meatballs or anything else with Sheriff Rameros. So why at six was I standing in the shower all lathered up with lemony-scented body wash? I told myself it was in the name of civic duty. A murder case needed my input. My off-key chorus of "Boot Scootin' Boogie," I can't account for.

Anyway, for Tony's, faded blue jeans would be perfect, along with a black, low-neck top and black high-heeled sandals that showed off the new pedicure. Too bad my feet would be under the table. To keep the look casual, I went light on the jewelry, just swingy silver earrings and my watch. Light on the makeup too.

I was still humming when I left the house.

A Eureka Falls institution, Tony's had been born a ma and pa restaurant and now the original owners' son and daughter-in-law ran it. The menu never changed, which suited everybody just fine. The interior didn't either. High-backed booths in dark wood, red and white checkered cloths and old-timey oil lamps on the tables made Tony's as cozy a getaway as could be found around these parts.

Seated in a back booth, Matt stood and came over to greet me, grinning like he'd swallowed the canary. "Thought you'd be a no-show."

"You think I'd let a little roadside hazing stop me?"

"Wasn't sure. This is kind of a test. To see how flexible you are."

"Funny, I have something like that in mind for you."

"Sounds like we need to talk."

Taking me by the elbow, he led me to the booth. We'd no sooner settled in opposite each other when Tony Junior hustled over, beaming a welcome and carrying a bottle of red. "Good evening, Sheriff." A little bow. "And lovely lady." He held up the bottle so Matt could read the label. "With our compliments."

"Thanks, but no thanks, Tony. We're both

driving," Matt said.

"A glass for each of you, then? This is our finest cabernet."

Matt nodded at me. "All right?"

No cold brewski then, darn it. "Wonderful."

Before Tony left us, Matt said, "Put it on my tab, Tone."

"But, Sheriff —"

"I insist."

Tony shrugged. "Very well. You're the boss." He hurried off.

"Are you always so honest?"

"Tony pays his taxes and runs a good, clean business. He doesn't owe me a thing. Taking freebies here and there isn't the way I run my department."

"A knight in shining armor?"

One eyebrow rose a fraction. "Is that a joke?"

"No, no, no. I meant it." I leaned across the table to squeeze his hand. "You're a standup guy, like somebody else I know."

A corner of his mouth quirked up. "Sam? High praise, indeed."

Oh. Lord, I'd said the wrong thing again.

Tony returned with two glasses of cabernet, hovering by our table to see if we were pleased. We sipped and nodded.

"Cin cin," he said. "I'll be back with

menus."

As soon as Matt and I were alone, I tried for damage control. "What I meant was you take your job seriously. That's no joke. Not at all. In fact," I twirled the stem of my glass, wondering how he'd react to what I was about to say, "your job is why I wanted to see you tonight."

"That right?" He eyed me, his look curious but wary.

"I have a proposal for you."

He took a sip of wine, half choked on it, and laughed. "The answer is yes."

Pretending I didn't understand his meaning, I took a deep breath. "Okay then, here goes. I want to wear a wire. Get Trey Gregson alone and tell him I know all about the senator's affair with Tallulah. Split the secret wide open. Get him so heated up he'll blow." A quick glance across the table told me Matt's lips were clamped together, not a promising sign, but at least he wasn't interrupting. I took a swallow, gulping it in my hurry. "If Trey doesn't open up, I'll threaten blackmail. Say I was in the cabin the day Tallulah was killed. That I hid in a back room, saw it all. Swear I'll go public, call CNN, the *New York Times,* you name it." I chuckled. "Definitely the *Eureka Falls Star.* That should get his juices flowing." I leaned

341

in over the oil lamp. "What do you say?"

The answer was painted on Matt's face in big, bold letters. NO.

"It's out of the question. Out of the question. No way are you going to take a chance like that." His jaw firmed into concrete.

It was "no" through the antipasto. (I left the pickled mushrooms.)

"No," through the linguini with Alfredo sauce. Though it's not nice of me to say so, that sauce tasted better than my grandma's cream gravy. Tony made his with truffle oil, whatever that was.

And though I argued my head off, "positively not" through the espresso.

"You play dirty pool," I told Matt. "You already said yes to my proposal."

Too feeble. He rolled his eyes. "I foolishly had something else in mind."

Not wanting to go there, I asked, "Is 'no' your final answer?"

"Absolutely. Having you killed while trying to learn why someone else was killed won't solve the problem. Far from it."

"So you do think Trey is guilty?"

He set his espresso cup down with far more force than necessary for that little bitty piece of china. "God, you're maddening. Never have I said Gregson was guilty or anyone else for that matter. Guilt hasn't been established in the case."

"My point exactly."

He finished his coffee and pocketed his credit card. "I think the subject has been exhausted. Now, if you're ready, Miss Ingersoll, may I escort you to your car?"

"So that's it?"

He sighed and nodded.

Out in the restaurant's parking lot, I unlocked the Lincoln then turned to him. "Dinner was way beyond good, Matt. Thank you."

"Don't mention it, Honey. For some reason, being with you, even when you're impossible, is a delightful experience." His smile gleamed in the moonlight. Then he moved in closer, blocking the light, giving me one of those warm, full kisses of his that I'll admit I always enjoyed.

With his "Drive carefully, sleep tight," ringing in my ears, I drove home through the quiet streets, relieved he hadn't asked to spend the night but disappointed he'd turned down my entrapment idea. Now I only had one choice left. Though I didn't want to go over Matt's head — really, really didn't want to — I'd have to call Detective Bradshaw in the morning.

CHAPTER THIRTY-SEVEN

Bradshaw barked his name into the phone. When I told him what I had in mind, he said, "I'd like to discuss this with you. I can be at the Eureka Falls station by eleven."

"Oh no, not the station. If you can come to my house, I'll explain everything there. And please don't let Sheriff Rameros know I called."

A pause. "Very well. I'll see you at eleven."

High on success, I hung up feeling like I could fly. Then, a minute later, my mood took a nosedive. What on earth did I think I was doing, playing games with the big boys? Palms damp, belly in a knot, I paced around my living room until my heart went back to its regular steady beat. It wasn't too late. There was still time to get out of this, but though scared, I knew I wouldn't.

With no weapon, no DNA evidence, no meaningful clues, only a sneaky affair as a motive, the odds were against any break in the case. So far, anyway. But a confession of guilt would change the odds, and Detective Bradshaw must think so too, or he wouldn't have dropped everything to meet with me.

At eleven on the dot, my chimes rang, and I raced to the front door. Bradshaw stood there as stern-faced as ever and not alone. By his side was a thin, forty-something woman with a face as serious as his.

"Miss Ingersoll, this is Detective Kotowski. Margery Kotowski."

She reached out, pumping my hand in a tight, no-nonsense grip that told me she'd never air-kissed anybody in her whole life.

"Welcome. Come in," I said, waving them into the living room. They sat in the club chairs, refused coffee, and listened to my idea without interrupting.

When I finished, Bradshaw asked, "How well do you know this Trey Gregson?"

"Well, we're not friends, if that's what you mean. We've met a few times. I sold him a condo a few days ago. That would give me an excuse to check back, bring him a new owner's kit or a housewarming gift, that kind of thing."

He glanced over at Detective Kotowski, who nodded. "It might work."

He rubbed his chin and stroked his faint

stubble. "Why don't you want Sheriff Rameros to know?"

"I ran the idea past him yesterday. He's totally against it. Said it's too dangerous."

"He's right. It is. If Gregson's our man, there's no way of knowing exactly how he'll react. Anyone who can kill twice . . . and what little evidence we have points to a single suspect . . . won't hesitate to kill a third time."

He stared across at me, stone-faced, not sugar-coating a thing, laying out the odds. Scared now, not quite as cocksure as earlier, I asked, "You'll be listening, won't you? You'll hear any signs of trouble."

"Listening, but not necessarily forewarned. He could pull a weapon on you, a knife, a gun. We'll know only if you say something, or scream. We'll break in at that point, of course, but. . . ." He shrugged.

I wiped my sweaty palms on my denim skirt. Yeah, I was scared but not ready to back down, not with Tallulah and Violet's killer walking around scot-free.

"This won't be a lark," Kotowski said, telling me something I already knew. "You have to go in with a full awareness of the danger."

"I understand."

"Do you, Miss Ingersoll? Do you really?"

"My father's a gambling man. Gambling

runs in my blood." Good Lord Almighty, where had that come from? I hated gambling.

"That's brave of you and foolhardy as well." Bradshaw drummed his fingers on the chair arms, making up his mind. He turned to his partner. "What do you think?"

"She could be our best break so far."

Coming out of the blue, Bradshaw's next question startled me. "You and the sheriff, are you involved?"

"You could say so. To some degree."

"I see. That explains a lot." He went back to finger drumming. "Rameros won't be happy when he hears about this, and that's unfortunate. But my job is to bring the case to a conclusion . . . if possible." He shrugged. "Who knows, you may make that possible. So, ergo, you're on, Miss Ingersoll. Now," he leaned forward in the chair, "you know this guy's schedule. When do you see this going forward?"

"Well, the senate's in session right now, so Trey and the senator spend a lot of time in D.C. But they're almost always in Eureka Falls on weekends."

Bradshaw slapped his hands on his knees. "Okay. Today's Friday. Tomorrow then. Now, let's get to work. There's a lot to be done." He upped his chin at Detective Kotowski. "Why don't you go over the preliminaries with her?"

She nodded, needing no more prodding than that. They worked well together, and my guess was they had for some time. For a second or so, I wondered if they ever played good-cop, bad-cop, but as she began her instructions, everything except the business at hand flew out of my mind. "What you'll be doing, Miss Ingersoll —"

"Please, call me Honey."

She smiled. "What you'll be doing, Miss Ingersoll, is acting as a CI, a confidential informant. But with a difference. Typically, a CI tries to entrap a subject into committing a crime. What the popular media call a sting operation. Your aim will be to secure the confession of a previously committed crime. It's perfectly legal as long as one party — you, in this case — consents to allow the recording." Eyes narrowing, she peered at me. "You okay with that?"

I nodded, aware of a bead of icy sweat trickling down my spine.

"Your approach to the subject will be the make-or-break factor. In other words, how good an actress are you?"

"Well, I'm not given to boasting, but I was voted second best actress in my high school graduating class. So if you're asking can I hide my feelings, the answer is yes."

"Excellent. That's vital. Should the subject sense you're nervous or fearful, he'll be wary. So, guard against talking faster than normal, or looking around constantly or showing agitated body movements. Just be your usual self." She tilted her head, sending me an eyeball-to-eyeball stare. "Think you can pull that off?"

"I surely can." I wasn't sure at all.

She wasn't through. "Don't initially jump into the situation. Establish some camaraderie. Be friendly, charming, disarm him. Lead up to what you're there for as naturally as possible. But if you think time is running out, go for it. Confront him with what you know. To get started, you have a built-in subject."

"His new condo?"

"Yes. Chat about it, get him talking, and gradually introduce your suspicions."

Bradshaw jumped in, "Pretend I'm Gregson. You've just walked into his home. What do you say? What do you do?"

For the next two hours, we kind of play-acted. While I pretended I had just dropped by for a friendly little visit, Kotowski and then Bradshaw took turns being Trey Gregson.

Finally, around two, Bradshaw said,

"That's enough. I think you've got it, Miss Ingersoll."

I'd given up asking them to call me Honey, so I just nodded, relieved to have the play-acting over with.

He glanced at his watch. "You mentioned something about coffee."

"Yes, I did, and I'll make us some sandwiches to go with it too."

They came out to the kitchen with me. Bradshaw sat at the table reading his messages, and while Kotowski made a pot of coffee, I fixed ham and cheese on rye. For sweets, I brought out a package of chocolate chip cookies I'd been saving for a late-night snack.

Lunch over, Kotowski said, "Let's talk about what you're going to wear tomorrow."

The wire.

"Sneakers, for one. . . ." She paused, maybe thinking the reason would scare me off, but I was already scared. "Sneakers are good in case you have to run. You know, get out fast. Jeans would work, and you need a tailored shirt with a pocket for the transmitter."

"That's it? No wires?"

Bradshaw laughed. A first. If I hadn't been so nerved up, I would have clapped.

"We still call it a wire," he said, "but the

technology's gone way beyond wires. Today we use a tiny transmitter. Small but powerful enough to stream sounds to a remote computer. Any nearby conversation will be picked up through your clothing. You can count on it."

"Supposing there's a problem. What then?"

"In all my years of police work, I've never known the device to fail." He held up a cautionary finger. "But in the unlikely event there's a problem on our end, someone will ring Gregson's doorbell. When he answers the door, the signal to abort will be —"

Kotowski offered, "How about, 'Sorry, I'm looking for the Joneses.' "

"Good enough." Bradshaw turned to me. "In case you have a problem, say 'What a hot day,' and we'll break right in." He fixed me with that eagle glint of his, the one that made me think he could see through walls. "However, despite our precautions, there's still an element of danger. I don't want to downplay that. Bottom line, it's not too late to change your mind." His voice was gentler than I would have thought possible.

"Thank you, but my momma didn't raise no cowards." That might have sounded tough, but I was trembling. What had started out as a risky notion was shaping up as the biggest gamble of my life.

CHAPTER THIRTY-EIGHT

By nine a.m., I was ready to roll. According to plan, I was wearing sneakers, jeans, and a dark plaid shirt with the electronic wire hidden in a pocket. Now all I had to do was wait till I heard from Bradshaw. Once Trey's car was parked outside his condo, they'd send a robo call to his house phone. Should he pick up or click delete, it would be A-OK, go for it, Honey.

I'd printed out a neighborhood guide for Trey with the numbers and addresses of local businesses. Bank branch, post office, library, and some basic retailers. Groceries, dry cleaners, fast-food restaurants, that kind of thing. I tucked the guide and a welcome card in a gift bag with a big, fancy box of Godiva chocolates and a bottle of Taittinger Champagne. Kotowski had picked the goodies up after our meeting yesterday. I'd offered to get some micro-brews and a few bags of salsa chips, but she'd frowned down that suggestion, which, so help me Hannah, was no skin off my nose.

Eager, sweaty, tense, I paced my apartment, drank coffee, turned on the TV, turned off the TV, read my company emails, made a gazillion trips to the bathroom.

When at ten after two the call came in, I nearly jumped out of my skin and hit "talk" with a shaky finger.

"Showtime," Bradshaw said. "You'll be great, and remember, we'll be outside listening."

He rang off without saying anything more. I closed the phone and dropped it in my purse. After hours of tension, damp palms, and a roller coaster stomach, I felt an icy calm come over me. Like a magic shield, it told me I was ready. I could do this.

Through light Saturday-afternoon traffic, I crossed town in twenty minutes. Overhead, gray clouds clogged the sky, the air heavy with unshed rain and summer heat. Near the Eureka Arms front entrance, a black Phelps Electric truck sat parked by the road. Cool as one of those television spies, I didn't give it a glance as I strode to the building's glass doors, pressed the lobby entry code, and *bingo,* hurried inside.

The detectives had told me surprise was important. Show up without warning, throw him off guard.

The elevator ride to the top floor was smooth and silent, no Muzak. This really was an elegant building. Gulping in a deep breath of the slightly perfumed air, I rang Trey's chimes.

Once. Twice. No answer. At three, he eased the door open. In a T-shirt, shorts, and bare feet, he hadn't expected a visitor and didn't look any too happy about having one.

As instructed, I said his name. "Mr. Gregson, surprise!" I held out the colorful gift bag dolled up with purple streamers and a big, purple bow.

He took it from me with a smile and a "Thank you. Most unexpected."

I didn't know if he meant the bag, me, or both. Anyway, he ran his free hand through his hair, the way a guy will when he doesn't know what else to do.

Figuring he wouldn't keep me out after I'd handed him such a nice gift, I risked asking, "Did I catch you in the middle of something?"

"Nothing that can't wait. Come in, Honey. Come in."

"Thanks, Mr. Gregson." Hah! I got his name in a second time.

"Trey, please."

"Oh, of course, Trey." Let him think I had forgotten. Mentioning a first name was important too.

Inside his condo, the high-ceilinged living room, with its wall of glass, was as gorgeous as I remembered. He had added a super-sized sofa in camel-colored leather and an oversized recliner in the exact shade, I swear, as the persimmons that grew in my grandma's yard.

"Fine-looking furniture," I said. "It suits the space."

"Yeah, I'm getting there, one piece at a time." A smile. A little strained but still a smile. "At least I have the big three. A bed, a TV, and a recliner." He placed the gift bag on the sofa. "I was about to have coffee. Care to join me?"

"I'd love some."

"Be right back." He left the living room for his sleek, galley kitchen. Needing to keep him in range, I followed and found him hastily sending a text message.

I leaned against one of the granite countertops. He finished texting and tucked the cell in a pocket. "Had to send a quick message. Sorry. Politics never dies. It doesn't fade away either." A laugh. At least it sort of resembled a laugh.

He reached into one of the nearly empty

cupboards for a couple of mugs. "I hope you like it black."

"It's the only way."

"Excellent." He poured a mug of brew strong enough to knock me into the next county. Already tense, I only took a few pretend sips.

Trey leaned against the front of the Viking stove and glanced around. "The problem is, there's no place to sit out here. I might get a butcher-block table and a couple of chairs for under the windows. What do you think?" He sounded like he really wanted my advice.

"That might do, but how about a glass-topped table instead? It would kind of disappear to the eye, and the room is a little narrow."

"Hey, I like that idea. The kitchen's cramped, but overall, the condo's great. Glad you suggested it."

"Just doing my job, Trey."

"Well, you picked a perfect spot for me." He sneaked a peak at his watch and rubbed a hand over his stubbly chin. A hint for me to leave? Did he have an appointment? Was he expecting someone?

Get to it, Honey. Get to it.

"I guess the real estate business is like any other," I said. "After a while, you learn what's hot and what isn't. A place like this is high on the list, but I've dealt with my share of lows too." I forced a chuckle. "Like the old Hermann farm. All that rocky, hardscrabble land. Lovely view, though."

As if suddenly scalded, he thumped his mug on the countertop. "I'd like to hear your take on that," he said, making a study of his watch. "But I have a meeting scheduled in an hour." He spread out his arms so I'd get a good look at his Saturday clothes. "As you can see, I need to shave and change into a suit."

"Do you remember the Hermann place?" I busted right in, not letting him go where he was heading. "Where Tallulah Bixby was murdered? Can't understand how anyone could kill a beautiful girl like that." I set my mug down carefully, slowly. "Can you, Trey?"

"I . . . I can't talk about her."

"Oh, I understand. You were so close it must be difficult for you."

He nodded. "Very. So if you don't mind —"

I ignored his politely spoken words. "Of course, you weren't as close to her as everyone believes." I met his gaze straight on. "Were you?"

Anger flared in his eyes. "What's that supposed to mean?"

"No way you could know, of course, but Tallulah told me what was going on."

"Told you what?"

Okay, here it comes. Undiluted. "That you were only a decoy, never her lover. The senator's the one she slept with, not you."

Every bit of good humor drained from his face. Hah, I'd poked a hole in his hide.

He took a step toward me. "Time for you to go, Miss Ingersoll." The hands fisted by his sides told me he wasn't joshing.

"Oh, I'll go. Don't fret about that." I backed up a ways. "Right to the nearest newspaper."

"Is that so?" He moved in closer, but I surprised myself by not flinching. "Then let me make something clear." He was whispering, his voice so low I hoped the transmitter could pick it up. "Repeat what you just said anywhere, anywhere at all, and the senator will sue you for defamation."

"No doubt, but I'm not worried." Chin raised, I faked self-confidence. "Senator Lott's political enemies will take care of me. For one simple reason. My story will take care of the senator's White House ambitions." I mocked him with an arched eyebrow. "And your career along with it."

His fisted hands came up, Rocky style. "Why you conniving little bitch. . . ."

Shades of Billy Tubbs. Afraid he'd sock me on the jaw, or worse, I dashed out of the tight kitchen into the living room. He followed me, and I whirled around to face him, head held high. No giving up now, not without a shred of information. "Call me names all you want, but Tallulah's sisters aren't fooled. They know what was going on between her and the senator. And what wasn't going on with you."

"Get out of here before I kill you." His face turned rage red.

Uh-oh. Bradshaw might come busting in any minute and ruin everything. I had to push on, spring my trap.

Keeping the sofa between us, I tried another tack. "There's something else you might like to know. I was there that day. In the back room."

"What day?" Quiet. Fearful.

"The day you murdered Tallulah."

"What?"

"I saw the whole thing. You had a gun at her back. She was crying, begging you to let her go. You lost your grip on her for an instant, and she ran across the room. That's when you shot her."

Looking furious enough to leap over the sofa and come after me, he had me scared. I stepped closer to the door, just in case.

360

But like he'd been bit by a stun gun or something, he didn't move. "You think I *shot* her?" His voice high. "You're insane. I never laid a hand on her. Not that day or any other. She wasn't my type."

He caught himself up short and stood staring at me, open jawed, shocked by what he'd just admitted.

I shrugged, making believe his confession didn't amount to diddly. "So she wasn't your type? That happens. But why kill her?"

"This is madness. I haven't killed anyone. Now get the hell out of my house." He grabbed the gift bag off the sofa. "Take your lies and your cheap gifts with you." He threw the bag, purple ribbons and all, across the room. *Crash!* The bottle smashed against the tiles. The champagne leaked out and puddled on the floor.

"Too bad." I eyed the mess. "It was Taittinger." I heaved a sigh. "But you don't have anything to celebrate anyway, what with your career in shambles and a murder charge hanging over your head."

Shocked into silence, Trey froze for a moment then he threw back his head and busted out laughing.

Oh God, I've overplayed my hand.

"You're sick. Bloody sick. You ought to be committed."

I'd squeezed one confession out of him, but not the one that mattered. At a loss about what to do next, I stood there, rooted to the floor with my mouth hanging open.

He pulled his cell phone out of his shorts pocket. "When the cops get here, tell them any damn thing you want. Your filthy accusations will never stand up in court."

"What filthy accusations?" In a bright yellow sundress, a big straw tote in one hand, a plastic shopping bag in the other, Lila Lott had let herself into the condo. She stepped over the shattered champagne bottle as if it weren't even there and stood staring at me, eyes wide with disbelief.

"Why if it isn't Miss Honey Ingersoll? What a surprise." Her voice was as cool as a long lemonade.

"Well hello, if it isn't Miss Lila Lott, looking as pretty as Little Miss Sunshine," I shot back in that bitchy tone women use when they mean the opposite of what they're saying.

"I sent you a text message," Trey said to her, kind of limp-voiced, I thought.

She held up a plastic grocery bag. "I didn't get it. I ran into a store with just my billfold. You must have tried then."

He shrugged. "Whatever. It doesn't matter. Her accusations are insane. I'm calling the police."

Fear, or something akin to it, leaped into her face. "Whatever for? Those mysterious accusations I heard you mention? Think of the publicity, Trey."

She lowered her grocery bag to the floor and shifted the straw tote to a shoulder. Strolling, sway-hipped, over to Trey, she put a hand on his arm and gazed into his eyes. "Has this naughty girl been saying bad things about my daddy's favorite aide?"

Oh my, talk about pouring poisoned molasses over your biscuits. . . . She was as sweet-nasty as any female I'd ever met.

With no intention of backing down, I took a deep breath and plunged on, "I saw Trey kill Tallulah Bixby. Witnessed the whole thing. You remember Tallulah, don't you, Miss Lott?"

Like someone trying to decide whether to lie or not, she hesitated. In that instant, I knew I'd never call her Miss Lott again. Not for as long as I lived. Of course, the way things were developing around here, that might only be for five more minutes. But before I got bumped off, I'd get in one final thrust.

"In case you've forgotten, Tallulah was your daddy's mistress."

She rewarded me with a gasp, full-blown

and right from the gut. "Well, I never."

"Trey's admitted he wasn't Tallulah's lover. So don't bother arguing about it. It won't do you no . . . any good. None at all."

Her mouth open, she went to speak, but I beat her to it. "The fact is, Lila, he's your lover."

Another gasp. Oh, Lord, I was enjoying this.

"How dare you?"

I stepped toward her, jabbing at the air with a forefinger. "No, how dare you? How dare you marry Sam Ridley? He's a decent guy. He doesn't deserve a woman who has sex in the backseat of another man's car."

She drew herself tall and sneered at me down her perfect little nose. I had to give her credit. The Queen of England couldn't have looked snobbier.

"Now you hear this, Miss Trailer Trash. What I do in my free time is none of your business."

"Most days, I'd agree with you," I said, forcing my voice into a tone as cool as hers, "except for one thing. Sam's my friend. Up till now, I had no intention of telling him about you and Trey, of breaking his heart. But your boyfriend there," I pointed a finger at Trey, pleased to see it wasn't shaking, "knows that when I leave here, I leave to talk."

I grabbed my purse off the sofa and tossed it over an arm. Where was all this tough-sounding talk of mine coming from? Not from the play-acting of yesterday. Ten minutes after getting here, I'd forgotten every darn thing the detectives taught me. Tallulah and Violet must've been egging me on, saying, "Go for it, girl. Go get 'em." Either that or I was in the grip of mind-blowing anger because I'd forgotten something else, something Daddy told me years ago when we played stud poker together. Never underestimate your opponent. And at the moment, that was Lila.

Stealthy as a mountain lion stalking its prey, she eased around the side of the sofa, narrowing the space between us. "You mean to tell me you'd sully my daddy's good name with cheap gossip?"

"Not with gossip, with the truth. I'm taking him down, Lila, and his aide along with him. Especially his aide. Before you arrived, he let me in on a choice tidbit."

"Don't listen to her," Trey yelled. "I'm calling the cops."

"No!" Lila shouted.

I challenged her. "Want to hear what he said?"

With a flick of the wrist, she swatted my question away as if it were a bothersome gnat. "You have nothing to say that I care to hear."

"Wrong. You'll care about this."

Her super long lashes fluttered.

Hah, she's hooked. Time to draw her in.

"Trey told me your daddy wanted Tallulah dead. When Trey shot her, he was carrying out your father's orders."

"She's a lying bitch," Trey shouted and lunged for me.

I raced for the door, forgetting to yell for help, forgetting everything but the need to get out of there *fast.*

I grasped the door handle, but not soon enough. He grabbed my arm and spun me around.

"Let me go!"

"In your dreams. Lila, call the police."

"I have a better idea."

She dropped her straw bag on the sofa and dipped her long, elegant fingers into it. They came out holding a pink Derringer, the business end pointing at my left breast.

"From Toys R Us?" I asked.

A corner of her lips twitched, knowing and nasty. "The Bixby woman learned otherwise." She giggled.

Elegant Lila Lott giggling? *Unbelievable.*

"Imagine my daddy married to that. He's headed for the White House. I couldn't let a tramp like her, or you, stop him."

This was it. The golden moment. Or almost. Now I needed to alert the cops. "Put the gun down, Lila. Don't shoot." I said that real loud. "I swear I won't say a word, not to anyone."

"That's correct. You won't. Let her arm go, Trey. Step aside."

"What the hell are you doing, Lila?" he asked.

"I don't want to shoot you, darling. Step aside."

"Don't listen to her, Trey. She's a killer."

Uncertainty flashed across his face. His hand on my arm eased. "Lila, put the gun down. That's not the way to solve problems."

"You want to debate?" Her voice was icy. "Like in law school? Don't be a fool. This little tramp will talk. I can see it in her eyes." Her attention riveted on me, she didn't even glance his way to knife him between the ribs. "And I can't buy *her* silence with sex, now can I?"

Beneath the stubble of his unshaven, Saturday face, Trey turned ashen.

"Before you shoot, Lila, there's one small problem you've overlooked," I said.

She cocked the gun, but, curiosity flickering in her eyes, she paused. "Your manicure doesn't match your gun."

She glanced down to check, and in that split second, I dove for the door handle. The gun went off, missing my head by inches.

"Get out of the way, Trey," Lila ordered.

"No. Don't shoot, Lila," he yelled. "I'll stop her."

He made a grab for my arm but got a fist full of fabric instead and ripped my sleeve out of the armhole. Fury distorting his features, he whirled me around and seized the front of my shirt. The pocket tore off, and the transmitter slid out, hitting the floor with a sharp whack.

"What was that?" Lila asked. "What fell?"

Eyes widening, Trey stared at the transmitter. Then a breath of air whooshed out of his lungs. His whole body sagged as if that one deep breath had taken his life along with it. Letting go of my shredded shirt, letting go of me, he went over to Lila, gently took the gun from her hand and dropped it into his shorts pocket. "It was a button, darling. Just a button."

CHAPTER THIRTY-NINE

True to his promise, in seconds that seemed like years, Bradshaw busted in with Matt close behind him.

Brandishing Glocks, they yelled, "Police, hands in the air! Hands in the air!"

I wasted no time reaching for the cathedral ceiling, but Trey, holding Lila in his arms, simply shook his head. "Sorry, officers, she needs me. I can't let her go."

"You're going to have to, Mr. Gregson. She's ours now," Bradshaw said.

Like the air in a pricked balloon, all the fake bravery drained out of me. I slipped to the floor, limp and exhausted, as empty as a roadhouse bottle at midnight. I tented my knees and laid my head on them, hiding my face, hiding from the truth. God, I'd messed up bad. So darn certain I knew who the killer was, I'd accused an innocent man of murder. How could anyone have been so wrong? So pigheaded?

"Honey." Matt's voice was close to my ear, so he must have been crouching by my side. I didn't raise my head to look at him. I was too ashamed.

"Honey, are you all right?"

"No," I murmured.

"No? What's wrong? She didn't shoot you, did she?" Alarm had leaped into his voice.

"She missed." With that, I threw my arms around him while he held me and patted my back.

Voices and footsteps sounded all around us, but I didn't give a good giggly.

"Sheriff, I have the transmitter." *Bradshaw*.

I didn't have the nerve to look him in the face.

"When you're through, ah, helping the CI, will you bring her to the station?" he asked. "We need a statement."

"As soon as she's able, Detective."

"Not too long, okay?" Kind of snarky.

I guess clinging to a cop at a crime scene wasn't considered a proper way of behaving, so as soon as the room emptied out, I yanked a tissue out of my jeans, blew my nose, and stood. "Thanks, Matt. I needed that."

"The pleasure was all mine." His eyes crinkled with amusement.

A strange time to be amused, I huffed,

and then I glanced down. "Oh, heavens."

"Very sexy bra." He sent me a big toothy grin.

"My best one." I said, drawing the ripped shirt together in front. "It's lacy."

"I noticed."

"I wanted to look good, in case I ended up in the morgue." Not true. I'd never given the morgue a moment's thought, but Matt didn't know that, and his grin disappeared. Temporarily.

"You're a remarkable woman, Honey Ingersoll, but there's one other little thing." The grin reappearing, he pointed to the back of my jeans. "I think you may have wet yourself. You know, being frightened and all. It's not uncommon."

I reached down and felt my bottom. Damp. "For your information, Sheriff, that's Champagne."

"Call it anything you want, sweetheart. Now, if you're good to go, we need to find you something to wear."

He disappeared into Trey's bedroom, returning with a starched white dress shirt.

"You're in luck," he said. "Custom made."

"That's stealing. I thought you were incorruptible."

"Not where you're concerned. But for your information, the county will reimburse

Mr. Gregson. Though a missing shirt's the least of his problems."

I shed my destroyed shirt, donned Trey's, and with the sleeves rolled up, the tail covering my wet rear end, drove with Matt directly to the Eureka Falls Police Station.

It was in chaos. Phones were ringing all over the place, and Deputy Ellie was going crazy fielding questions from curiosity seekers lined up at the front desk. As we hurried past, Todd Stevens, editor of the *Star*, hustled in with his photographer in tow.

"I don't have a story for you," Ellie told him. "No, you cannot photograph Miss Lott. No, I don't know if the senator has been informed of her arrest."

How on earth has the news escaped so quickly?

Zach met us outside of Matt's office.

"Get up front," Matt told him. "Clear the building. Tell the press they'll be informed as soon as Detective Bradshaw is ready to make a statement."

As Zach hurried off, we went into Matt's office and closed the door.

He said, "I'm going out front to give Zach a hand. You'll be okay in here for a while?"

"Of course."

"Bradshaw will be in as soon as he's filed formal charges."

Against Lila, the love of Sam's life. Oh, God, what had I done? He'd be heartbroken when he found out about her, though chances were he already knew. From the noisy excitement here in the station, the whole town knew.

The last thing in the world I ever wanted to do was hurt Sam, but who could have guessed that privileged, lovely, and oh-so-correct Lila Lott was a serial killer?

Serial killer? I bolted upright in the chair. *Is she?* During my little sting operation, Violet's name hadn't come up once. But since the same gun killed both victims, it was unlikely anyone else was involved. Though, as I'd learned this afternoon, without proof positive, you shouldn't assume guilt or innocence.

I heaved a sigh that bounced off the walls of the tiny room. What with so much floating around in my head, it felt too heavy to hold up. I wanted to go home, take a hot shower, and go to bed. Tune out today and what I would see in Sam's eyes the next time we met.

He'd never forgive me.

Oh boy. I laid my head on Matt's untidy desk and closed my eyes. It wasn't a bed with a duvet, but it would have to do.

The rattle of the doorknob startled me awake.

"Sorry we took so long, Miss Ingersoll." Bradshaw, his face full of shadows, strode in.

Matt followed and closed the door behind them.

I pushed back from the desk. "Your seat, Sheriff."

"Stay where you are, Honey." He took a stance by the filing cabinet.

Bradshaw sat across from me in the only other chair in the room. He took a recorder out of his pocket and laid it on the desktop. "If you don't mind, we need to verify a few facts."

I nodded. Would I refuse at this point?

"The suspect's testimony is on the transmitter. We heard every word." He permitted himself a small smile. "Just a few questions remain."

The operation had only lasted a short time, but it was a blur of accusations and denials and confessions. Though my recollection was shaky, I answered everything as best I could. When we were finished, he pocketed the recorder and leaned across the desk to take both my hands. "On behalf of the citizens of Yarborough County, may I extend our deepest gratitude?"

"Oh, that's not necessary."

"Oh, but it is." He let go of my hands, gazing across at me with that dark look I'd found so off-putting just a short while ago. "You stopped a serial killer, Miss Ingersoll."

"She killed Violet Norton too?" I whispered.

"Yes."

"Why? A harmless old woman like that."

"Apparently she saw Miss Lott on the Hermann farm the day the Bixby woman was killed." He shrugged. "She was silenced."

Though I had guessed at a motive for Violet's killing, if not the killer, I didn't say so. This was a good time to keep quiet. I'd said enough already today. Besides, Bradshaw wasn't through.

"Without your help, there's no telling when we would have cracked the case. However, that said, I must tell you that you took terrible chances in there today and went way beyond our instructions. You're lucky to be alive." He stepped away from the desk. "So, my advice, young lady, is never again volunteer to be a CI. Not if you intend to live as long as Sheriff Rameros here wants you to." With a wink — *a wink!* — he marched out, slamming the door behind him.

I blew out a breath and sent Matt a shaky smile. "Now what?"

"Now Bradshaw tells the press what went down. It'll be all over the evening news. You're going to be famous, Honey." As if he needed to rest a while, he sank onto the empty chair. "Not only have you stopped a sick woman from killing again, you've altered the course of a national election." A big, proud grin took over his face. "And how many realtors get to do that?"

CHAPTER FORTY

Yup, Matt was right. NBC, CNN, MSNBC, Fox News, they all carried the story. I guess it had everything a media hype could want, murder, sex, money, and politics. Even the underhanded casino deal came in for an airing. I hoped to God all this negative publicity would keep the casino backers from going through with their plans. For clearly, they wouldn't have Senator Lott's influence to rely on.

Lila's photographs, in which she looked gorgeous — what else? — and as innocent as a flower, appeared on every news broadcast and a special Sunday supplement in the *Eureka Falls Star.* My picture was in the *Star* too, with some flattering copy underneath it. Headshots of the senator, Tallulah, and Trey were also featured above the headline, SECRET LOVE NEST.

By Monday morning, the frenzy hadn't died down a bit, and I still hadn't heard a word from Sam.

Though dreading our meeting, I dressed with care, hair shiny straight and makeup in place. But I left off mascara in case I cried when I saw him. No sense in walking around with tire tracks running down my cheeks. And no black clothes either. Blue, I decided. It was my color, after all, and today I'd need every bit of help I could get.

Pulse pounding, I drove around the corner of Main Street into Ridley's back parking lot, wondering, hoping, afraid. Yes, Sam's car was there in its usual slot. Before getting out of the Lincoln, I sat clutching the wheel for a while, hoping my knees wouldn't turn to rubber when I stood.

Finally, hands trembling, I picked up my purse. On the second try, I managed to open the car door and get out.

The weekend's humidity had fled, leaving the air dry and crisp and sweet. Good, clean mountain air. So, why couldn't I fill my lungs? Gulping, panting for breath, I leaned against the side of the Lincoln until the panic eased away. Then I stumbled across the tarmac to the back entrance.

The moment I walked in, Mrs. Otis spotted me and leaped up. Well, sort of leaped — first she had to heave to her feet — and came fluttering over to me.

"Land sakes, I'm so relieved to see you. I tried calling all weekend long but never got an answer."

"Sorry about that. I turned off my phones."

"I understand. How are you, darlin'?"

"I don't know. It's too soon to tell." I gave her hand a squeeze. "Talk to you later. I have to see the boss."

She nodded, sympathy welling in her eyes. That was dear Mrs. Otis all over. She always knew more than she let on.

Sam's office door was closed, so I knocked. At a dim "Come in," I squared my shoulders and entered. Having to face the one you loved, knowing you'd dealt him a body blow, was like facing a firing squad. It meant the death of all your dreams. Even though your dreams had been foolish, up till now they had held a tiny ray of hope. No more.

As I stood in the doorway, my heart sank to my shoes. In the few days since I'd seen him, Sam had aged ten years. Dark circles ringed his eyes, and he was thinner. His brilliant white smile, the signal that life was an exciting adventure, was nowhere to be seen. Like a man who had lost everything that mattered, he had a droopy, hound-dog air about him.

"Honey," he dropped his pen.

"I, uh, I just came to tell you two things, Sam. First, how sorry I am for what's happened. Truly, truly sorry. And second, I'm leaving. You won't have to deal with me ever again."

His gaunt face — yes, he definitely had lost weight — registered shock. "Does what I say matter?" he asked softly.

"Well, of course, but —"

"I don't want you to leave." He got up from behind his desk and came over to me, standing so close I could count every one of his impossibly long lashes. "I want you to stay forever."

I gulped. "Forever?"

"Yes." A smile lifted his lips, and my heart leaped up with it. "I've done a lot of thinking this weekend. Thinking that I should have done long before now. I've been thick as a brick, overlooking signs of trouble, telling myself they didn't matter, denying the truth."

"You don't have to explain."

"Shh." He put a finger on my lips. I thought I would die. "I do have to. Lila had me fooled, Honey. Hornswoggled. Her looks, her money, her position. I bought into it all and forgot the common horse sense my momma taught me." His voice became tender. "That you've taught me too. I've been blind, but you've made me see past the lies and the glamour. Can you ever forgive me?"

His hands on my shoulders, his sapphire eyes, his lips, were so close, so very, very close. Everything I'd longed for was touching me, begging for forgiveness, for acceptance. Could it possibly be true? Or was I in some kind of strange but exciting universe?

I had no way of telling. The surprise was too great. I'd expected a firing squad and was being embraced instead. His arms tightening, he drew me to him, and bending down, gave me the kiss I'd been dreaming of, aching for, and had despaired of ever knowing.

That's when I got the second biggest surprise of my life. The gorgeous, wonderful, unattainable Sam Ridley didn't kiss a single bit better than ol' Billy Tubbs.

I was free.

ABOUT THE AUTHOR

Jean Harrington swears she ingested ink as an infant, for words are in her blood. Her first job was writing advertising copy for Reed & Barton, Silversmiths, and she claims she has the spoons to prove it. Then for seventeen years, she taught forms of discourse and English literature at Becker College in Worcester, Massachusetts. For several years, she also directed a peer-taught writing center at the college that was available to any student with writing problems. After Jean and husband John moved to Naples, she began dreaming of murder, and the award-winning, tongue-in-cheek Murders by Design Mystery Series is the result. *Murder on Pea Pike* is book 1 in the Listed and Lethal series. Jean is up to her knees in dead bodies and loving every minute of it.

Jean is a member of Romance Writers of America, having served two terms as president of her local Southwest Florida chapter;

International Thriller Writers; and Mystery Writers of America.

For more information, go to www.jean harrington.com.